PRAISE FOR ANN HOWARD CREEL

"*The River Widow* grabbed me from the first page. Ann Howard Creel's elegant and vivid prose brings to life a remarkable woman's struggle against oppressive forces during one of the darkest periods of American history. Haunting and ultimately uplifting, *The River Widow* is one of the best books I've read this year."

—Olivia Hawker, author of *The Ragged Edge of Night*

"*The River Widow* by Ann Howard Creel shows a mother's fierce love for a child of her heart."

—Laila Ibrahim, bestselling author of *Yellow Crocus* and *Mustard Seed*

"*The River Widow* paints a vivid picture of life on a 1937 tobacco farm under the shadow of one family's corruption and exploitation of others. A page-turner from the start, the story draws you in with a simple but compelling question: After murdering her husband in self-defense, can a young woman save her child from the cruelty of her in-laws?"

—D.M. Pulley, bestselling author of *The Buried Book*

"Ann Howard Creel's accomplished, fluid storytelling makes for a pacey, page-turning read."

—Gemma Liviero, author of *Pastel Orphans* and *Broken Angels*

the
RIVER WIDOW

OTHER BOOKS BY ANN HOWARD CREEL

The Magic of Ordinary Days

While You Were Mine

The Whiskey Sea

The Uncertain Season

the
RIVER WIDOW

ANN HOWARD CREEL

Published by Lake Union Publishing, Seattle
www.apub.com

Amazon, the Amazon logo, and Lake Union Publishing are trademarks of Amazon.com, Inc., or its affiliates.

ISBN-13: 9781503904699 (hardcover)
ISBN-10: 1503904695 (hardcover)
ISBN-13: 9781503903340 (paperback)
ISBN-10: 1503903346 (paperback)

Cover design by Faceout Studio, Lindy Martin

Printed in the United States of America

First edition

For Neil

Chapter One

1937

Her hands were lined and scarred and looked older than her thirty-one years. They had read cards and cooked and scrubbed and carried wood. They had turned the pages of books, touched love, and been betrayed by it.

These hands now dragged her husband's body to the river to let the flood take it away.

Now they had touched death, too.

December had been as mild as autumn, but in January, winter blew in cold and icy. An ominous haze lay on the horizon, iron clouds streaked across the sky, speared icicles hung from the barn eaves, and frost on the ground spread like a savage web.

The sleet and rain started and wouldn't let up, day after day, and then the flood warnings came. By the time they heard, the Ohio River had overrun its banks and inundated their lowland cornfields. She and Les raced with his daughter to Les's folks' farm on higher ground near Lone Oak, left Daisy there, and then came back to free the livestock and salvage what they could from the house, as everything inside was sure to be ruined.

While Les aimed for the livestock barn, Adah Branch ran through the driving rain up the creaking, peeling front steps to the house, flung open the screen and the door, and then stood inside looking around her loveless home while holding a big burlap bag in her hands. They should've evacuated days earlier; it was almost too late. Paducah was flooding, and swollen creeks had made many of the icy roads impassable. This would be their last chance to salvage anything before the water rose, perhaps high enough to submerge the house and everything else along the Ohio.

Eyes slowly adjusting to the darkness—the electricity was out—she perused the room while her thoughts spun. The fraying rag rug wasn't good enough to save, the old blown-glass lamps too fragile, the sagging furniture too big. Their best piece, a polished oak secretary, was too heavy, as was the potbelly stove. What did one take from a house that had seen so little happiness?

She grabbed their old Atwater Kent radio and then headed to Daisy's room and gathered her stepdaughter's stuffed bear, Shirley Temple doll, some clothes, and her other pair of shoes into the bag, then hurried into the bedroom she shared with Les. Everything about that room a reminder of moments that sickened her. She stripped the bed and pushed the sheets into the bag, which was almost full. Lastly, from the closet she took the folded Lone Star quilt, the only thing she had left of her parents. Her mother had stitched it by hand, and every time Adah gazed at it, she longed for love so deeply it felt like the hunger she could only imagine came from starvation.

She dragged the bag to the front door, hoisted it up on her hip, and then plunged back outside into rain pellets, lightning forks that illuminated the fields and fences and trees with quivering bursts of blinding brightness, and wind that rattled the wood-frame house as if foretelling the arrival of a blustery demon or the lowest sinner. Blinking and gasping, she slipped across the saturated soil and flung the bag into the back of Les's black Model A truck and grabbed another, now-drenched burlap bag and fought the slant rain back inside to get Lester's and her clothing.

When she trudged outside with the second bag, Les was loading the back of the truck. She could barely see through the rain but discerned enough to gather that he'd carried tackle, saddles, and tools up from the livestock barn. The milk cow moved past them, trotting faster than Adah had ever seen her move before. The only hope for the livestock was for innate sensibility to drive them to climb higher and farther inland from the river. Maybe when it was over, she and Les would find at least some of them. One of their Plymouth Rock hens fluttered by. Then she noticed something else—the first burlap bag she'd packed sat sagging on the muddy ground beside the tools Les had yet to load.

Les lifted a saddle and threw it into the truck bed. "What the hell were you thinking? My guns is in the house. Why'd you go and pack clothes and pillows?"

Adah wiped her face. "Daisy's toys are in there, too, and my mother's quilt."

Rain sluicing off his worn brown hat and falling on his shoulders, every inch of him except his face sopping, he yelled, "You ain't taking them. Get yourself back inside and get my shotgun."

Adah dropped the bag she held and pushed her drenched hair away from her face.

"Get the frying pan and some of the dishes, those good ones the old folks gave us. Are you some kinda idiot? Everything you brung out here is made of cloth, it's going to get ruint by the rain."

"We can cover it with a tarp or dry it later." She stumbled toward the first bag on the ground. She would just grab Daisy's doll and her mother's quilt, then put them in the truck cab. Les always got his way, and despite the true words she had said—of course they could dry those things—there was no use arguing for the rest of it.

She dug into the bag for both items and then stood and turned.

A flash of Lester's fist, and then a beam of light cut across her pupils, bringing on a familiar feeling rooted in her groin, the blow expelling the air from her lungs. Time lengthened and then froze. Something liquefied the bones of her knees and numbed her legs and mystified the world in front of her, all of it nothing but a moving periphery. She held on but swayed, vision blurring. Then the world turned upside down and on top of her at the same time.

"Ain't you heard what I said? You leave that junk be and go git some things that matter."

He was behind her now, pulling up her head by her dripping ropes of sodden hair. Visions inside her eyelids, small streaks and spots of light, shooting stars or fireflies, strange sparks and flames. He jerked her head—hard—and then a shot of pain, a hot, throbbing stab over her left eye, where he must have landed the blow. Her heart thumping high in her throat, her breaths ragged, bile rising in her mouth.

He dropped her back into the mud, and then came brutal kicks to her side, each blow delivering its own excruciating pain to her ribs. She lifted her head, and there, within her grasp, the pile of tools he'd gathered. She lunged. A heavy iron shovel in her hands, she scrambled to her feet and then struck out with all her might.

When Les staggered back, swayed, and then fell face-first into the muck, it took a moment to register. She had hit him. She had landed a good blow. She'd never fought back before; he'd probably kill her now.

Run. She should run. But where? She wouldn't dare take his truck.

Lester wasn't moving. Heaving and swiping at the wet hair plastered on her face, pressing rain out of her eyes, she slumped down on the ground and nudged him. He still didn't move. She rolled him over.

Crouched beside his body in the mud, she must have blacked out for a moment. And then, as the rain pelted the earth like falling bullets, she came to. Though still swimming upward back into the moment, not believing where she was or what had happened, struggling to make herself see straight, she did, however, know this: his temple was not shaped the way it had been shaped before, and Lester was not breathing.

Dear God, what have I done?

She had endured his tirades and temper, his foul mouth and coarse hands, his slaps and fists and shoves for three years, and now something had cracked open inside her on this storm-soaked, wild night. Now she had murdered her husband, and either she would go to jail or his family would kill her.

Later she would have no notion of how long she sat there, her body filling with stunned, conflicting emotions: she had loved Les, she had hated Les. She had killed him, she was free of him. Better, perhaps, that *she* had died. And yet an inborn instinct to survive still burned.

Get rid of the body.

She lifted him from behind, under his shoulders, and, hunkering low to the ground, dragged his body toward the swollen river into utter blackness, feeling her way with her feet, backing downhill until she heard the raging and foaming snake of a river already over its banks and bleeding onto the land.

She was already composing a story. She could say Les went too close to the river or some such, and then he was just . . . gone. The truth would never do. It wouldn't matter that he'd hit her so many times she'd lost count, that she had to cover her bruised body with long sleeves even in the summer, that she wore makeup from Kresge's Five and Ten Cent Store to mask discolorations on her face. It wouldn't matter that she was pretty certain he was widely known as a bad man, that his family were equally well known as menacing people. She had killed Les, and someone would make sure she paid.

And yet there was hope. Hope was something she always kept close, held in her hands, and spread over her body like a balm. It had saved her from despair. And now the flood, this gift, would provide her with a story.

River roaring in her ears now, trees snapping, the smell of soil and death rising from the muddy water surging forward with surf like the ocean. Her next step was into shin-high freezing water pushing her and trying to suck her down. She dropped Lester and trudged to his feet and began to push. He didn't budge. The water was swirling around him, but it wasn't deep enough to take him away. She slogged back to his head and pulled him up again by the shoulders, stepped back a few more feet into thigh-high rushing water, almost lost her balance, checked herself, dropped Lester again, and then sloshed her way back to his feet, knelt down, and shoved.

Another blow, and her first thought was that Les had arisen from the dead and was well enough to strike her again, but instead it was shockingly cold water, the river raging like a beast of purest evil, taking her away from her sin and into the very bowels of the place the killer in her deserved to go, into a frigid and water-ravaged version of hell.

Chapter Two

Bitterest cold and blackness and no air and the powerful force of a river turned furious. Unable to gain purchase on the slippery ground below her, not knowing which way to go, she clawed at the water and kicked and flailed, and it made no difference. The river had her in its almighty grip, as if God had ventured down with the rain to make certain she would never gain redemption. Her head above the surface for a moment, she screamed, but only a wave replied, filling her mouth with putrid water, the current pulling her in deeper.

The river would not let her go. She would drown.

There hadn't been much for her in the world anyway, and she'd felt only snatches of happiness since being left at Saint Mark's Church in the Bowery, in New York City, when she was but thirteen years old. Her sweet, loving parents had perished in the influenza epidemic of 1918 to 1919, and her only living relative, an aunt, couldn't take her in and had instead taken her to the church. Then there was a year of learning from Father Sparrow, and it had been magical, a book always in her hands.

Happiness disappeared after his death. Not even during a brief period of adoption by a barren couple was it better; that family lasted only until what they felt was a miracle happened—the woman was finally pregnant—and they didn't want another mouth to feed. After that, Adah lived among thousands of other young people who worked and prowled and slept in street corners, eking out meager existences often within sight of New York's famous Broadway. They roamed Manhattan's Lower East Side and earned a few coins working as newsboys, trinket peddlers, flower sellers, and shoeshine boys, among assorted other pitiable occupations that Father Sparrow had once said didn't require any learning or expansion of bright, young, and impressionable minds.

One summer day at the railyard, she met two brothers, Chester and Henry Nash, and some exciting moments followed as they jumped trains together, but it lasted only until her newfound friends made their way to a town in Virginia, where relatives took them in.

Adah continued hopping trains alone until she reached Kentucky, where the land was green and spongy like the reaching fingers of a massive crawling creature, and she began to see that maybe this was what she'd been looking for. A place grounded and verdant and unending, growing so abundantly that she could reach down, touch it, and pull it up by the roots for examination.

Now the river she also loved was killing her. She was slender but strong—hard work on the farm and housework had given her muscles—but she was no match for this water.

Back in Louisville, Adah had kept company with some carnival types, and a kindly woman named Jessamine made Adah finish her high school education and also taught her how to read the tarot cards, a way to make a living. Jessamine said that a smart young woman with a New York accent, serious eyes, and pleasant looks could glean coins from country yokels looking for work in Louisville, as well as from city people down on their luck and seeking prosperous predictions to keep their spirits afloat. Adah discovered she had a knack for reading people. She took that God-given talent and further developed her observational skills. Everyone had a tell, and she used that more than anything else to survive by fortune-telling. Jessamine had taught her the ropes before she, too, died suddenly, and Adah picked up the practice, going around the city and its outskirts with a band of peddlers and other misfits, setting up gritty little camps in parks, empty lots, and open spaces.

People began to fascinate her, not as scientific objects of study but as vessels of soul and desire and spirit, each as unique as an individual leaf or a sparkling stone. She learned that a person's emotional needs were as important as physical ones. Never disingenuous, she tried to dole out hope, even a glimpse of it.

In Louisville, she met Lester.

Three and a half years ago, he had pushed aside the flap of canvas that made the door to her fortune-telling tent and stepped in for a reading. Adah's eyes had traveled from the dungarees up to the leather belt at his waist, to the shirt, unbuttoned at the collar, to his neck, Adam's apple dominant, to his face, nicely boned. He was approaching thirty, she guessed, not tall, but built compactly like a boxer, with a cinched waist and steel-rail limbs. His hair was thick, black, and curling; it would never thin out, but instead would turn into distinguished silver. One long lock spooled down his forehead. His eyebrows were curly, too, but looked as if they had been combed in one direction, out toward the temples. An attractive man.

For a moment, she remembered herself as the girl who had once wanted to become a teacher or a nurse—someone who might appeal to such a handsome man. She had never intended to make the reading of cards into an occupation. But she was alone, and the Depression had changed everything. One had to make a living any way one could. And during tough times, the demand for fortune-telling was on the rise.

People doing well rarely came to her, and sometimes she stretched hope to its limits for the downtrodden, painting as rosy a picture as possible and even declining payment from a few.

"Sit down," she said to the handsome man.

He slipped into the chair, clearly comfortable in his own presence. But he kept his hands folded beneath the table, where she couldn't see them.

"Your hair is unusual," said Lester. "Right pretty, it is."

Adah fingered wisps of it on the nape of her neck. Her hair was short because lice from hand-me-down clothes had taken up in her once-long chestnut-brown hair, and she'd had to shave her head a few months back. At first, she'd worn an old flapper hat to cover her baldness, but now her hair was coming back in, fingery about her head, and she'd given up the hat. Her hair was still short enough to set her apart, but Adah didn't care. It gave her a bit of a spooky look. Good for business.

"Thank you."

From a person's eyes and clothing, from their skin and hair, Adah could often come up with revealing details. But the most telling features had always been a person's hands. Not the palms, as one might guess, but the backs of the hands and fingers. The condition of their skin could tell her a person's line of work, and the size and cording of the veins was a good indication of age. But more importantly, the way a person held their hands, how they managed them during conversation, how they moved and quieted, gave her clues.

Adah gathered the cards, forming one pile. "You must cut. Use your left hand to cut twice, leaving three stacks."

"Why the left hand?"

"I assume you're right-handed."

He nodded.

"The right hand is the hand of labor, our occupations, our business with the outside world. The left hand is more akin to what goes on in our personal lives and minds."

"I see," he said, looking a bit amused.

Lester cut the cards as Adah had requested, and she finally saw a working man's hands—weathered, chafed, and callused, but clean. Then he settled his hands back below the table and looked at Adah as if he were sitting back in the theater, waiting for a play to begin.

Adah pushed the cards back together to form a single stack and then scooped them silently before her in one fluid movement. Her hands were fast and efficient with the cards, her skin was still young looking and unblemished, but her cuticles were chewed up out of anxiety, ragged and inflamed in spots. Her hands gave *her* away, too.

The cards were mainly props, but they sometimes gave her insights, and she read them as best she could.

In this case, the first two cards she turned for the handsome man showed favorable things. But now she rested her hand on the most important card, the third one, the card that would pull all three together and focus the reading into a cohesive picture.

She turned it, and a stone dropped into the vat of her stomach. She had to hold herself from instinctively drawing away.

The hanged man, reversed. Upright, the card showed a male figure hanging upside down by one foot, tied by a leather strap to a living wood gallows. The man's hands were bound, but his expression as he faced outward was peaceful, not in apparent pain. Even upright, the hanged man was the most confusing and mysterious card in the deck. He could represent any number of things, but reversed, he signified selfishness of the worst kind, self-interest of the greatest magnitude.

Adah looked into the handsome man's lovely doe-brown eyes, then gazed back at the three cards before her, and finally, steeling herself, perused his face again. There was something there below his skin, something seething beneath the surface, a secret, something not exactly frightening, but unsettling anyway. His face was peaceful, yet there was a twitch on the outside corner of his left eye, one he didn't seem to notice, or else ignored. Jessamine had once told her that everyone had a secret, and sometimes the cards revealed it. What was this man's? What secret could command such power?

As she studied him, her back instinctively stiffened, and the stone inside her stomach dug in deeper, but she didn't hesitate to tell him what she saw.

She centered her head and her gaze. "Nothing is as it seems here. All the rest, all the previous things I've related to you—the comfortable life, the healing, the happy home—it's but a façade. I think you're quite miserable. And as for your future—I'm sorry I can't say . . ."

He held her stare. Then, slowly, a smile began to form at the corners of his delicious mouth, spreading to encompass his entire face. He had a thoughtful face, a compassionate face, and this confused Adah. He had pulled the hanged man, reversed, as his final and most important card. It had never before come up this way. A reading had never affected Adah this way before, either. Once in a while she'd felt moved—as though something true and helpful had been revealed—but not normally. This reading, however, was powerful. A gut reaction told her the bad signs were true.

The man's face became relaxed, the skin looser, as if he was relieved instead of angered by her reading. He said, "You're right."

She had hoped she wasn't. Adah let her eyes fall to the tabletop and pushed the three cards together.

"Is that it?" he asked quietly.

"Yes."

He hadn't moved. Adah glanced up. "Please don't ask for another reading. I can't do another one until some time has passed."

His voice was mild, quiet, summer wind–like. "Why would I ask for another reading if I believe the first one?"

"Many people do." She glanced around the interior of the tent she had worked in since Jessamine died, then faced him again. "Times are tough for most people, and I hate to give out dire predictions. On the other hand, I relay the truth. Often people don't like what they hear, so they ask me, sometimes even beg me, for another reading."

His eyes softened. "I'm fine. I'll just pay you and be on my way."

In her confused state, Adah had almost forgotten to ask for payment. Normally she requested a nickel or a dime, but she wanted more from him. "Twenty-five cents, then."

Lester stood, reached into his right hip pocket, and left on the table a crisp and neatly folded one-dollar bill.

She breathed out gratitude that he was gone. He was a different breed of man—part self-assurance, part curiosity, and part pure animal need, which unnerved her.

Adah always made note of her transactions in a ledger, and after this one she listed: *Handsome man, many secrets. $1.00.*

Later that night as she looked over her ledger, her eyes fell on the line occupied by the man she would later know as Lester, and she underlined his entry with a wavy stream of ink. Something about him called to her with a hooked finger and an alluring smile.

If only he had never come back.

In deeper water now, she could no longer reach the bottom and went under again. Her head surfaced for a moment, and she pulled in a desperate breath, then was sucked under once more. Beneath the surface, it was as if all the muddy, swollen streams were joining in and magnifying the flood—her muffled, thick grave. She pushed back up with her arms and legs and found air, just as something hit her hard in her bruised ribs. Debris, logs, branches, pieces of metal, plywood, tires, and railroad ties flew along the surface; she grabbed for something to hang on to, held tight for mere moments before it got free of her and then vanished like some phantom friend.

Hit again, this time on her shoulder, she clutched a slablike thing that seemed to be a door and clung to it. She worked to slide up on it at least partway, the air hitting her trembling body with a blast of cold that took her breath away. But she was above the water now, and though still flying downstream in the deluge, she had a chance. She could hear people shouting, either nearby on the banks or also caught and flowing with the river to nowhere. Maybe they would all eventually end up in the Mississippi and then the broad, wild sea.

She shimmied farther up on the door that had become her lifeline and thought the frigid air on her wet body would surely freeze her to death. At one point, something slammed into her door, and she teetered to the side, but Adah held on, trying to keep heading lengthwise down the drowned valley. Exhaustion poured out of her marrow, and it took all her might to keep clenching on and blinking and breathing. Sticks flew into her face, and she pushed them away until she realized she had just passed the top of a tree. She was over what used to be dry land. If only she could work her way to the edge of this monster and out of its reach.

More and more branches and twigs slapped her as she swept past them. She clambered all the way on top of the door and began to paddle to her left, hitting treetops. Maybe she was passing what had been a riverside orchard or a wood. Sitting on her feet, she dragged both arms through the water, trying to get out of the current, but it was of no use. The river would take her to a painful death, whether by trauma from a passing object or by drowning in that roiling, cold, and clotted abyss for all eternity.

The door slammed into something that held it in place for a few moments, and Adah reached out into branches and felt bark. Something large and steady and strong. She put one arm around what was indeed the trunk of a tree, held on, and gathered her wits about her. *Don't let go of the door.*

Without movement, her body stiffened and numbed; she would surely die of the cold. The tree had thick, long arms reaching out, and she found a way to control herself by grabbing its branches and moving along until she reached some kind of structure. Probably another farmhouse near the riverbank. She was working her way out of the river surge and farther onto the floodplain, where the flow had quieted to an insistent whisper and birds shrieked overhead. She could paddle and steer the door somewhat now, making her way into more slowly moving water and into what seemed to be a lake. Then paddling for what felt like hours, miraculously going in the right direction until the door slid to a stop.

Adah put her foot in the water and found land. Nothing had ever been so life sustaining and hopeful as finding that muddied but firm earth beneath her feet. Still holding the door afloat beside her, she got off and walked into shallower water until she was completely out of the flood's grasp, on soaked but solid ground. She left the door floating and walked into darkness, bleak and cold.

And then she remembered what she had done.

Even on land and with smudged moonlight offering some scant visibility, she saw herself as lost to humanity, forever doomed to wander alone. With little awareness of her surroundings, she plodded onward until a murky mass loomed ahead out of the gloom, one of man-made dimensions. Likely some kind of farm structure. Drawn closer, she reached a barn, doors open. Inside, she collapsed into what felt like hay and covered herself with it. Then she curled up and prayed to whoever might be listening.

It looked as if her life might be spared. But why? She, of all people, probably deserved to die. If Lester had not taken away her cards almost as soon as they'd married, would she have been able to read the signs and know this was coming? No, she could never have foreseen this.

Freezing cold, hiding in an old structure that might still become flooded, its walls lashed by wind and rain, somehow, some way, she drifted off to sleep.

After their first encounter in Louisville, Lester had returned a week later to her tent and taken her out to dinner. He presented himself as a moderately successful farmer despite the Depression, a man whose wife had died six months before, leaving behind a baby girl. He explained that his misery had come from losing his wife and from loneliness. His elegantly boned face, which summoned imaginings of actors and singers rather than farmers, gave him a special charm. And how he had turned it on! His laugh was deep and rolled like thunder. His hands, which he'd stopped hiding, moved like lightning through the air when he talked. So it was no surprise that love struck with the strength of a sudden storm.

After a swift courtship, he offered her a comfortable life in a comfortable home.

But the cards! Over the years, she had learned that at times they revealed pasts and predicted the future correctly. Yet Lester assured her they were nothing but hocus-pocus, and Adah had known them to be wrong at times, too. By then she was fiercely in love, and so she ignored her doubts, grasped her chance, and married Lester in a church. She and Lester stood before God and pledged their lives to each other. The wind was still, like a wild thing holding its breath, but a chill strapped the morning air, and the sky refused to surrender to blue. Outside, a strange bird called out with a high-pitched caw that seemed to ask a question rather than announce an event.

On her wedding day, she stood as thin and strong as a strip of rawhide, wearing a trembling white dress and carrying a bouquet of wildflowers—lupine, daisies, and Indian paintbrush. After the wedding, she moved to the farm, where she met and began to care for Daisy, who was then about seven months old. Daisy, who fit perfectly in the curve of Adah's arm. Daisy, whose innocent trust and need for Adah made her believe for a short time that this was exactly where she was supposed to be. But it wasn't long before Lester endured some bad harvests, and he took up drinking and gambling in between banging her around. Love left in spurts with each push, shove, slap, and hit.

Once, she had thought there were a thousand good things ahead of her. But after she married Lester, her dreams, which had at one time seemed so close she could stretch out her fingers to touch them, drifted away like dying stars—shining brightly, then blinking and blinking slowly away into nothingness.

She should've believed the cards.

Chapter Three

Icy spears of torture, surges of pounding pulsations, coming one after the other, increased, then grasped on to Adah as iron fangs that released venom into her body and invaded every cell. Waves of blood-stilling cold rocked her, too, and yet she could not move. She could not even open her eyes. The only movement was her own breathing, and she could not control that, either. Her body inhaled and exhaled on some primal level, directed by the most basal area of the brain. It was all out of her hands now.

No sense of how much time had passed; a new day came. The dawn began to break out of blackness into purple and pink, the pastel light before sunrise bled into the sky, and she observed its many shades, so many degrees of darkness and brightness. She lifted herself up from her makeshift bed and peered down at her body. Her shoes and socks and coat were gone; her legs and arms were scraped, scratched, and bloodied; and her head felt full of sharp spikes. Her torn and ragged dress still clung to her body, and all of her was coated with hay. She was too cold to shiver now.

Beyond the open barn door, the rain had stopped, and the air wafting in was warmer.

After cranking herself up to a stand and shaking off the stiffness, she brushed away the hay. The flood hadn't dissipated. Water could still be seen in the distance but getting nearer. She searched out any objects she could find—an empty crate, blocks of wood, a fragment of rope—and fashioned them to make something of a way up, then climbed and clawed to the barn roof while the water crept closer.

The river was still at war with the land. Above the water, mists formed and reformed like the ghostly remains of the tribal hunters that had once roamed here. Nothing but flooded plain and the tops of trees, their branches glazed with shimmering ice. No homes or buildings in sight. It was as though the rest of the world did not exist or had forgotten this place.

Surely she would die before help could arrive. Surely this pain and thirst would kill her.

Did she want help? She deserved to die; she had killed her husband, and even worse, she had tried to cover it up. How could she live with that?

With a pulsating head, she recalled the early days with Lester. He had treated her like a free bird he'd captured and tamed for his pleasure. During the first year, a few times he'd taken her to the Arcade Theater, hosted by uniformed and brass-buttoned ushers, and the White Oak Diner, with its delicious five-cent hamburgers. Thinking of Lester in those early days—his sparkling eyes, the smooth glide of his movements, his smile as he dug into supper—nearly collapsed her. She'd appreciated and grown to love the farm—its orderly rows of burley tobacco, each plant a large green flower; the smoky tang that drifted in the air during firings; the warmth from a mule's flank when she lay her hand against it. These things had pleased Les, and she'd instinctively taken to cooking and housework as if a mother had taught her from an early age.

Most of her life had been spent in bustling cities, surrounded by others, but the day after her marriage, she woke to an almost-silent morning, looked beyond the window, and gazed at a world run not by people but by nature. In between the lovely silences, there was the snapping of sheets drying on the line, the hammerings of something Les was repairing, the rumbling of the river, and the shrieking of hawks.

There was a sense of comfort as she walked the land entrusted to her as Lester's wife. The shade of old trees, the smell of turned earth, and the unmistakable spirits of other lives before theirs floated on the pollen-rich air. She and Lester shared that same sense; they tasted it daily and allowed its weight to fall upon their shoulders. This, they had in common.

For a time as a couple, they had worked.

And yet there were ominous signs. One day a bird with a broken wing foundered in the grassy area before the house, and Les had taunted the bird, laughing at its helpless plight. It sickened Adah. As the Depression deepened, they couldn't afford to make improvements to the house, which was showing its age. Les became easily frustrated and irritated, drank more and more, and the first few shoves became harsher and more hurtful. Then came slaps and pushes to the floor, and finally his fist.

She squeezed her eyes shut and covered them with her elbow, remembering: Once, in a panic, she'd tried to get away from him on foot, but Les had tracked her like a bloodhound. He'd plodded over the land that spread downriver, his head low, his expression grim, and moved closer, slowly but surely, in her direction. He had hunted her, then forced her back. He would never have let her go.

She dared not cross her husband, but it had never been her nature to cower. It required extreme acts of will to keep her mouth shut and move about lifelessly while Lester worked himself first into a state of supreme self-pity and then rage. After making her own way in the world for so long, she had no intention of letting someone master her.

And yet that was exactly what had happened.

Little Daisy had borne witness to it all.

In December, Les had been rechinking the old log curing barn, furious that he hadn't been able to afford a new one made of wood planking and tar paper. Adah had been disgusted. They weren't going hungry; tobacco growers in general were holding their own better than others, as people found relaxation in smoking and chewing. But she said nothing. Anything she mentioned that was contrary to his feelings was met with fury.

When a beam of sunlight poked through a slip in the clouds, she opened her eyes. Her eyes stung and her throat constricted. She sat on the slant roof, cranked her knees into her chest, and buried her head between them. At that moment, an icy wind swept in and captured her guilty soul, dumping it in a place of shame so intense that it paralyzed her, and she could not move, could barely breathe. Hell was not a place of fire; it didn't burn. Hell was the opposite: arctic air so brutal it could break every bone. Numbness everywhere, no longer human, only a husk of a being. She was already dead.

But still she breathed and her heart kept beating. She creaked open her eyes. She was alive even if she didn't want to be. In her mind, Les's body, that dent in his temple, the absence of breath, all of it by her hand. That truth would scream and reverberate in her head from this day onward.

And yet there were so many shades of right and wrong, and who was to say which shade made the turn from goodness into sin? One thing was certain, however: no judge or jury in McCracken County would've let her off the hook with a self-defense exoneration. If she hadn't floated the body away, the well-connected Branch family would've exerted all the pressure they could to make sure Adah was convicted of murder.

Lester's family history in the area went as far back as the first election for trustees in 1831, and distant relatives had had a hand in the construction of the Paducah market in 1836. Their forebears had been present when Grant occupied the town during the Civil War and had remained staunch supporters of the Confederacy. The limb of the family tree that led to Lester had never given up its prejudices, and Lester's grandfather had been one of the first Ku Klux Klan members in Paducah.

And now God or someone else had intervened, sending that surge of water to come at the very moment she was releasing Lester to the Lord. It swept Les away and had also delivered a nature-made indictment of its own, whisking Adah down the river, too. So why had she lived?

Daisy. Thoughts of her stepdaughter made Adah's chest clench, as if a hand had reached in and squeezed the blood right out of her heart. Affection for Daisy had grown slowly at first, but then love had struck like a thunderbolt.

Daisy was dark haired and dark eyed like her father, and although she was but four years old now, she had a soft, sweet soul. She loved to pet the ducklings and chicks and handled the hens' eggs as though they were precious gifts. She had cried when Les had to shoot an old mule gone lame. Adah had taught her to press wildflowers between the pages of books, and Daisy did so, only to cry afterward and exclaim that they had killed the flowers. No matter how Adah explained that a picked flower was already in essence dead, it did no good. Daisy must have inherited her gentle nature from her poor dead mother.

What would happen to Daisy now?

Adah carefully managed to lie back, and as the level of water below her steadily rose, she ignored the pain racking her body and watched the sun cross the sky through the patchy clouds that changed shapes over her head. Below her, icy, mucky water carried everything from bloated dead bodies of goats to power poles, window frames, and what looked like a car door. Above her, birds streaked fast across the patterned gray and blue beginning to break through. The sight was lovely—a gorgeous after-the-rain day—but the weight of a million rivers lay on her. What would she do now that she harbored a secret, one as dark as the depths of the river on no-moon nights?

A hum of low voices reached her ears, and Adah sat partway up to look around. Two men in a johnboat were drifting by her, no more than a hundred yards away. They had not seen her. Were they looking for people who needed rescue or just surveying the flood? Either way, if she called out, no doubt they would come to her aid. Exhaustion seeped out of her pores, and she wasn't sure she could make a sound pass beyond her parched lips. Was it worth the effort to go back and face a life in which she had committed murder? Could she live with such a secret?

Swimming up from the murk of her brain, more thoughts of Daisy. The little girl would be left alone with the Branch family.

The johnboat was almost out of sight.

"Help!" Adah cried with less strength than she'd hoped. "Help!" she yelled louder and louder, over and over, until she was heard.

"Ho, there. We're a-coming," said the man in the stern as he dug in the oars and glided in her direction.

She tried to answer but could form no more words. She gave them a feeble wave instead.

"We've seen a goat in a tree, a dead dog on top of a house, and now you," the older of the two men in the boat said as they reached her.

The younger one helped her slip down, her bones groaning in protest, while the older man held on to the side of the barn. She sat in the bow facing the men. They introduced themselves, a father and son from the higher-ground Heath area, out to help those in need. They were strangers to Adah. The city of Paducah was home to thirty-five thousand residents, and in the three years she'd lived just outside the city limits, she'd met few others beyond Lester's family and the people who attended their church.

The father, who introduced himself as Chuck Lerner, took off his olive-and-red-plaid jacket and handed it to Adah. She slipped her arms inside and into the heat remaining from Chuck's body. Heaven to be somewhat warm again.

He said that workers had built two hundred of these johnboats in just one day for search and rescue. Then he pummeled her with questions she hadn't the strength to answer. Her first encounter with humans since the dawn of a new life, and she was struck dumb. She wanted to say the right thing but couldn't pull anything out of her brain or heart or even the frigid air.

The two men exchanged glances.

The boy said, "She's scared out of her senses."

"Confounded, I'd say," replied the older man.

Adah swam upward into more complete awareness as her body warmed, and she found the strength to study the men who had rescued her. Clearly related, both had boxy faces, kind gray eyes, and soft brown hair—features that came together into comforting assemblies. Flannel shirts and wool pants, and the boy still in his hefty jacket—these things indicated they were better off than she and Lester had been, but the muddied work boots and callused hands showed they also worked hard for a living.

The boy stared at her as if suddenly mired in a fog of wonder.

The inside of her mouth was so thick and dry, she had to work to revive her vocal cords. "Do you have water?"

Chuck pointed to a can in the bottom of the boat. Adah grasped it with both hands, twisted off the top, and drank heartily.

"How did you make it?" asked the son, named Hugh, his eyes still gleaming amazement. He was probably only eighteen or so.

Her throat thawed, then burned. Then her body stung and burned, too. "I just held on."

"How long you been out here?"

Her lower lip quivered. "I don't know. I passed out for a while."

"You got bumps and lashings all over. Looks like you took quite a beating."

Beating? A wave of nausea made her sway in the seat.

The older man peered closer. "You don't look so good. What happened to you?"

Adah gulped back bile jumping into her throat. "The river rose so fast. I got too close."

"Where're you from?"

Adah blinked and focused, suddenly more mentally alert, although she was achingly tired and had to fight for each muffled breath. Their impression of her would matter later. "My husband . . . ," she said with forced sad desperation, although it took all of her attention and abilities to do so. She had to make herself into an actress. "He was swept away the same time I was. Have you seen him?" Raising her voice now as best she could. "Have you seen him?"

They shook their heads. "What's his name?"

"Lester Branch. I'm Adah."

Father and son glanced at one another.

The older man said, "We haven't seen no one but you so far out. We been rescuing people from the second stories of their houses in town. Decided to take a look out here just to be sure no one got trapped in these lowlands."

She twisted her hands together. "We have to find him. He must be near." She swept her gaze around.

The two men didn't speak at first. Then the father breathed out slowly, a sad slack about his jaw. "We'll be on the lookout for him, ma'am, but right now, we got to get you someplace safe."

"And dry," Hugh added.

"I don't want to go anywhere without my husband."

They kept paddling hard.

Adah clutched the dress over her heart. "Listen to me, please. I have to get back home. I have to find my husband."

"We're heading back to Paducah now, but the town's underwater. After all the power went kaput, we were cut off from the rest of the world. People that was flooded out holed up in the Cobb Hotel until the power failed. Lots of people now staying in the Southern Hotel. And the sick ones are at the Clark School."

"Others are going down yonder to Mayfield," said the boy.

"You got a place to go?" asked Chuck, but Adah didn't answer.

The two men had to fight a ferocious current and dodge floating debris to slowly make their way back to the city. There, the extent of the devastation shocked Adah. The streets had become canals, and downtown buildings were flooded with filthy water almost to their second floors. Eerily deserted hotels and grocery stores, barbershops and drugstores, banks and laundries were battered by waves and beginning to smell of death and decay. Telephones, telegraphs, and even the local WPAD station were out. No power, no drinking water, and no sanitation had turned the city into a cesspool. No sounds save for sloshing water, not even a breeze or a birdcall, as if Judgment Day had already arrived and deemed this place done. Chuck Lerner and his son had to dodge semisubmerged cars and wooden pieces of houses, even an oil tank riding on the current.

The boy told her they were taking her near Twenty-Eighth Street to transfer her to one of several small barges, which were being hauled out to dry land by tractors. A makeshift dock three hundred feet long also reached into the icy, murky water on Broadway, gathering the homeless and taking them all by truck to the Arcadia School, which had become a clearing station for refugees.

"By the way," said Chuck Lerner. "What were you and your husband doing down there so close to the river?"

Her head became a hollow chamber echoing with his question. *Think fast.* "We were going for our milk cow. Sweet thing was down at the edge lapping at the water. We went to get her, and then it was some kind of surge. Took both of us down."

"Are you sure it knocked your husband down, too? You was being swept off, so how do you know?"

"We were right together in the water for a few seconds, then we weren't."

"What happened then?"

"I-I guess I don't know."

Neither the old man nor the boy said much after that. They had stilled, and Adah didn't know whether it was because they were filled with sorrow for her or they doubted her story. Or because they knew the Branch family.

She hoped she would be taken away to Mayfield. It suited her just fine not to have to face Lester's family yet. Based on what had just happened, she needed to work on her story.

Chapter Four

On the Avondale "hill," eight hundred people had been relocated from the Cobb Hotel and other points in the city, and others like Adah were streaming in from rescue boats and barges. Red Cross volunteers were handing out mattresses and blankets, giving typhoid inoculations, and sending people to homes, schools, churches, and—once those places had filled—to trains and buses headed for Mayfield, Fulton, and Murray.

A mass of slow-moving, stunned humanity filtered everywhere. People who'd fled with only the clothes on their backs were hungry and thirsty and often rank smelling, stumbling about in shock. Paducah had survived the 1913 flood, so no one had imagined anything this horrific could happen. And yet no one complained.

Adah pulled Chuck Lerner's jacket, which he'd insisted she keep for now, close around her. The wind cut through her as harshly as a shovel cleaving frozen ground. *A shovel.*

The sun sent down occasional spears of light to the water-soaked land. Gazing about, Adah was waiting her turn to be checked in. She didn't know these people, as she'd almost never left the green fields and dark crumbs of earth on the farm. She'd gone to Rudolph's Grocery on Saturdays and the First Baptist Church of Paducah on Sundays, but hadn't ventured much farther. Lester hadn't wanted her to have friends.

Around her now were the downtrodden people of Paducah. The women in simple cotton dresses covered by worn coats, wearing soggy boots and holding the hands of young children. The men in overalls, threadbare jackets, and damp hats, carrying a baby or a hastily packed suitcase. Some city workers in hip waders. Younger people helping the elderly. Few people wearing rings or wristwatches. And as always, the colored—in even worse shape—kept separate from the whites.

As her eyes drifted over the horde, Adah became weightless, not really alive, not yet one of them. She blinked against the haze and the bitter drizzle that had started again, and then filled her lungs with an expanding breath of air. These people were kinder, more honest, and more giving than she had ever been. And they had never killed anyone. They were not murderers.

A relief worker from the Civilian Conservation Corps was peering at her, and Adah realized the man was asking her a question. He wanted to know if she had any family or friends with whom she could seek refuge. All she had to say was *I killed my husband*, and it would be over. The police would lock her up, the truth would be out, she would pay the price, and the lives of these good people would be unaffected.

Did she have family?

Daisy. Only Daisy. Each day under Lester's domination, Daisy had lost more of her innocence. She already knew the most painful things in life, and her face often resembled that of a skittish kitten separated from its mother. How Adah had wished to escape with Daisy! But as a stepmother, Adah had few choices. She'd tried to make up for Lester's meanness by being a loving and attentive mother, and she had helped, she knew that.

But not enough. Not enough to provide a full antidote to Les's poison. Nothing could do that. Adah closed her eyes and pictured Daisy— rag doll held loosely in the crook of her pudgy, sweet elbow, her knees scabbed from running after goats and falling. She loved trinkets, so Adah had made her little bracelets using string and tiny buttons and beads. The bracelets had become Daisy's most prized possessions. She kept them on her dresser, laid out in perfect circles. Adah had felt the same way about the buttons her mother had collected for her.

And then Adah recalled the way Daisy managed to disappear, as though the walls could absorb her, when her father's anger began to rear its ugly head. All the years Adah had watched Daisy, seeing her suffer, it was like witnessing the death of joy and hope.

But Lester was gone now.

Adah focused on the relief worker's hands—fleshy, soft, kind—and then his eyes. Telephones were a luxury, but Lester's folks had one. Maybe some of the telephone lines had been restored. People were also communicating by ham radio, and some of the helpers were delivering messages and giving people rides to friends' and families' homes.

"No," she said. "No one to go to."

Not yet. She had already heard that, as expected, Lone Oak was fine, but she couldn't face Lester's family this soon, even though that meant she wouldn't see Daisy yet. Like Lester, his father and brother harbored no kindness in their hearts; his mother was only barely better. Adah had overheard enough whispered conversations to know: the Branches were reputed as landowners who broke the backs of their farm labor, cheated on business deals, and sought revenge on anyone who crossed them. They brought to mind a flock of vultures feeding off the lives of others. No wise man would ever choose to cross them. The family had never accepted her, and she had once overhead a comment about *Lester's little witch*, concluding they meant her, based on her former fortune-telling occupation.

Now she asked if Lester had passed through this station and relayed her hastily assembled story. The man said he would check for her.

When the relief worker returned and told her that Lester had not been seen, Adah's grief and remorse were not disingenuous. The relief worker said, "People are still coming in. He'll show up." He patted her shoulder. "And I'll tell him you've passed through here."

"Thank you," she said.

On one of the white buses, she sat in the midst of misery, even as some tried to find humor in the situation. A woman was saying she'd seen a cow on someone's second-story porch, and others were scoffing at that claim.

As they moved through the countryside, Adah stared through the window at barren and frosted farmlands that held perfectly still, as if trapped during an ice age. A man nearby said in a more somber tone, "Nothing's going to be left of the town after this."

"No reason to go back there," someone replied.

"Where'll you folks go?"

"Not sure yet, but I do know it'll have to be nowheres near a river." The man smiled.

Adah closed her eyes and for the first time let relief wash over her like a wave. She was free now. She could likewise leave and never look back. In Mayfield she could send word to Lester's family about what had happened and tell them she was moving on. Or she could just disappear. The Branches could probably find her name on the refugee lists at some time in the future, but she would be long gone by then. In the midst of this chaos, she could vanish like smoke swept away by the wind. She had no money or possessions, but she had survived that way before. She could go anywhere and never make contact with the Branch family again.

Many times, as she'd lain in bed next to Lester while he snored, she'd dreamed of walking away, taking nothing but herself to go find her life again, beholden to no one, free of the land she didn't own, the endless work it took, and the shame of being conquered.

She was sharing a seat with a young married couple. Bonnie, a petite redhead, said, "We was renting. House didn't belong to us anyway, so we might as well make a clean break." Bonnie wore a thin gold wedding band—a sliver of treasure.

Her husband, who said he'd worked as an usher at the movie theater, said, "Nothing's going to be working for a while. Can't see too many people going to see a picture show anytime soon. I got what little money we've saved out of the bank before the water rose, so we've been thinking of heading out to California."

Bonnie addressed Adah. "What are you going to do?"

Adah gave them a brief version of her story, then said, "The first thing I have to do is find my husband."

"Maybe he's already in Mayfield."

"That's what I'm hoping."

She was keeping up the façade of a woman desperately searching for her husband, but inside, the prospect of another life, one of her own choosing, thrummed hope through her veins, until another image emerged, again. Daisy, of course. A sweet little bluebird surrounded by circling birds of prey. Would the Branch family destroy her spirit? Would they make her mean? Would they beat her? Adah suspected that Lester had been beaten as a child and therefore had been infused with an illness that drove him to treat others the same way.

No. Adah's body jerked involuntarily.

She had to go back, even though turning around and going backward had never been a part of her being. But now she had to do it. She had to go back, for Daisy.

In Mayfield, all evacuees were directed to the Graves County Courthouse, where those who had not already done so were to receive typhoid vaccines. Adah learned that the town was already overflowing with refugees, and volunteers and city officials had no immediate plans for where to send the people still coming. Many homes were packed with as many as forty refugees, eight or nine crammed into one room, most all of them relegated to the floor.

She couldn't take up the space that others so desperately needed, so resignedly she asked one of the workers to contact the Branch family.

The volunteer said, "We'll send word, but you're probably going to have to spend the night here."

Adah was sent to a church, where she slept curled up on a mattress in a hall occupied by entire families, couples, children, and assorted loners like herself.

During the night, grief came like a fever. Lying flat on her back, searching the ceiling for answers, she balled her blanket and held it against her mouth to muffle her cries. Lester was dead. Her husband. A mean man, a tortured man, but one she had once loved and given herself to fully. She had known the contours of his body, the hair on his chest, the way he breathed as he fell asleep, and the sounds of their intimacy. At one time, she had loved his body. And now she'd ended his time on this earth. She hadn't deserved his beatings, but he hadn't deserved to die an unnatural death. Over and over she had to remind herself that it was done, that it could not be changed, that death was permanent.

In the morning, she received notice that Jesse Branch was waiting to pick her up.

Outside, he stood backed up to another Model A truck, this one newer than Lester's. His arms crossed, his eyes that always seemed as if they were in a permanent squint staring hard at her, and his rigid stance like a bull about to charge. Most of the time Jesse didn't bother to groom himself or try for a pleasing appearance. Eternally stuck to his bottom lip was a burning hand-rolled cigarette that suffused the air around him with the smell of scorched ruin. Today his hair stood out in fuzzy tufts from under his hat brim.

"Where's my brother?" Those were his first words. Not "How are you?" or "Glad you're alive." He looked as if her presence were about as welcome as the flood itself.

Jesse was Lester's older brother by five years, his parents' favorite, set to inherit the family farm outside Lone Oak, where he still lived. Bigger and bulkier than Lester but less handsome, he was devoid of humor, rarely smiled, and had never married. Once, she'd overheard a young girl at church describe Jesse Branch as *a big, bad bear*.

No warmth had ever been aimed in her direction from Les's family, as they disapproved of her previous life and occupation, once proclaiming it the work of the devil. And yet she had been expected to endure tension-charged Sunday suppers after church for three years, during which Lester and Jesse sparred in not-so-subtle ways for their father's favor. Lester always fell short—he'd had to buy his own place and start over, whereas Jesse was all set up to inherit the much larger, more prosperous family farm on higher ground. Jesse's future was secure—he'd won the big prize. And yet these brothers had remained in competition. Lester had managed to get two women to marry him, something that Jesse hadn't been able to do, plus Les had produced an heir—albeit female, but still an heir—and so beneath Jesse's slow and deliberate exterior, Adah had always read a seething envy.

Adah walked up to Jesse, tears blooming in her eyes. Despite her dislike of Les's family, it was still an awful thing to have to give them bad news. "I haven't seen him since the river . . ."

"The river *what*?"

"The river . . . it rose so high, so fast. We'd let out the livestock, but the poor milk cow went in the wrong direction. We were trying to save her . . . and then the river took both of us down." Adah almost believed her own story now.

His narrow eyes never left hers, and he shifted his weight. "Are you telling me my brother is gone?"

"I was hoping he'd already made his way to you. He can't be gone, I know it. You haven't heard anything?"

He stared off, and Adah was pretty sure he was fighting tears. But Branch men would never cry. When he turned back to face her, however, there was an unexpected hardness to his face, his mouth a stern, tight line. "Not till this morning, when I heard about you. We been waiting for word and asking around. Ma and Pa have been pacing the floor. Nobody could sleep."

"Have you checked at other places? I've heard people are scattered everywhere."

Jesse's face paled and his eyes reflected shock, as if the gravity of the situation was deepening and gripping him even tighter. "I just told you we ain't heard nothing till this morning—and it's only 'bout you. Where the hell is my damn brother?"

Adah wrapped her arms around herself. She remembered why she was subjecting herself to this. Daisy's face floated unbidden in her mind, and Adah resisted the urge to bring her up so soon. If her story were true, her only concern now would be finding her husband. "Maybe he's hurt. Have you checked at the Clark School? I heard the sick and injured are there."

"I been checking everywhere."

He kept staring her down, searching, apparently not the least bit interested in how she had survived. She must have looked a fright. Still wearing Chuck Lerner's jacket over her dirty dress, unbathed, unshod, covered with scratches and bruises she evidenced no reason to doubt her story. It was obvious to anyone that she had been in the river. And yet Jesse's eyes showed doubt. He tossed his cigarette into the mud, then ground it under his boot, his eyes never leaving hers.

"Get in the truck, then" was all he said.

He drove with his hands clenching and unclenching the steering wheel, steely eyes focused on the road ahead. The veins on his large-knuckled reddened hands were bulging.

They crossed a land of moving, ghostlike mists; spindly trees swaying with the wind; winter-bare fields; icy creeks; frozen ponds; slick roads; and the occasional inviting farmhouse, yellow lights in its windows and curls of smoke from its chimney.

"How's Daisy?" Adah finally asked, unable to wait any longer.

"Fine and dandy," he answered in a flat voice.

Adah focused ahead. What would she be doing if her story were true? What would she be talking about? "Can we go to some of the other places Lester might be? I'm dying to see Daisy, but we can't stop looking for Les."

He breathed out slowly, as if fighting every ounce of this release. "You and I both know my brother is dead."

"No," she said. "If I got out, he could get out, too. He's stronger than I am. I just know he's alive. Have you looked around our place?"

He didn't respond for a long time. "We cain't get there yet. Water's too high."

"What about the police?"

His head jerked in her direction. "You think we're idiots? Of course we been to the police and the sheriff's department, too."

The skies were drifting down snowflakes that stuck to the windshield and turned to ice. Jesse exhaled audibly again and spoke to the road. "If he got out, I would've found him by now. Where you been all this time?"

"I made my way to land, slept in a barn, then got on the roof. That's where they found me."

"When was the last time you saw my brother?"

"When the water hit us."

Jesse wiped his brow with the back of one hand and then gripped the steering wheel again. He looked as if he was restraining both grief and rage. "So now I got to go tell the folks their youngest is gone."

"I don't think we should do that. He could be anywhere, even farther downriver. I've reported him missing, so others'll know to keep on the lookout. He could be fine but have no way to get word to us. Everything is such a mess right now. He has to be okay, I just know it."

He drove the rest of the way in silence, and Adah sensed true grief emanating from her brother-in-law. Jesse and Lester had competed for their father's favor, but for people like the Branches, blood was everything. They stuck together. When one of the Lone Oak farmworkers took off with tools and a good quarter horse, Lester had joined his father and brother to hunt the man down. If not for the intervention of a nearby county sheriff, the Branch men would've lynched the thief.

Despite it all, Adah's heart went out to Jesse. She had taken away his only brother and a son from his mother and father. A sob rose in her throat, and Adah made no attempt to suppress it.

Jesse seemed aware of her silent crying but made no comment. Adah could tell he was still sorting things out in his head. Still letting it sink in that his only brother was likely dead. Maybe for the first time something in his life had struck him deeply, into a vulnerable space that he'd always protected.

But any vulnerability was quickly replaced with anger. Adah could sense Jesse's pain and rage gathering from the very center of his soul. The air between them went icy despite the warmth from the engine.

"Something that don't make sense to me," Jesse eventually breathed out. "Lester's no idiot. Why'd he go down to the river when it was all a-rising and rushing like that?"

She managed to say, "It was the milk cow."

A stony silence and then, "I don't know much yet, but I do know this: Lester didn't go down there for no cow."

Fear leached from the roots of her hair. Adah sat completely still.

"No," he said as Adah now broke out in a quick sweat. "Lester was too smart to let himself get caught like that. There's something you're not telling me."

The sky shifted duskier and started swirling heavier snow. Adah told herself to stay calm. Not to get carried away defending herself, which would only make her seem guilty. "I-I'm telling you what happened."

He jerked his head. "Just don't make sense."

She rubbed at her eyes and whispered, "I can't believe it happened, either."

A long hush followed, during which Adah stole a glimpse sideways. Jesse's facial features were coming together hotly. His neck looked monstrously thick and red. He spoke through his teeth: "There's something more to this story."

"Th-there's nothing else I can tell you. We were caught unaware."

Jesse was driving under control on roads that were icing over. He seemed far away for a moment. What was he thinking? Was he thinking about Les, or was he thinking about his parents? Was he thinking of himself, or was he thinking about Adah?

She couldn't read him.

"I don't get it," he uttered with a cold fury. His lips twitched, and he gripped the steering wheel so hard Adah expected blood to come oozing out of his hands. "There's something else, something you're not saying, and you better believe I'm going to find out what it is."

Now the land was a wide swath of stark white glister. She kept silent, her heart gripped with a hundred new fears. What would they do to her? And what of Daisy, the innocent in all this?

If family history held, there was no telling. The Branches had always let it be known that Adah wasn't one of them. Les's mother, Mabel, had always refused Adah's help in the kitchen, and his father, Buck, had once corrected Daisy when she'd called Adah "Mama," insisting, "She ain't your real mother." Yet her in-laws had always remained civil. Could she count on civility now?

Adah's breath snagged in her throat. The idea of escape was still there, like a whisper—soft, yet insistent.

"When we get to the house, you ain't putting one step into the room where my folks is waiting. First thing, you go on and get yourself a bath." He glanced in her direction. "You smell like shit."

Chapter Five

The Branch house, a well-kept white two-story with dormer windows and an inviting wraparound porch, sat on a low rise overlooking empty fields ringed halfway around the back by an unlogged hardwood forest. Off to the side of the house stood a livestock barn, a new wood-plank curing barn, an old log-sided curing barn, and a shed that housed farm equipment. Adah had never been prone to romanticizing the rural life, but the Branch place was the picture of pastoral loveliness, complete with painted wooden rocking chairs with rope seats spread across the sprawling front porch.

Jesse parked the truck at the top of the long gravel driveway in front of the house. Adah looked up to see her mother-in-law standing in the doorway with Daisy hiding behind her grandmother's housedress skirt and thick-stockinged legs. The Branches' two large hunting-type dogs bounded forward but didn't bark.

As Adah opened the truck door, Daisy sprang down the front-porch steps, crying, "Mama!"

Adah stepped down onto the wet ground and immediately had the sensation of being stuck there. But Daisy, wearing the same woolen jumper she'd worn the last time Adah had seen her, threw her warm and pliable body at Adah, and her heart took a turn. The little one clung to her, burying her face in Adah's filthy clothing, and Adah stroked Daisy's hair, silky as fine threads. But tangled. When was the last time someone had combed her hair or put it in pigtails? She pulled in a deep breath.

This was why she had come back.

Daisy lifted her tear-streaked face and gazed at Adah. Her eyes were wide set and open, and a circle of dried milk ringed her mouth. "Where'd you go, Mama?"

Adah leaned down, smoothed Daisy's hair, and tucked the sides behind the girl's ears. "The flood took me away for a while," she answered, "but now I'm back."

"Where's Daddy?"

Adah glanced at Jesse, who shooed her away like some annoying insect, and Adah determined to do exactly as he wished.

The Branch home was one of the first outlying farmhouses to have indoor hot and cold running water due to the New Deal. And still there were parts of town without sewers, which the Works Progress Administration was working on, and most rural homes had no running water. The Branches could afford to install the plumbing and buy toilet paper and towels for the bathroom.

In the second-story bath, Adah stripped out of her clothes and sank down into the claw-footed cast-iron tub full of warm water. Finally the remaining numbness in her toes and fingers seeped away into the fluid around her.

When she had finished bathing and wrapped herself in a towel, her hair dripping down her back, she wiped the tub clean and picked out tiny twigs and pieces of hay that must have come off her body. She wanted to leave no trace of her filth behind. Only then did she realize she had no clean clothes to put on.

She tiptoed down the hallway and peered into her mother- and father-in-law's bedroom, where a chenille bathrobe hung on a hook behind the open door. It was her only option, so she took the robe and wrapped it securely around herself. The robe almost swaddled her twice around, as Mabel Branch was as stout and stocky as any man. Her soft fleshy features and silver-streaked hair pulled back into a bun were the only things that made her appear feminine.

And yet of all the Branch family members, Mabel seemed the only one with charity in her heart. Mabel often gave old clothing, shoes, and coats to the poor through her church, though always making sure people noticed her altruism. If only Adah could get her hands on some of that old clothing now. Adah had long ago taught herself to sew; she could take in and refashion Mabel's discards.

Outside, another storm was gathering, and a gloomy haze crept over the farm, pressing in against the walls of the house. Every sound from within and outside was dulled, the air itself thick with foreboding.

Adah stepped silently down the staircase and into the hallway below, then gazed into the parlor to her right. A well-sized room with tall windows, sofas and chairs that were rarely used, and polished tables on which sat frozen bouquets and dusty figurines.

Mabel was sitting straight backed on her sofa, a Queen Anne look-alike, her eyes muddled with grief, the flesh under her eyes swollen so full it appeared she could scarcely see. Buck Branch sat beside her patting her hand, while Jesse stood over the both of them. Daisy was nowhere in sight, and Adah could only assume the little girl was taking a nap.

She took in a deep breath and held it. Preferring to face the lions as soon as possible, Adah stepped into the room.

When he saw Adah, Buck stood to his full height, his chest thrust forward, and said, "Git on in here. We got some questions for you."

Lester's father was also large, making it curious as to where Lester's litheness had come from, and his height and demeanor meant he had a powerful presence. His ruddy complexion made it evident he'd spent most of his life out in the elements, and his chest and shoulders were still broad and formidable, as though they could carry the world, despite the ample hard belly that protruded in front of his body like a watermelon. He had steely gray-tufted hair, and age spots on his bald pate and on his arms and hands. Buck's large hands, knobby knuckled and braided with large blue veins like rivers, were clenched on his hips. Adah had always read dominance and anger in those hands. For a man his age, he commanded respect, but today a stench of sweat blended with the sour smell of fear.

Adah stole a look at Mabel. "I borrowed your robe."

Mabel leaned back, waved off her comment, and peered askance, as if unable to speak.

Buck commanded again, "Come on in here."

Her head ringing, Adah did as she was asked and stood before her seated mother-in-law and her standing father- and brother-in-law.

"What's this I hear about you and Les going down close to the river?"

Adah gulped, trying not to show it. She and her story felt as flimsy as one of *Good Housekeeping*'s paper dolls. "We did. Lester and me. He freed the livestock and was gathering up tack and such while I was inside. We were loading up the truck when we saw the milk cow running off in the wrong direction. So we went down to save her, and before we knew it, we were in the water."

Buck surveyed her with a skeptic's crinkled eye. Sizing her up, making her sweat it out. "It must have been your idea."

"Maybe it was. I don't remember."

"Say what?"

"I don't remember. I mean, not all of it. It was so . . . quick."

"So you ain't no help," Buck said. Then he pulled himself up even taller, breathing harder, faster. His stare a brutal arrow of hard sunlight. "My son ain't no damn fool. He'd have known where the water was."

"It was pitch dark. We knew we were getting close as we searched out the cow."

"It was so dark you couldn't see the river, but you could see a cow?"

Adah hadn't thought of that. Naturally, the Branches would look at her explanations with the harshest scrutiny. Thinking fast, she scrambled. "Our cow's white. We could spot her especially when light-ning flashed, and we could hear her sloshing in the mud ahead of us. Then a big ole wave came. We both went down with it."

Buck didn't move except for a narrowing of his eyes. He let long tense moments pass, then spoke with a croaking but loud voice. "Jesse and I ain't buying it."

Adah touched her wet hair. "You saw for yourself I was in the river. I was picked up way down."

"No doubt you was in the river. That much is true. Jesse's been hearing that some folks is saying it was a miracle."

Adah shrugged. "Just good luck, I guess."

"Good luck for you. Too bad my son don't seem to have got any of that good luck rubbed off on him." Buck's eyes flashed with rage. "I want the damn truth. I want it now!"

"I've told you everything I can remember!"

"You've told me nothing that can help me find my own God-fearing flesh-and-blood kin out there in the freezing cold."

"He's alive."

"You don't know what you're talking about."

"I feel it!"

Buck's brow went flat, and his eyes burned. "You *feel* it? Like you got some kind of special way of *feeling*? Like the abracadabra nonsense you once used to get poor fools to part with their hard-earned money for?"

There was no use defending herself as Buck stood there studying her, and the weight of three pairs of eyes nearly buckled her knees. She was an impostor pretending to be human, playing a role. "Listen to me. I was in shock. I was fighting for my life, too. I wish there had been some kind of magic to intervene, and maybe I did get lucky somehow. I don't know where Lester went, but my gut tells me he's okay."

Buck said, "Like I said, no doubt you was in the river, but how you got there and how my youngest got in there is still a mystery to me. A mystery I'm damned sure to solve."

Mabel was sniffing and wiping her eyes with a handkerchief. "Why didn't you two stay together in the water?"

Hoping to glean one shred of kindness, Adah turned to Mabel. "We tried. But the river was too strong for us."

Jesse broke his silence and interjected, "It weren't too strong for you."

Buck glanced at his wife and then back at Adah. "For now, I gotta make one last search for my missing son." He flicked a finger at Jesse, indicating that his son was to come along; then he looked at Mabel. "You hold tight." And then to Adah: "You stay put."

After the men left, Adah took a step closer to Mabel and whispered, "I'm so sorry."

Mabel sat rigid for a few long moments, then lifted herself and walked slowly off. Reluctantly Adah followed her to the kitchen area, which was much larger and better equipped than most with plumbing against one wall, an icebox and stove against another, and a checker-board linoleum floor. Mabel was already pulling out potatoes to scrub and had put a pot on the stove to boil. As usual, she declined Adah's offer of help.

After gathering her strength Adah asked, "Where's Daisy?"

Mabel flinched, but she breathed out an answer. "She's down for a nap."

Adah lightened her voice, if only a little bit. "That girl hates her nap these days."

"That girl's been a bunch of trouble since you left her here that night. On top of not knowing where my son is, I been running around like a chicken with its head cut off, trying to take care of her."

Adah's brain recoiled. "That girl is your granddaughter. And thank God we brought her here, Mabel. She would've probably ended up in the flood, too." No response. "I'm sorry she's been an added burden, but I'm here now. I'll look after her."

Mabel's head snapped up. "Like you done looked after Lester?"

Adah took a step back, determined not to become defensive. "What does Daisy know?"

"We told her you two was gone and would be back shortly."

Adah said, "I understand."

Wiping her hands on her apron and then chopping onions, Mabel shot a hate-filled glance at Adah. "Reckon you got no other place to go now, do you?"

Her *do you?* felt like a shove. Adah stood still, then slowly nodded.

Mabel tossed a rotten onion into the bin. "I'll fetch you an old dress."

Buck and Jesse, like animals drawn by innate hunger at the smell of food, appeared just as Mabel was fixing to set the table. By now Adah was wearing one of Mabel's old housedresses, so large on her it was like a cape with sleeves. After she'd helped Daisy wash her face and then gently combed the girl's hair into a ponytail, she had gotten down on the floor with her to play with blocks that were too young for the girl. But the Branches kept no other toys in their home for their granddaughter.

"Let's make a house," Adah whispered.

"A new house," Daisy replied. "With flowers out front."

"And a white picket fence?"

Daisy gazed down at the blocks. "We don't have a fence."

"So we'll pretend," Adah said and gulped. Her life now was all about pretending.

Buck headed for the kitchen while Jesse climbed the stairs. Adah could overhear Buck tell Mabel, "He ain't turned up now, he ain't never gonna turn up."

Then Mabel's wrenching sobs.

Over supper everyone seemed to find their plate in need of focused attention. No one looked up except when passing the platter of fried calf's liver with onions or the bowls of mashed potatoes and green beans or the basket of biscuits and crock of butter. Adah made Daisy's plate and set it before her, then made her own.

"Everything okay, sweetie?" Adah said. Daisy was staring into her food as if she saw some kind of riddle on the plate.

"I don't like beans," Daisy replied.

"I know, honey," said Adah. "That's why I gave you a small serving. Just take a few bites."

A moment of strained silence hovered in the air, then Buck turned to Daisy. "Hold on, there, little lady. In this house, you'll eat what's put on your plate. Every bite of it, you hear? We don't put up with no complaining."

Daisy looked down, her soft little lips quivering. "But I don't like—"

Buck's glare remained fastened on Daisy. "What'd I hear you say, girl?"

Daisy peered up at Buck. "I didn't say nothing."

"Exactly. But now that you're living in this house, you better start saying 'yes, sir' and 'no, sir.'" His gruff tone and the rising color in his cheeks held everyone still.

"Eat what you can," Mabel whispered.

"Yes, sir," said Daisy to her grandmother, but no one laughed. She turned her face to Adah's. "Do I have to eat it, Mama?"

Before Adah could decide how to answer, Buck nearly yelled, "Listen here, girl. You don't need to ask Adah there nothing. This is the damned hard truth, and you best hear about it now. She ain't your mama, and your daddy's dead."

His color had reddened, but he remained still and in command—the captain of his ship, despite it all. He motioned with a butter knife to himself, Mabel, and Jesse. "The three of us—this here's your family now."

Chapter Six

The high-water level in Paducah wasn't reached until February 2, the river eight miles wide at that point. Seven-eighths of the town was underwater, as were cities and towns all along the Ohio, including Cincinnati and Louisville. Now Paducah was a ghost town of foul water, broken-windowed buildings, submerged cars and trucks, and floating trash.

Adah's life among the Branches was just as desolate.

While the nearby town festered, the Branch men had to keep working, focused on the new year's crop, while Adah concentrated on appearing helpful with the farmwork. The seedbeds were prepared by burning brush, wood, and bark, which provided ash—a good supplement for tobacco seedlings—then tilling and fertilizing the beds. The main fields had to be broken up, disked, and furrowed.

Buck said to Jesse one night over supper, "We're gonna have us a tractor this year. Oughta be coming any day now."

Jesse quirked an eyebrow. "How'd you manage that?"

Buck waved his fork in the air and, still chewing, said out of the corner of his mouth, "That Harper boy sells John Deere tractors now, and ever since last harvest he's been at me to buy one of those new ones with rubber tires and a diesel engine." Buck's face twisted into an ugly smile; then he chuckled and wiped grease from his mouth. "I told him I wasn't buying anything I hadn't tried out yet, said I wanted one on approval. But he goes and says the company don't do that, so I said fine, no deal, then. Damn fool said he's so convinced I'll want the thing, he'd go ahead and buy the tractor himself and let me use it and then pay him once I've 'fallen in love' with it or some such hogwash."

"You gotta be kidding," Jesse said. "He went ahead and bought it?"

"Yep, he thinks I'll be convinced to buy it from him. But I never had no wanting of buying a tractor, 'specially when I can hire help for nothin'. Boy's gonna end up with a tractor he don't need."

Jesse gave off a snort. "A used one at that."

"Yep," Buck said with a sly smile. "He's got no use for a tractor; he lives in town. Right smart little house he has with his whore of a wife. Too bad it's probably ruint now, like so many others."

Shocked, Adah had stopped eating. With so much suffering and loss around, Buck was trying to take advantage of people's goodwill.

Mabel appeared to be astonished, too. "He'll tell people what you done."

Adah had a difficult time believing that even Mabel could think the family was held in the slightest bit of high esteem by others. She obviously had no ability to read people.

Buck harrumphed. "Like hell he will. He'd be admitting to being duped. Mark my word, he won't say a damn thing about it."

Adah's words slipped out before she could stifle them. "Why would you want to do that to someone?"

Buck pointed his fork at her. "None of your business, now, is it?" Then he dropped the fork and dug his hands into the ribs and tore meat off with his teeth, juices sliding down his chin. A moment or so later, he dropped the rib, cleaned down to the shiny bone. "Come to think of it," he said, gazing across the table at Adah, "you might as well know: me and that boy's father go way back. Let's just say we once had a major disagreement."

Adah's back went rigid. Buck had no reason to give her this explanation unless it was meant to serve as a warning, making it clear that he could hold a grudge forever. Was it meant to scare her? And still she couldn't stop herself. "But that was his father."

His face hardened as they both stared at each other. "Don't matter. All them Harpers think they're better than everyone else 'round here. Truth be told, I never cared none about any of that bunch. Bad pennies, all of them. But they go prancing around like they're all shiny and clean."

"What have they done?"

"The old man's a banker. Ain't that enough?"

"I still don't see what this has to do with his son," she said. "He'll probably lose his job."

"Am I supposed to care?" Buck sat back, patting his belly. "If he's fool enough to fall for the deal I made, he deserves to lose his job." He looked over at Jesse, wearing that ugly smile again. "In the meantime, we're gonna have to learn us how to drive a brand-new tractor."

Jesse bellowed with laughter.

After that, the voices at the table were like whispers from far away. Shocked, Adah became deaf. It was one thing to have heard from others how unethically the Branches conducted their lives, but it was another thing to have to bear witness to it in person.

Would she now be seen as one of them? Or had it always been this way? Had she been seen as theirs from the moment she married Lester? Adah remembered trying to befriend some of the farmwives who lived nearby. The women had been civil but never warm, and nothing had ever developed. Adah dropped her hand into her lap and grabbed her skirt, bunching it into a ball. People were too smart to get close to a Branch.

Paying them some wary deference seemed to be the status quo. Later that night Buck said he'd been asked to be a part of a February 19 Paducah town meeting to discuss the possible construction of a floodwall. He had no expertise in construction or engineering, so Adah concluded that he'd been asked out of respect for his family history in the area and because one of his sons had apparently perished in its waters. By then three bodies had been found, one man having fallen out of a boat and two others discovered in the kitchen of their three-room house. More were sure to come.

From then onward Adah lost herself in her daily chores and playtime with Daisy, deciding that raising her with a sense of fairness and kindness was the best thing she could do to counter the Branches' lack of character. That was the only thing she could do now, until she came up with a plan for them to live elsewhere.

As both February and the floodwaters receded at an agonizingly slow pace, the Branch men had to continue to prepare for the next season's crops, some of the time allowing Adah to help. As bad as it was to exist in the same space as the men (Mabel's company was little better), the fields provided fresh air for both Adah and Daisy. Especially since the family hadn't left the farm yet except to attend makeshift church services.

Outside, Adah could breathe. On the porch, as she stretched her back, she looked out to the dawn—its blossoming colors of blue and salmon and silver; its cool, crisp air that spoke of new beginnings. Pulling her coat closer, she exhaled a long frosty breath as if she were releasing demons, and she allowed herself to briefly relish the glory of a rising sun over the hazy fields. Those moments provided only a brief reprieve from the torment of her entrapment, however, and each day she awoke with renewed purpose, racking her brain for a way out.

The day the Harper boy, Ben, came to deliver the new tractor, Adah lingered outside in hopes of saying something to the man, who was young, still baby faced, and had dressed well for the occasion in a suit. He had the wide-eyed look of someone whose life loomed ahead as full and sweet as June days to come, and it wrenched Adah's heart to observe his obvious excitement. Even his hands looked fresh and innocent. Ben

Harper had no idea he was soon to receive a swipe from Buck Branch's poisonous claws.

Adah longed to whisper to him, *Don't do this. Buck won't buy no matter what*, but there was never an opportunity, and when Ben Harper left, all smiles, she was left with a sadness she couldn't suppress.

Only two kindly women had come by to deliver condolence casseroles, and one lady, once she learned the flood had left Daisy and Adah with nothing, came back with some hand-me-down clothing and shoes she had packed inside an old and faded needlepoint bag. She looked friendly but declined Adah's invitation to come inside.

"Thank you so very much," Adah said as she opened the top of the bag and glanced inside, where she could see a flowered housedress, some walking oxford shoes, and more things underneath. "I'll take the clothes upstairs and bring the bag back down to you."

"No, of course not, honey. You go on and keep the bag, too."

Adah held it close. Any small possession was now a precious thing. "But it's so nice."

"It was a donation, came in. Some folks' trash is another man's treasure, or some such. And I couldn't think of anyone who needed something nice as much as you."

"Thank you." Before the woman left, Adah asked her, "Do you know Chuck Lerner?"

The woman nodded, and Adah fetched the jacket, which she had laundered, ironed, and folded. "Please return it to him with my deepest gratitude."

"Will do."

Adah whispered to the woman, "Do you think you could get ahold of a doll? Any ole doll would do."

Flipping her coat collar up against the wind, the woman looked hesitant but eventually said, "For the girl, yes. I'll try my best." She turned to leave, then swiveled back, giving Adah a strange stare, one of pure sizing up. "You're not like them, are you?"

Adah only gulped, afraid to answer but grateful for the woman's words. She had the feeling that Father Sparrow's spirit had guided the woman to her. With an aching chest, she thanked him in her heart. She also thanked her hardworking parents, who had taught her right from wrong.

The woman gazed down at the jacket she held in her hands. "Nice job on the jacket, by the way."

One day Adah found Mabel in her favorite parlor chair, knitting. Gathering her strength, she said with determination, "Mabel, may I have a moment of your time?"

Mabel looked up and waited.

"Daisy needs new shoes. She's outgrown the pair she's been wearing. I was thinking I'd borrow the truck or the car and go to town."

Mabel dropped the knitting in her lap and gazed upon Adah with disdain. "She has new shoes, those hand-me-downs, isn't that right? I don't like taking charity, but you done took it, didn't you?"

"They don't fit right, Mabel. Her old pair is getting too small, and the shoes given to us are way too big. She needs to wear shoes that fit her feet right. It could cause damage—"

"Damage?" Mabel picked up her knitting again and stabbed the needle in and out, in and out. "How dare you talk to me about damage when the town is near ruint and my son hasn't been found? You know nothing about *damage*. You talk to me about *damage*?"

"I'm talking about the girl's well-being, about his daughter. Your granddaughter, Mabel." Adah shot a glance toward the window. "The men are out there working. They know the farm must go on, their work must go on. People are getting back to their houses now, and they're talking about rebuilding. At least that's what we heard in church. Daisy's life must go on, too."

"Hers, yes. That seems to be all you care about." Mabel's eyes looked as if they could shoot flames. "Lord knows I'm the only woman in this household who's grieving for Lester."

Adah steadied her voice. "I am grieving for Lester, too. But I feel the best thing I can do for him right now is look after his daughter. I can alter the clothes that don't fit, but I can't fix the shoes."

Mabel batted her eyes a few times. "No businesses have opened again yet. Where do you reckon you could find shoes for a little girl at a time like this?"

"I was thinking about seeing what the Red Cross has to offer, or maybe the churches have been collecting things?"

"You ain't going out of this house begging for charity! We always done taken care of our own, and we ain't gonna start asking for handouts now. It's embarrassing you took clothes and shoes already. If I'd have known what you was up to, I'd have put an end to it, but I didn't want no scene in front of that lady done come out here." She pulled in a ragged-sounding breath. "You cain't understand people like us. And never will. I knew it the first time I laid eyes on you. Knew Lester was making a big mistake."

Ignoring that comment, Adah said, "What do you expect me to do? Let her go barefooted? I only want what's best for the girl."

A strange resolve entered Mabel's eyes. "That girl is fine. You go and spoil her with every little thing she thinks she needs or wants, and you'll ruin her, turn her into a brat. Believe you me, that's not going to happen in this house."

"I've never wanted to spoil her or turn her into a brat."

"We done seen your influence. We sure has. And it's gonna stop."

"Are you refusing shoes for your granddaughter?"

Mabel dropped the knitting. "You ain't too bright, are you? You best leave well enough alone."

During the day, Adah helped the men with the seedbeds, while at night she slept with Daisy tucked in at her side, the girl sleeping soundly, having not once cried for her father or even barely mentioned him.

"Where's Daddy?" she finally asked one night as Adah was reading a book, one that Adah had found in the bottom of the needlepoint bag. *The Cat Who Went to Heaven*, based on an old Japanese tradition, taught a gentle lesson about compassion and goodness. It contained lovely illustrations, too. Obviously the nice lady had intended it for Daisy.

Adah rested her hand on the page, then closed the book and turned Daisy around to face her.

"Honey, I have to tell you a sad truth. Your daddy's not coming back, and I know that's a difficult thing to hear. Most people would say he's gone on to a better world, up in heaven. That's what they tell you in church. But the truth is, we don't know for sure. It's nice to think of him in some better place, though, isn't it?"

Daisy shrugged, and she looked down. "Daddy was mean."

Adah blinked hard. "Why do you say that?"

"He hit you."

Adah sighed. "Yes, he did." There was no use in denying it; Daisy had seen. "People do bad things sometimes, but it doesn't mean they don't love you. Your father loved me and he certainly loved you, I'm sure of that. And now he's looking down on us from what we can only hope is a better place."

"Can he come back?"

"No. No, he can't come back."

Daisy shrugged again.

"I'm sure you miss him."

Daisy said, with no expression on her face, "Can we finish the book now?"

"Of course."

After that, Daisy had spoken no more about him. Adah lay awake wondering about Daisy's reaction and also about the scant appearance of friends and supporters for the Branch family during their time of loss. People had always spoken to the family at church, remaining somewhat distant but polite. The Branches were polite in return and then complained during the drive home. Buck had once fumed that a woman had brought her baby into the sanctuary and the infant had cried during the sermon, and Jesse often made fun of an extremely shy young man who attended with his grandmother, calling him "that dimwit."

But the Branches kept that side of themselves hidden as best they could. How many people really knew them? Why had there been no gathering of people offering comfort, no clusters of women coming over to cook, no men offering to help Buck and Jesse in the fields during this difficult time? Had the Branches turned away charity before and so no one offered it this time? Or was there something else? What did they know that Adah didn't?

After the fields were prepared, Jesse and Buck often disappeared during the day. Adah overheard them talking one night, gleaning enough to realize that the men were going out on a boat in search of Lester. It seemed that the flame of hope, even one so tiny, was too intense to smother.

One day Buck and Jesse returned from searching, clumped inside to the kitchen, and looked past Adah to Mabel. Buck simply shook his head.

Mabel grasped the edge of the worktable in the kitchen. "I need to find my son. I need to put his soul to rest proper."

Adah had been cutting up an apple as a snack for Daisy. Her hand stilled. So the men had been looking for Lester's *body*. So they *had* lost hope of finding him alive.

Buck said, "We ain't giving up."

"We ain't giving up, never," Jesse added.

Mabel breathed out. "I want him to have the finest gravestone in the county."

"Don't you worry about it none. We'll find him and return him to his maker, alright." Buck turned to leave the room and suddenly seemed to realize that Adah was in the kitchen, too. She handed Daisy the apple slices on a small plate and then looked up. Buck had stopped dead in his tracks, and his back had stiffened. "This is all your fault."

An ire she couldn't suppress rose in Adah. Not this time. It was out before she knew it. "The flood wasn't my fault."

The old man caught her eyes in a stare as squeezing as a vise. "Did I ask you a question?"

"You made an unfair accusation."

He pointed his finger. "Listen here. Don't you never talk back to me, you hear me? It's bad enough we have to give you a roof over your head cuz you don't have another goddamn soul willing to take you in, but I'm sure as hell not going to listen to your comments about anything. I don't give a rat's ass about your opinions, neither."

Adah zipped her lips.

Buck made as if to move away; then he spun back and laid his harshest stare on her again. "A funny thing we saw today. Looked like your old milk cow out loose roaming around down close as we could get to your farm."

Adah almost gasped.

"Funny thing the cow you was aiming to rescue survived, but Les didn't, 'specially since the cow was supposed to be down by the river with you."

Adah scrambled. "Don't cows swim?"

He squinted. "I reckon so. Maybe. But it sure casts some doubt on your story, don't it?"

Desperate to not appear rattled, Adah asked, "Did you bring the cow back? Les and I were hoping to find her and the mules after the flood passed."

Buck barked, "You think I care about a cow at a time like this?"

Adah simply looked away.

"I ain't seen too much sadness from you, like one would 'spect from a grieving widow."

Turning back, Adah met his gaze. Shakier souls would've wilted under his scrutiny, but Adah faced it straight on. "I grieve in private."

"You grieve not at all," he said. "You look all fine and dandy to me. Look like the cat that swallowed the canary, if you ask me. You're as slinky and crafty as those barn cats out there, eking out a life from stalking mice and birds."

"Scaredy-cat," Daisy said out of the blue as she picked up a slice of apple and plopped it into her mouth.

The hair on Adah's arms lifted. Where had Daisy heard that expression? Even though Adah had tried to conceal her fears and worry around Daisy, had she been too transparent?

Adah recalled one day when she'd been sewing a romper for Daisy and had lost track of the time. When Lester came in from the fields, the meal wasn't ready. He stomped into the house and took one look at her as she abruptly remembered the time, set aside the sewing, and rose from sitting in front of the machine.

His face full of scorn, Les said, "You care more about her than you do about me." Daisy was a toddler then and had just learned how to stand without holding on to furniture or someone's hand. Adah glanced at the girl as she lifted herself to stand, and, seemingly oblivious to the tension in the house, the toddler beamed a smile of self-satisfaction, seeking Adah's approval. For a moment, it was just the two of them, intertwined against the enemy. Adah had to tear her eyes away.

By then she should've learned to keep her mouth shut, but there were times when the urge to defend herself burst through her carefully constructed wall of reserve. "She's a child. She needs more."

Les's face went tomato red, and he breathed like an inhuman beast. He looked ridiculous, and she had to tamp down a grin.

"I need more!" Les shouted. "Lately I don't get nothing from you."

Unconsciously she shook her head, grateful that the education her parents and Father Sparrow had provided allowed her to speak correctly more often than not. She quipped, "If you never get nothing, that means you get something."

Les looked confused for a moment, then his expression quickly turned. "Don't be smart with me."

"Not to worry. I haven't made a smart move since I met you."

He raised his arm. And that was the first time she remembered cowering. He had taught her to cower. "Scaredy-cat," he said, smiling deviously.

Could Daisy remember back that far? Were the most powerful memories of our childhoods the bad ones?

Buck's booming voice brought her back to the present. He pointed at Daisy. "Now we're talking. Now you're talking like the Branch you are. You better believe she's a scaredy-cat, one that's scared for a damn good reason."

Face burning, Adah summoned her willpower and held her tongue.

She didn't think it could get worse, but later over dinner, Buck asked her out of the blue, "How're you planning to earn your keep 'round here?"

Her fork nearly fell out of her hand. She had to remain here with Daisy until she could hatch a plan. Trying to appear unfazed, she said, "I'm looking after Daisy. And I'll help even more in the fields, if you like. Les and I worked together some of the time. I know a bit about tobacco farming."

Buck stabbed a piece of pork roast and stuffed it in his mouth. Still chewing, he said, "Is that all? That don't bring in any money, now, does it?"

Adah searched her brain. She must do something to earn her keep. The Branches weren't hurting for money; they simply wanted to make her as uncomfortable as possible. Then she remembered the woman who'd complimented her work after she'd laundered Chuck Lerner's jacket. "I could take in laundry."

"That's it?"

Adah's thoughts spun. "That's all I can come up with at the moment. But I'll give it more thought . . ."

Buck snapped his fingers. "Come to think of it, that ain't such a bad idea. You can take over doing our laundry, too. Then we can fire that old colored washerwoman we been using." Buck gave a slow blink. "Yep, I reckon you could take in laundry."

"I'll get to work on it right away. I can put up a note at church and ask around, too."

"You do that," he said, a bit of spittle at the corner of his mouth.

That night her mind fought sleep as it had been doing every night since the flood. The cow swirled in her brain. She doubted Buck or Jesse had ever noticed the cow before, but perhaps they had, and since the cow had never been branded, no one could ever prove it was the same one. It was nothing, she told herself. But the search for Lester's body terrified her. Although if Lester was ever found, it would be in the water or where water had been. The dent in his temple could be blamed on debris having struck him while he was being swept away. It would corroborate her story rather than contradict it.

Only then did she remember something else Buck had said: *Looked like your old milk cow out loose roaming around down close as we could get to your farm.* Your farm. Of course. As Lester's legal wife, she would inherit at least part of it, unless Les had a will that denied it to her. But Lester had never mentioned a will, and Adah thought the chances were slim to none that he had executed one she hadn't known about.

The farm, useless as it was now, could still grow corn and other crops less labor intensive than tobacco. They'd always grown corn in the lowest of the lowlands anyway. She would probably own some of the property, which had to be worth something, even if it did flood from time to time. It would explain why the Branch family had been keeping her around. All along Adah had wondered about that and then had concluded that it would reflect poorly on the Branches if they threw their homeless, widowed daughter-in-law out on the street. Mabel cared about appearances, and besides, she disliked looking after Daisy. Adah was useful as a caregiver for the girl. Also, if they wanted to someday pin Lester's death on her, they would need to keep her close at hand.

But the farm—that made even more sense. No doubt at some point they'd ask her to sign over her portion because they could use it and she couldn't. It was true; she couldn't run a farm on her own, and the house would probably be unfit for living. They would probably try to convince her of that.

As she lay there at night, the house talked to her; it moaned as if some benevolent creature had been trapped in it. Perhaps it was the good soul of a former family member who had wanted to escape the stigma of being a Branch. During harvest time, the Branches had always hired colored field-workers, who dotted their fields, backs bent, the sun pounding down. Everywhere they went, these colored workers were paid almost nothing, but it was widely known that the Branch farms paid even less than smaller spreads.

Two years earlier, when one worker had dared to question his wages, the man and his family were visited at their dilapidated shack a few days later by mounted Klansmen wearing white masks and robes and waving burning torches. They hadn't set anything on fire, but the message was clear. The *Paducah Sun-Democrat* published an article about the rare KKK incident but didn't name any suspects, and yet it was widely known—Adah had heard it whispered in church—the Branch clan meant to send the direst of messages: *Don't no one ever cross us.*

The problem with still, dark nights was their witchy emptiness, which allowed all manner of fears to form and grow.

Chapter Seven

A late-February thaw brought a few unexpectedly warm days. One morning, when the day broke, sunlight beamed through the lacy curtains and filled the bedroom Adah and Daisy shared with a yellow glow.

After breakfast Adah let Daisy play on the front porch with her doll, which had been given to the girl the day before by a woman who also came bearing even more hand-me-down clothing and shoes for both Adah and Daisy. Finally Daisy had a pair of right-sized shoes: black patent leather ballet flats with a strap.

Adah, despite protests from Mabel, helped clean the kitchen and wash and dry dishes. As she glanced out the window and saw that Daisy was no longer on the porch, she quickly put aside the coffee cup she'd been drying and went straight to the front door. Stepping out, she turned her head frantically in both directions, then breathed again when she saw Daisy trudging toward the house, cradling her doll.

Adah rushed down the steps. "Where did you go, honey? You weren't supposed to leave the porch. I was worried."

Daisy's perfect little forehead folded down as Adah reached her. Daisy said, "Dolly fell in the mud, and now she's dirty."

Taking the doll from Daisy's muddied hands, Adah saw that its faded blue polka-dot dress was smudged with brown sludge. Adah studied the doll's solemn embroidered face. "Did you drop her?"

"Yes, but it was an accident."

Adah sighed. "I know it was, sweetie. I think I can get her clean again. But you shouldn't have gone . . ." Adah then noticed that Daisy's shoes were coated in brown sludge, too. Smears and clods also ran down the front of her dress, where Daisy must have tried to rub her hands clean.

Adah's mistake hit her like a flat wave; she should not have turned her back for a moment. The sunlight and warm air had been too tempting for a little girl, and now Daisy was a mess.

Mabel would be furious. "Come here," she said and led Daisy up the porch steps, set the doll on the porch floor, then helped her out of the shoes. Crouching down, Adah used the hem of her apron and tried to brush off the partially dried mud from Daisy's dress.

The door flung open. "What's this I see?" Mabel said, but Adah kept her head down and continued trying to remove as much mud as she could, hoping to limit what might fall off onto the floor inside. Daisy didn't answer, either.

Mabel barked, "You done thrown that doll down into the mud?"

"No, she fell," Daisy answered after only a moment's hesitation.

"And look at you now!"

Adah glanced up. "It was my doing. I let her outside because it was so nice, but I didn't realize how much mud was still around."

"What you been teaching her?" Then to Daisy, she hollered, "You pick up that doll right now. Someone done given you something nice, and you best be grateful for it. The same with what you're wearing. I see you disrespecting gifts again, and you'll be getting a beating. You hear?"

Daisy shied away like a hunted animal. Adah put her hands on Daisy's upper arms, holding her steady and sending a message as best she could. *It's going to be okay.*

Mabel's breaths emerged in huffs. "I got a hundred things to do this morning, and now I gotta run you a bath."

"I'll do that, Mabel," Adah said calmly.

Daisy looked down at her feet. "I don't want to take a bath."

Having done all she could, Adah stood and took Daisy's hand. "I'll take care of this," she said to Mabel's folded face. She handed the doll to Daisy, who, still scowling, took the doll and touched its red yarn hair. Her face looked as tortured as Adah felt. "Let's go inside now," Adah whispered.

"I took a bath last night!" Daisy whined.

Mabel's hand whipped down, grabbed Daisy's arm, jerked the girl away from Adah, and then shook her with a force that drained all color from Daisy's face and hung her mouth open. Her eyes were wide with shock. It happened so fast. Mabel had a brutal grip on the girl, while Adah stood there in stunned disbelief.

"You don't never talk back to your elders," Mabel yelled at Daisy. "You hear me?"

Daisy seemed unable to speak, but Adah soon found her voice. "Mabel, stop. You're being too rough."

Mabel jerked Daisy one more time and glared at Adah. "How dare you question me and what I do? I'm teaching this girl here to be an obedient child." She shook Daisy again. "You let her talk back like that, and there'll be no end to it. You gotta be in charge, and obviously you ain't. You let her go outside in the mud like a wild animal. I reckon I gotta be the one in charge, or you'll ruin her. And I'm not letting the only thing left of my dead son get ruint."

Adah resisted the powerful urge to push Mabel away and take Daisy in her arms. "Please, Mabel. Let her go."

"Let her go? To you? So you can go on treating her like a baby?"

"She's just a little girl. Like I said, it was my fault. I must not have made it clear enough that she wasn't supposed to leave the porch." Mabel seemed to be wavering, if only a tiny bit. "I'm so sorry, Mabel. It was my doing. I wasn't watching her as well as I should have."

"You can say that again," Mabel fumed and then drew in a deep breath, finally dropping Daisy's arm. "I see one tiny smear of mud inside my house, and there'll be hell to pay. Got that?"

"Of course, of course," Adah said to Mabel, although she couldn't tear her eyes away from Daisy's face. Daisy didn't speak, instead simply stared ahead into nothing, a look of fear on her face that rent Adah's heart.

Throughout the process of bathing and re-dressing her, Daisy's expression didn't change, and she refused to answer any of Adah's questions or respond to her gentle touch. What could Adah do? As she slowly and gently bathed Daisy, memories of her own parents flooded in. Even an admonishing stare had been punishment enough when Adah had done wrong. Her parents had been gentle souls, her mother sickly and barren ever since Adah's birth, but still she made evening meals a celebration every night, during which her father, a postal worker, relayed the events of his day and Adah relived her time at school. Her mother had perished from the flu first, and within days, her father had fallen, too, and Adah often thought back on the inevitability of it. Her mother had been susceptible to every illness, and her father's purpose in life had been looking after her, protecting her. Once his wife was gone, he couldn't push forward.

Why hadn't Daisy been born into a family of loving, sweet souls like hers?

As the floodwaters had slowly receded from Paducah and other ravaged cities, towns, and farmlands, so had any of Adah's hope that this family could form a loving home for the young girl. Was this to be Adah's punishment? To watch Daisy's eyes slowly turn icy and hard like dark stones in the snow? To witness the ruination of a pure little soul and be unable to stop it or undo the damage?

No! Adah recoiled.

After the bath was done and Daisy was clothed again in a laundered dress and pinafore, the girl sat on the edge of the bed while Adah slowly cleaned her shoes with a cloth.

"I was bad," Daisy said.

Relieved that Daisy had spoken at all, Adah moved closer and looked her in the eyes. "You weren't. You're still learning."

"Because I'm bad."

Adah sat on the bed next to Daisy, putting an arm across the girl's shoulders. "You're not. You're a good, sweet girl. Maybe you made a little mistake, but you're still—"

Daisy quickly jerked her gaze to Adah's face. "You were bad."

Managing to swallow while also gazing into Daisy's eyes, Adah searched for words, then asked, "Why are you saying that?"

After a sigh, Daisy said, "Daddy said it."

"He said I was bad?"

A moment later, Daisy nodded.

Adah rubbed Daisy's back. "Your daddy was wrong. He made a mistake about that."

How to explain something to a little girl, something she should never have had to witness?

"And your grandmother made a mistake today as well. She shouldn't have done what she did."

Daisy shrugged. Adah glanced at the doll, which Daisy had gathered into her lap.

"I have an idea," Adah said. "Maybe we can make Dolly some new clothes. Would you like that?"

Daisy shrugged again, but her distance was waning, and she was coming back into the moment. Adah could see it in the loosening of her face and posture.

Daisy let her gaze fall gently on the doll now, and she touched it where a heart would be. "Dolly doesn't want to live here."

Adah whispered weakly, "She doesn't? Why not?"

"She doesn't like it here."

Adah asked "Why not?" although she knew the answer. It was important for Daisy to be able to say these things, to talk to someone who would listen. Adah had watched Father Sparrow counsel church members and had witnessed the benefits when he'd managed to get them to open up and speak of their miseries. She'd seen how even one gentle, caring ear could make a difference. It was about all Adah could do now. Until . . . she figured out how to get Daisy away from here.

Daisy shrugged again. "She doesn't like Grandma and Grandpa. She wants to go to another house with you and me. She wants to leave here."

Adah couldn't have said it better. Determination to remove Daisy from the Branch house was turning into desperation, but Adah had to keep her head.

Now that she knew she might be the legal owner of at least part of the flooded farm, that prospect shone like a beacon of hope. If the farm could be sold and Adah received her share, it could be her means to get away from the Branches and make a new start with Daisy. Or, if the house hadn't been completely destroyed, perhaps it could be cleaned up and made livable again. Maybe the Branches or a judge could be persuaded to let her share of the farm include the house. Then perhaps she and Daisy could live there again, just the two of them. Perhaps Adah could find work in town and lease her part of the fields to other farmers.

The farm was the key to a different life, one centered around Daisy. The only reason the Branches were letting her stay had to be the farm, too. Most likely they wanted it all, and she had to stick around long enough to put up a fight. She had to wait it out and be as little trouble as possible while still protecting Daisy as much as she could.

Every time Adah closed her eyes, she relived the brutal force Mabel had used against her granddaughter, and reexperienced the horrified expression on Daisy's face. Buck's words were almost as toxic as Mabel's actions. Daisy needed to be removed from this situation as soon as possible. But Adah had nowhere to go, no safe place to take the girl, and, more importantly, no money and no job. She'd survived with little or nothing before, but that was before she'd become a mother and had a child to take care of. She needed some luck, and then she could make a break. The farm was her best hope.

As February turned into a torturous early March, the old church building reopened, and the Sunday service was Adah's only outing. Yet a sense of wary distance existed between the church members and the Branch clan. The congregation looked like an alliance of those who'd rather ignore anything that didn't directly involve them. Just let it alone. They would carry on, unbothered by the bone-dusty history of the Branches. Adah slid her weary eyes over the lot of them and found no glimmers of hope.

During the first service held after the storm, she went through the motions of praying, singing hymns, and listening to the sermon, while at the same time dreading what was to come that afternoon. After church, all of the Branches would be heading over to Adah's old house to see what, if anything, could be salvaged. Buck and Jesse had agreed to take a break from the laborious process of preparing the main fields for transplanting. Even with the tractor making it decidedly easier, it was still grueling work.

Adah doubted that anything not in ruin would be found at the house, but she had a plan. Lester had kept his cash in a locked box in the secretary, and before they'd taken Daisy over to his parents' farm the night the flood hit, he'd grabbed it and put it in the truck cab. With a little luck, Adah would find it in what remained of the old truck, if it hadn't been swept away. Her goal was to be the first to check its interior and grab the box without being noticed. Now convinced that she had to somehow engage the help of a lawyer, she needed to come up with the money to pay for it. She had to find out if she really did own any of the farm and, even more importantly, if she had any rights to custody of Daisy—or if she could fight for it. Adah had never adopted Daisy and might have no legal leg to stand on. Whether Adah liked it or not, she would have to return to the scene of her crime, with Jesse and Buck beside her.

Although there was a chill in the air, the sun was a bright white coin in the sky, and Adah cracked her window as she and Daisy sat in the back seat of the Branches' four-door Dodge sedan, reserved for use only on Sundays. Back at the house, they all changed out of church clothing, and Mabel decided to stay home and start Sunday supper instead of seeing the place where her son had perished. Now, with some burlap bags and empty crates in the truck bed, Adah had to ride in the cab, holding Daisy in her lap, squeezed between Buck and Jesse.

"Did you lock up your house that night?" Buck suddenly asked. His words had the feel of sharp little stones, and it was obvious he had to force himself to address her at all. But he had said *your house*. Adah registered that.

"No," she breathed out. "We hadn't gotten to that point yet."

As soon as the farm appeared in the distance, Adah spotted the house. With all its windows broken, the front door hanging open on one hinge, and debris everywhere, it was a pitiful survivor of nature's wrath. No one spoke as they took in the sight.

Then Daisy said flatly, "Is Daddy here?"

No one answered.

Adah finally whispered "No, not here" in Daisy's ear as Jesse brought the truck to a halt in front of the carcass of what had once been their home.

In a rush, it all came back—how this place had stolen her life, her happiness, her hope, and finally had taken her innocence with one reflexive swing of a shovel that would leave its scourge on her soul for the rest of her life.

And then elation—Les's truck was still there. It listed to one side and was jammed against the house as though the flood had pinned it and kindly kept it there for her.

After Buck and Jesse stepped out of their truck, Adah slid out with Daisy, then stood looking at the house as if still absorbing the damage. Both Buck and Jesse were climbing the porch steps and entering the house, so Adah quickly turned her attention to Les's truck. Despite its position up against the house, she would be able to get inside by way of the passenger-side door.

She grabbed a burlap bag and searched the soggy, mud-covered interior that smelled of mold, and there it was, wedged under the seat. Glancing up at the house, she saw that the men were inside, and so she grabbed the locked black metal cash box and put it in the bottom of the bag. While Daisy stood waiting for her, she looked around for something to place on top of it. The trick would be to hide the cash box until she could retrieve it later. On the ground were pieces of sodden lumber, tree branches, assorted trash, and a crumpled soggy blanket that didn't belong to them. Nothing of use. Nothing to take. The burlap bags she'd packed on the night of the flood were nowhere to be seen. Quickly changing plans, she pulled the box back out and then slid it under the seat of the truck they'd come in. Tonight, after everyone went to bed, she could slip outside and retrieve it.

Everything both outside and inside the house was covered in brown and black sludge. When she went in the front door, the smell of mold and mildew assaulted her, and she told Daisy to remain on the porch. As they had expected, there was very little to salvage. Most of the dishes, lamps, and glassware were shattered, and the curtains and slipcovered sofa were stinking and unfit even to wash. The plastered walls were crumbling, and the wood floor had buckled. She found a coffee cup and some of her pots and pans and placed those in the bag. Buck and Jesse had been surveying the damage in the bedrooms and emerged wearing scowls, bringing only Les's shotgun with them.

"Nothing else," Buck said simply. "You find anything worth keeping?" Again, he addressed her as if it were torture.

"Just a few things from the kitchen."

"You go on and keep looking around. I'm fixing to walk the property." He turned toward Jesse. "See if there's anything in that truck out there."

Remaining in the house, Adah looked outside to check on Daisy and then quickly assessed the rest of the rooms. She found her brush and comb and decided they could be soaked and cleaned. The mattresses were foul smelling and waterlogged, as were the remaining clothing and bedding. Knowing it was probably hopeless, Adah searched for Daisy's bracelets but found no trace of them. She pulled open some drawers, and then a thought hit her. *The attic.* Perhaps the water hadn't risen to the level of the attic, which Les had used for storage.

Adah climbed the steps and pushed back the slab of wood that covered the opening, then lifted herself and, crouching over because the ceiling was low, stepped onto the wooden beams.

The attic was dry. She found a large basket of fabric scraps, a broken chair, and Daisy's cradle. She'd forgotten it was up here. Thinking Daisy would like it for her dolls, Adah stepped closer. The cradle was too large to get down on her own, but she managed to move it to the top of the stairs, then spotted a crumpled burlap bag pushed into the far corner of the attic, where the ceiling was even lower. It was so far in the shadows one might never know it was there. From a distance the bag looked empty, but Adah decided to investigate.

She had to cross over the rafters on her haunches, crablike, to reach the bag. Inside was a small brown box full of letters, all of them addressed to Betsy Branch, Les's first wife and Daisy's mother. Adah pondered whether or not to take them. Why were the letters up here? Quickly thumbing through, she found that almost all had come from the same woman, Doris McNeil. Perhaps Betsy's mother or a dear friend? Adah slowly closed the box, taking it with her when she descended the stairs. Perhaps one day when she was older, Daisy would want to read the letters.

Back outside, Buck was nowhere to be seen, but Jesse helped her retrieve the cradle and basket of fabric scraps from the attic. He put them in the truck bed, where he had also placed some things from the barn.

While Daisy played on the porch, Adah and Jesse waited for Buck.

"What's in the box?" he asked her. Adah had placed the small wooden box full of letters inside the larger basket of scraps.

"Nothing," she lied. "But it's a nice box. I think it belonged to Daisy's mother, and so I'm taking it for Daisy."

Jesse asked "Where'd Les keep his money?" as he shaded his face with the flat of his bearlike hand, watching Buck walking back toward them. Obviously Jesse had conducted a search inside for cash but had come up empty handed.

"I don't know," Adah answered. Jesse had no idea that she'd found another box—the cash box—and had hidden it from them.

Jesse harrumphed. "Figures that my brother would have kept it from you."

She ignored that, and as Buck moved closer, she asked, "What now?"

Jesse stared out over the farm. "We'll have to come back and clean out all the junk, then you can scrub the place down. House is still in one piece. Once it gets aired out, someone could probably live here again."

Someone? Adah sensed an opening. Maybe she could negotiate with Jesse. As awful as he could be, he did seem the most reasonable. Adah said, "Do you think Daisy and I could ever come back here?"

He stared at her hard, eyes turning to slits. "You and Daisy?"

"This was our home. Her home. If the house becomes livable, of course we'd want to come back."

Jesse lifted his head, and his lips curled in contempt. "You best put thoughts like that out of your head. You think we're going to let his murderer live in Lester's house?"

Murderer? It was the first time any of the Branches had actually spoken the word. The sound of it like abject terror. *Just ignore it,* she told herself. *They have nothing on you.* But hope fell from Adah's chest into her gut. Bringing up ownership of the farm with any of the Branches was out of the question now. Even so, a small sense of promise surged through her. Jesse thought the house could be lived in again.

She followed Jesse's gaze as he looked past her then. Buck was approaching, carrying some things. As he drew closer she could see that he'd found a saddle and, in his other hand, something that chilled her blood. The shovel.

"Found these caught up in a tree over there near the property line," Buck said as he heaved the saddle into the truck bed and then slid in the shovel.

"Anything else?" Jesse asked while Adah tried to slow her breathing and squelch the panic tightening the skin all over her body.

Buck said, "Not a damn thing."

The drive home was tedious and tense, and it seemed no one had the urge to speak, not even Daisy, who fell asleep in Adah's lap.

As soon as they arrived back at the Branch home, Mabel lurched down the porch steps. Her face tear-streaked and pinched, she scurried to the driver's side of the truck as they pulled up.

"What happened?" Buck asked through the open window.

"Lester," Mabel said with a sound like a moan. "They found Lester."

Chapter Eight

The morgue door opened, and the first thing to hit Adah was the smell. Beneath the antiseptic overlay was the unmistakable scent of death and decay, one she had never smelled before, but she recognized it for what it was. She stifled her gag reflex and forced herself to step inside the cold green-tiled walls of the morgue, which was located in the basement of police headquarters. Bright lights overhead hurt her eyes, and a buzzing sound seemed like a warning.

Jesse and Buck followed one step behind her.

As Lester's wife, she could have identified the body alone, but her brother- and father-in-law had both wanted to come and do so as well. Adah could've let them do it without her, but her survival instinct drove her to attend. If anything came up about Lester's death, she wanted to hear about it firsthand and be there to defend herself. As dangerous as it felt to go with the men, it was better than drowning in fear, waiting for them to return without knowing what had transpired.

They had ridden to town in total silence, Buck's eyes never leaving the road ahead and Jesse staring out the passenger-side window intently, as if even one glance at Adah would amount to agony.

As she moved farther inside the morgue, her eyes were drawn to only one thing. On a metal table, the contours of a man's body lay covered head to toe with a white sheet, that body as still as the tile floor beneath her feet.

The coroner, who wore a black suit and a concerned expression and exuded enough apprehension to make Adah's worse, waited for her to approach. When she stood before him, he introduced himself, and then he addressed only her: "Because the body spent so much time in near-freezing-cold water, it's well preserved, considering. That's not to say it's a soothing sight. I have to warn you, Mrs. Branch, identifying a body in this condition can come as a shock. It's not for the faint of heart." He gestured to Jesse and Buck. "Are you sure you don't want the male family members to identify the body?"

Adah nodded. "I'm sure."

"No shame in letting the men do it for you."

"I have to see for myself."

The coroner looked reluctant for a moment and then gave a single nod. "Alright, then."

She stood with Jesse and Buck on either side of her now, clamping her in as if with a wrench, as the coroner pulled back the sheet, exposing Lester's head and upper torso. Again, the smell of death hit her, and she rocked back on her heels. And then there were the open glassy eyes, waxy skin the color of a pale bruise, and lips an opaque purple, almost black. But his face! Oh so dreadfully familiar. Yes, it was her husband, or what was left of him. The man she had once loved, the man she had grown to despise, the man she had killed.

As if someone had reached down and pulled the pins out of her knee joints, her legs gave way and she sank into herself, slumping down, down, down, a sickness in her stomach, until a pair of arms lifted her back to her feet. Jesse released her while expelling an almost-silent disgusted snort. She had momentarily stopped breathing. Quickly she sucked in big lungfuls of air. Blinking against white stars swimming and dipping in her vision, she realized that the Branch men had identified Lester, and, taken together with her visceral response, the coroner had determined that the task required of them on this day had been completed.

A policeman escorted her to the truck and made sure she was alright before leaving her alone. Still gasping, Adah reentered the world in which she had committed the worst of all crimes. Her secret, her cross to bear. She had somehow managed to put it out of her mind most of the time, but now it was back with the fervor of a pouncing wildcat. Her humanity was in question, her very essence.

Over the course of her life, she had learned that people could hold inside the brightest peaks and the darkest pits, and there were those who straddled the break—half of them drawn to evil, half drawn to beauty. Those people could step from one side to the other and back again as if the line were as thin as a strand of hair. Her husband had been one of those people. Was she one of them, too?

She sat for what felt like hours, gazing out at the sunny, slightly breezy day, at boys riding bicycles, women strolling by pushing baby carriages, and working men eating lunches out of paper bags. A scene as peaceful and promising as this new spring day. The still-bare trees made a mesh of shadow and light on the brown ground, which was urging toward green. It seemed impossible to grasp what had happened, what she'd done.

But the world would go on and waited for no one to catch up. She would have to go on, too. And Lester's body having been found west of Paducah on the floodplain after the water receded left no reason to ever doubt her story. The facts surrounding the discovery of Lester's body had been revealed to them when they'd first arrived at the police station. It had all worked to her advantage. She should've been relieved. She should've felt safer.

So why were Jesse and Buck staying so long inside the police station?

A crushing sensation in her chest brought on rapid breathing and threatened the return of the swimming white stars, but Adah told herself to stay calm. Knowing the Branch men, they probably wanted every detail about how and where Lester's body had been found, details she didn't care to know. And still, she had the urge to lurch from the truck and go back inside the station, to bear witness to what was transpiring instead of waiting exposed and alone, a sitting duck. If anything suspicious had come up, would the policeman have led her to the truck? Would he come back with handcuffs and tell her she was being charged with murder?

Adah talked herself out of another episode of near panic. Minutes elongated, and the inside of the truck cab grew warmer, but she kept telling herself not to worry. The police would've included her if they'd had anything further to say. She was going to get away with murder.

And yet when the Branch men finally emerged, Buck's face was bloodred, and he wore a look not of grief but of rage. Jesse looked little better.

They slid inside the truck cab without a word, and Buck drove away. Adah glanced at her father-in-law once and saw that beads of sweat had gathered on his upper lip even though it was pleasant outside. Something other than the weather had clearly pervaded Buck with a mad heat.

The spring warmth was only just beginning to urge life back to the land, and the scenes beyond the window were as bleak and barren as Adah's thoughts, and yet as they drove away from the station, she started to relax.

Until halfway back to the house, when Buck let out a long stream of air Adah could feel on her arms and said, "That was quite an act you put on in there."

She gulped silently, panic already beginning to grab on to her gut again. How quickly could only a few words or a look from one of the Branches toss her like a small boat surrounded by angry seas. "What do you mean?"

"Nearly fainting and all that. Yeah, that was damn good."

Adah remained facing forward and didn't move a muscle.

"You might have fooled some idiot in there, but don't you go and think you've fooled me and Jesse." Buck released an angry huff. "What I saw in there sure weren't no comfort. No, sirree. Do you know what I saw back there?"

She shook her head.

"Any ideas? Any guesses?"

She shook her head again.

"You of all people know what I saw. What I saw looked like my son's head had been bashed in."

Adah's heart froze in midbeat.

"Them fools in there kept on saying there's no telling what Les done bumped up against while he was in the water, that all manner of things could have hit him in the head, full as it was with junk, but I don't think nothing happened to his head in the river. We Branches ain't no fools. You best believe that's not what I think happened."

"You got something to confess?" said Jesse.

Adah wouldn't answer, too afraid of the terror that her voice might reveal.

Jesse continued. "Come on, now. Ain't you heard that ole saying that confession is good for the soul?"

Adah sat still, her muscles tensed like taut wires, spine tingling, scalp tightening.

"You must think you're some smart cookie," Jesse said. "Thinking you done tricked everyone with your swooning spell back there. You're not no actress, that's for sure."

"It wasn't an act," Adah breathed out.

Jesse laughed menacingly. "Sure was a good one. If'n we'd been in there alone, I would've let you fall straight down on the floor. But then again, you might've caught yourself and saved yourself the fall, right? Somehow no harm never comes to you. Now, why's that? I wanna know. You're one lucky little bitch, ain't you?"

"It's alright, Son," Buck said with a snorting sound. "We know what happened. We saw it, didn't we? You don't have to say nothing," he said, addressing Adah now. "Today I saw what really happened to my son, and I know who did it, too. Happens to be sitting here in my truck betwixt me and my other son, happens to be living in my house that's been in the family for generations, eating my food, sleeping in one of my rooms."

Jesse interjected, "Les once told me he was sorry he'd ever married you. Said you weren't to be trusted."

Still not moving, Adah became aware of her right leg trembling. Why had Lester said that to his brother? But then again, what had she expected of a wife beater? Her husband had probably convinced himself and his family that she was a bad person; therefore, in some sick way, he could justify what he'd been doing to her. She pressed down on the ball of her foot then, willing the trembling to stop. Never show weakness to people like the Branches.

Buck went on. "Even if I cain't do nothing about it right at this moment, you best be sure that I will. Don't you never go fooling your-self that we believe your cock-and-bull story. Don't think you're making the fool out of us."

"No more lucky breaks for you," Jesse said.

And Buck finished, "Don't never go thinking you got off scot-free."

Sleep was impossible that night, and well after midnight, when all was silent except for the scratching of mice and the songs of night birds, Adah slipped out from under the covers, leaving Daisy, and tiptoed down the stairs, wearing only a nightgown. Her feet whispered across the wood floors. She was barely breathing as she eased open the front door silently and slipped like smoke to the truck, the air outside as frosty as if it were inside the morgue. Both of the Branches' dogs approached her but didn't make a sound, since they'd been trained to bark only for strangers, fire, or other dangers and to keep quiet at all other times. She reached down and scratched both dogs' heads to be certain they would sense nothing amiss and stay quiet.

After carefully and slowly opening the passenger-side door, she searched for the cash box and found it where she had placed it. It had shifted position a bit but otherwise was easy to find. Taking the box with her, she retraced her steps and hid the locked box under her bed, then lay down again next to Daisy and thought through once again what had happened and what she needed to do.

Obviously Jesse and Buck, even with their influence in the community, hadn't been able to convince the police that foul play had caused Lester's death; otherwise she would've been arrested or at least questioned. They were well connected but not enough for the police to charge someone for a crime without evidence. So she was off the hook as far as the law was concerned. But Jesse and Buck had seen what she hadn't wanted them to see, and she had no idea what they would do with that information.

Would they tell Mabel? Would they tell others of their suspicions? Would they tell Daisy? What did they have in mind for her when Buck said, *Don't never go thinking you got off scot-free*? Would they take matters into their own hands and hand out vigilante justice as they had against the farmworker who had stolen from them? Would they slit her throat in the middle of the night or stage a fatal accident?

Now at least she had the cash box, although she had no idea how much money was inside. She'd never had a key, hadn't found any keys at the house, and the police had found no possessions on Lester's body. She would have to bang it open, and how would she do that without making too much noise and calling attention to herself? Even though the money was rightfully hers, she didn't want the Branches to know about it. She would have to figure out how to break the lock later, and then, with some cash in hand, she would go to an attorney in town and get him to work on custody of Daisy and at least partial ownership of the farm. Once out of the house and with nothing proven against her, she could begin her life with Daisy anew.

"Time," she breathed out. It was only a matter of time now.

The next day, Mabel and Buck gathered themselves to drive the sedan to the funeral home in order to make plans for Lester's service. Now that a body had been found, there was no need to wait any longer. Plans were made, Adah not once being consulted.

She was sincerely pleased she didn't have to go with them. She hated funerals and funeral homes, and playing the grieving widow while so consumed with her own thoughts and plans would have been difficult at best.

Buck had made no eye contact with her since the coroner, but before he and Mabel left, he glared at her hard and said, "Nothing here means anything to you. Not even that girl you pretend to care about."

Adah rose to her full height. Buck was the kind of enemy who knew just where to strike. Accuse her of anything, but not about her feelings for Daisy. Stunned by his cruelty and surprised that it still stunned her, Adah stated firmly, "That's not true." She was showing vulnerability. She had to arrest the resentment in her voice.

"You're not her mother. Don't never forget that," Mabel said, and Adah paused. These two were capable of cruelty even on the day they would take the first steps in laying their son's body to final rest. Pain and loss made some people kind; others became even more susceptible to their own demons. They would go to the funeral home and make the necessary arrangements without fuss, never once letting even one sign of vulnerability escape from their shallow souls.

Buck turned on his heel and opened the icebox door, then took a swig of milk from the milk bottle. He said not another word to her before leaving abruptly. Mabel followed solemnly behind him.

When Buck and Mabel were gone, Jesse fired up the tractor and started a second tilling of the main tobacco fields. While he was far away and out of sight, Adah grasped the opportunity to break the lock on the cash box. She put Daisy down for a nap and found an ax in the shed, then took the box with her to the barn, set it in the straw on the ground to muffle the sound, and then swung the ax against the front of the box. The lid broke off easily.

Adah fell to her knees and pushed the lid aside. Inside, a lot of dry bills. The box had remained watertight. She counted out the bills: $122, a small fortune. She'd had no idea Lester had been able to save so much. He'd once told her he kept an emergency fund, but this amount was surprising. Another thing he'd hidden from her.

She folded the money into her apron pocket, determined to later find a good hiding spot in her room, and then half ran to the wooded part of the farm, through a thick stand of maple, ash, and buckeye trees, and finally to a small creek that crossed the corner of the property. Overhead the tree limbs and branches wove a lacy net, blocking all but occasional flashbulbs of the sun. She was alone. This would be a good place to commit a murder. Dump the body and no one would find it.

The water was running high, full of spring runoff dancing and singing over stones and carrying away debris. Now it would take the damning box away from here, so she tossed it in, saw the current catch it, and watched it float away.

Now she had money. Not as much as she still hoped to receive from the farm, but enough to take steps in the right direction. Money could make things happen. Money meant everything. It could buy her freedom from this family. Freedom for both Daisy and her. It was like the glory that preachers promised the poor and downtrodden every Sunday. Maybe now there would be mercy, even for Adah.

Chapter Nine

Lester Branch's funeral was held in the sanctuary of First Baptist Church, a closed-casket service, followed by burial in Oak Grove Cemetery in a family plot that had held the remains of Branch men, women, and children for almost ninety years. Lester was to be buried beside his first wife, Betsy.

A couple of days earlier, after Buck and Mabel had returned from the funeral home, Mabel had cried for an hour and then appeared to bury her grief with baking, cooking, and cleaning. She had said to Adah, "My son's funeral is in two days, and I don't want no trouble. As far as anyone else is concerned, we're a family. You act right or there'll be hell to pay."

So there was Mabel's secret. She worked hard to paint a rosy picture to the outside world, hiding the fact that the family was awash in strife and probably always had been. Competition between brothers and wary treatment from the outside world aside, what else was hidden under the farmhouse façade? What other secrets?

Adah wandered through the funeral like a lost lamb. Most of the attendees—church members, businessmen from town and their wives, and farm families from the surrounding area—acted as if they were frightened of something, and no one spoke much to Adah. While some lent comfort to Mabel, Jesse, and Buck, Adah kept her head down, almost shaking. By all appearances she was with the family; they were at peace and she was one of them, for the moment.

It was a glorious afternoon. The skies were a charged blue, and a cool breeze carried the sweet scent of early spring and the surging river sweeping down the wide Ohio River valley. After the service, the funeral procession made haste to the grave site, while above them birds sang. It was the first perfect spring day, and yet a sticky film of perspiration encased Adah.

The cemetery grass was still brown with only a few hints of the green to come. Headstones made of fieldstone, slate, limestone, marble, and granite leaned and reached in orderly rows, along with the occasional obelisk and statue. All of the mourners had dressed in black, even Daisy—Adah had sewn her a black pinafore. Everyone had to walk to the Branch section, where a large rectangular hole had been opened in the ground next to the grave of Betsy Branch.

Betsy's blue granite gravestone gave the dates of her birth and death, her name, and then simply, "Loving wife and mother." Lester's matching gravestone had been ordered but had not arrived yet.

With the Branch family standing together and a gathering of mourners behind them and at their sides, the minister shared his final words on the matter of Lester Branch's demise and asked Adah to come forward. She moved as if sleepwalking, letting go of Daisy's hand and stepping up to the grave's edge.

After her husband's body was lowered into the ground, Adah tossed the first clumps of crumbling sable-brown earth on the casket, willing time to pass quickly, needing this to be over—this last step in saying goodbye to her husband. Despite her resolve, her hands were trembling so badly that a woman moved forward from the gathering of mourners to put her arm around Adah's shoulders.

"Tough to lose a husband," the woman whispered in Adah's ear. "I lost mine, too."

Adah turned her head and gazed into the weathered face of an older woman who, although dressed primly, looked capable of kindness. Smile lines tracked her face, and her soft olive-green eyes were surrounded by fleshy lids. The woman had probably once been beautiful.

She had long, tapered fingers like that of a pianist. Elegant fingers, and hands that had seen little harsh sun or hard work. Did this woman own a piano? During the cleanup, more than 2,500 of the estimated 3,200 pianos in the city were found in ruin—only one of the devastating effects of the flood—and would be dumped on the east side of the Illinois Central roundhouse. All that music, silenced.

Adah stood still for a moment under the touch of a human hand. Then, as she looked closer, she recognized the woman. She lived on the same road as the Branches in a large stately farmhouse surrounded by lovely lands. Adah took a step back from the grave, and the woman seemed to instinctively know to steer Adah farther away, that she had had enough. The service was ending anyway.

"Thank you for your kindness," Adah finally said.

"Of course, of course," the woman said and took a small step back while still holding Adah's arm, then glanced at the Branches. Was she surprised that no one in the family had come forward to offer comfort to the wife of the deceased? Was Mabel's attempt at making them look like a happy family failing?

Gathering her wits, her thoughts in disarray, Adah said, "You live near us, don't you? I've seen you out in front of your house."

The woman said, "I'm Florence Wainwright, and yes, I do live down the road."

Adah's mouth was dry and she was still trembling, but she had to make use of this rare contact with the outside world. "It was so kind of you to come."

Florence nodded once. "It was the right thing to do."

Adah had to fight the urge to bite her nails. She glanced around and saw that others were out of earshot for the moment. Turning back to Florence, she said, "May I ask you a question?" Without waiting for an answer, she continued. "I need to find some work. Would you have any need of help with laundry or mending?"

A frown and a questioning expression rode over Florence's face. "Well, no. But why do you ask, my dear?"

"I need to keep busy these days. I'm trying to find some laundry customers in the area, people nearby if possible."

"I'm sorry, but it's just me and my youngest son now, so not much to launder. I have a man who does the little bit we need done. He's a good worker, and I have no reason to replace him."

Adah glanced about. "Would you know of anyone else in the area who might need help?"

Florence finally let loose of Adah's arm and placed her right forefinger against her chin. "Well, let me think on that for a moment." She began tapping her chin. "There's a family up our same road that's full of kids. I think there's eight of them, at last count." She brightened. "Oh, come to think of it, an elderly couple live nearby, too. They've sold off the land but still live in the house. Both of them're getting frail, so you could check with them. See if they don't already have a laundry man or are willing to switch over to you, especially if your rates are lower. And I just thought of a bachelor man farming on his own, too."

"I'd be much obliged if you could tell me where to go to meet them. And since I'm new to this type of work, how much do you think I should charge?"

"Well . . . let me see. If you'll do a week's worth of laundry for two dollars, that would make your fee dirt cheap, and I'd be willing to bet you'll get some customers."

Dirt cheap sounded just right to Adah. "Thank you."

Florence was staring unabashedly now. "Sure, honey, but are you certain you should be thinking about working at a time like this? Maybe you need to let it all sink in. Take some time to work through it all, get all your sadness out of your system. You have to have some really hard cries, I know. We all reckoned Lester was lost for good a while back, but it still must have been a shock, finding him like that . . ."

A flashback of Lester's body on the coroner's table, and a shiver rode up Adah's arms. She rubbed them as though she could banish memories that way. "That's exactly why I need to do something with myself."

The kindness hadn't left Florence's face, and Adah found herself mesmerized. Other than the loving looks she received from Daisy, Adah hadn't experienced a single sweet expression since the Lerners and relief workers had helped her after the flood.

Florence said, "Follow me to my car, and I'll write down those folks' addresses for you. I have a pencil in the car." She turned and started to walk away, and Adah, not caring about the Branch family or what they thought, followed in Florence's footsteps.

"Will I be able to walk to see the folks you have in mind?"

Once they reached the car, Florence wrote down some names and addresses on a piece of stationery. "Funny thing, I just bought a box of stationery the other day and forgot to take it inside." She handed over the paper, then stopped and looked at Adah with a baffled expression. "Why would you need to walk?"

Adah shrugged.

"That family of yours has a truck and a car. About the only people in these parts that have two vehicles. Why can't you use one of them when need be? Don't you know how to drive?"

Adah hesitated, then answered, "Yes, I learned from my . . . my husband way back, as soon as we got married. I can drive just about anything, I think, but I'm trying to be as little trouble as possible to the Branches."

Florence stared at Adah for a few long moments, then breathed out, "Well, if that don't beat all." She lowered her voice and leaned in. "Though if I lived in that house with those people, I'd want to be as little trouble as possible, too."

Adah had to tamp down the urge to tell this nice woman all of what she'd been enduring. She longed for some sympathy but knew better than to reveal anything. The Branches had to have some friends in the community, and Adah didn't know whom to trust. Even though Florence seemed nice, it was possible she was a gossip, and anything Adah said to anyone could come back to bite her.

Florence sighed. "Never saw a whole lot to like, truth be told."

A little burst of triumph. She had been right. Not only did many people steer clear of the Branch clan, they downright disliked them. And Mabel seemed to have no clue. "So why did you come today?"

Florence glanced about. "I'm a neighbor, and I don't want to get on their bad side. You know, it's just the way we do things around here. A family loses one of their own, and we tend to gather 'round, no matter what. Even if we're not the best of friends . . ."

Adah would've loved to hear more, but by then she could see that Buck, Mabel, and Jesse were waiting for her, standing outside the sedan with Daisy and looking annoyed. "Well, thank you for the information. I sure appreciate it."

Florence was studying Adah and tilted her head to one side. "You take care of yourself, now, you hear?"

All Adah could do was shrug again. She had to contain her quivering chin. Her plan had to be carefully, cautiously enacted—appease the Branches by bringing in some money from laundry, wait for the ownership of the farm to be determined, get advice from an attorney in town about both Daisy and the farm, and don't let anyone know. For now, she had to remain alone in her plight. But solitude had never been a stranger to her. In many ways, it was her best friend.

Chapter Ten

The next day, Adah asked Jesse if she could borrow the truck to go to town and post notices about her laundry services. Which indeed she would do, as well as oh so much more . . .

"Your husband ain't even in the ground one day, and you wanna go prancing about town?"

Jesse's attitude no longer surprised her, and he had always been less terrifying than his father. She had even risked defending herself with him. "I'm trying to bring in some money. That way I can pay your parents back for some of the funeral expenses. I heard the casket they chose was costly."

He harrumphed. "You bet it was costly. They wanted the best for their dead son, or should I say murdered son?"

The word *murdered* burned through her like a hot staff. But she was learning how to let words fall away and show no expression in response. If they knew for sure, she would be a dead woman. Did they think they could somehow pull it out of her? Was that one of the reasons they were keeping her around? Jesse seemed too single minded to ever give up on an idea, and she wondered if he was even the slightest bit intelligent.

She ignored his question and stood still.

After staring her down for a while and sneering, Jesse finally handed over the keys. "Don't be gone long. And you best make it worth your while. Don't come back here with nothing to show for it. Pa expects you to start bringing home some bacon. And I mean real soon."

"That's why I'm going to town, Jesse."

He looked to be searching his brain for a new threat to make but had to settle on one already stated. "Like I said, don't be gone long."

Adah took the keys without touching Jesse's hand. "I wouldn't dare," she said and dropped the keys into her pocket.

Jesse let that go. Although there was no tempering toward Adah, he and Mabel seemed to be tiring of the tension they'd created in the house. But Buck, why, he flourished on it. His line of the Branch family had a deep history of slave ownership, and his treatment of Adah reminded her of what it must have been like to be an indentured servant taunted by her master.

If Adah ever had reason to smile, he quickly said, "Wipe that grin right off your face, girl. You best be showing the signs of a wounded woman 'round here."

Once, she had asked if she and Daisy could listen to a radio program, *The Bob Hope Show*, on the Blue Network, and Buck had retorted, "We have no time to listen to no programs. Pretty soon, come growing season, there won't be no time for anything but going to bed after night falls, and you best be prepared to do your share of the work. When your head hits the pillow, you'll be so tired you won't know what hit you. That is, if you can still sleep after what you done."

After she'd gotten the keys, Adah dressed both Daisy and herself in the best of their hand-me-down dresses and then drove away as Mabel labored in the kitchen, making a big pot of stew, and Buck and Jesse disappeared inside the old log curing barn. Often they went inside it for hours at a time, and Adah had no idea what they did in there, since the curing barns wouldn't be put to use until after harvest.

Whatever it was, Adah frankly didn't care. The more moments without them the better.

The sun was already tracking downward through a cloudless sky, but a chill in the air reminded them that winter had not completely come to an end. As Adah drove out of sight of the farm, a compulsion entered her. She could just keep driving. Past the town, out of the county, or across the river at the nearest bridge, into another state, into obscurity, and start a new life with a new name, Daisy as her daughter. Both of them away from the Branches.

But that would amount to kidnapping, a federal offense that would put even the FBI on her trail, and with that thought the urge left slowly, like a dying flame. Better to seek a legal course.

In the truck Daisy said, "Where are we going?"

Adah glanced sideways at the girl. "To town."

"Why?" This was one of Daisy's newest words.

"We're going to talk to a man, but it's kind of a secret."

"Why?"

Adah debated with herself about what to say, but if she managed to talk to an attorney on this day, Daisy would be with her and would hear anyway. There was no way to hide it from her. Besides, she wanted to give the girl some hope. "We're going to talk to a man about helping us go back to our old house, just you and me."

Daisy sat up taller in the seat. "Me and you?"

"Yes. Would you like that?"

Daisy nodded and then broke into a sunshine smile. "Can I get some candy? Oh puh-lease, Mama."

"Listen, sweetie. This is important, what I told you. For now, it's our secret, okay?"

But Daisy was already gazing beyond the window, awed by the outside world they rarely got to see.

In town Adah parked and enacted her cover story by placing handwritten notes on church bulletin boards and grocery stores that had reopened. By then the town was in full rebuilding mode with most businesses in various stages of restoration, some already completed. The sound of hammers against nails, the scent of sawdust, stacks of lumber and glass, and plenty of men working told the story.

How were some of the businesses able to rebuild so quickly? And then came an idea. Probably these buildings had been insured by their owners. Could Lester have taken out an insurance policy on the farm? And if he had, would the other Branches know about it? And if so, would they even tell her? Doubtful.

One more thing to consult the attorney about.

Despite her spinning thoughts, she somehow noted everything around her: the way the more prosperous people in town walked using longer steps and a more languid posture, the way the purveyor of buttons touched each one he set out on his cart as if it were a precious stone, and the way the owner of a diner swept the street just outside, looking for potential customers like an eagle. All these glimpses of life beyond the Branch farm she collected like gifts.

Since she'd found the money, she had seen herself as a new shoot of spring grass beginning to emerge from the cheerless, frozen earth. She had been reborn with a new purpose. But she had to conceal her smile.

A few women whom she was acquainted with from church, wearing smart hats and street clothes, spoke to her, saying, "Sorry for your loss," "He's in heaven now," "If there's anything we can do . . . ," and so on, all of which reminded Adah to appear solemn and move slowly. She was supposed to be mourning her husband.

At first, she had hoped for customers she could walk to, but now that she'd been allowed to borrow the truck, she was aiming to broaden her search. Being able to drive away from the farm had brought on a feeling of reprieve. After finishing her postings, she crossed Main Street, holding Daisy's hand, and headed for an attorney's office she had spied.

Something twitched in the far corner of her vision: a man crossing the street a discreet distance behind her. She slowed her steps, then stopped for a moment to gaze inside a dress-shop window and stare at a black evening dress with a silk overjacket, then daring a glance behind her. Yes, there was a man following her and not doing a good job of keeping himself hidden.

Jesse! He must have driven the sedan and been trailing her through town. Why? Despite having no clear answer to that question, there was no doubt that her plan had been foiled. She couldn't be spotted going into an attorney's office. The Branches would then know too much. They would certainly figure out at least part of what she had hoped to accomplish there. During all of the time she'd been with them, the legal ownership of Lester's land and house had not been mentioned. Nothing since Buck had said *your farm* and *your house.*

She had to abort. Taking Daisy again by the hand, she perused more windows of recently reopened shops, feigning interest in a green dress that flared on a mannequin's calf and pretending to be interested in the return of the veiled hat. The attorney's office, which occupied a storefront, came into view. So close; but she had to return to the truck and get back home. Daisy never asked why they hadn't talked to the man, and Adah assumed the girl had already forgotten what they'd spoken about only an hour or so earlier.

Despite not getting to see the attorney, at least she had spotted Jesse and halted in time. She'd outfoxed the fox that had been hunting her. There was a quiet sense of having, for once, beaten the Branches. She felt relieved.

Only she shouldn't have.

At dinner that night, over meatloaf, mashed potatoes, and canned sweet peas, Mabel asked Daisy, "How was your trip to town?"

The girl shrugged. "We didn't do nothing."

"We didn't do anything," Adah corrected softly in a whisper.

"We didn't do anything," Daisy repeated.

The sound of a utensil dropping made Adah jump in her seat. "You telling that girl what to say?" Buck fired.

Adah looked over the table at him. "No, I'm just teaching her how to say things the correct way."

"The correct way is the way I tell her." He glared at Daisy. "We don't talk no New York City 'round here. You say 'we didn't do nothing' like us farmers do."

Daisy said, "We didn't do nothing."

Adah wiped her lips with her napkin and gazed down at Daisy. "In truth, we did do some things. We looked in the store windows and posted notes, remember?"

Daisy shrugged. "But we didn't get to see the man."

"What man?" Buck barked.

Adah reluctantly moved her gaze up and into the steaming face of her father-in-law.

Daisy answered, "A man to help us go back to our old house."

Something came over Adah now, a stone cloak. Each second dragged. Outside the sun winked down beyond the horizon, and the daylight dimmed.

"Going back to your old house?" Jesse nearly shouted, pinning Adah with his eyes. "Like I already told you, put that idea right out of your head. That ain't going to happen."

Jesse's threat chilled her, but Buck spent long moments simply staring Adah down, as if he could peer into her soul and see her sin as plain as day. He stabbed his fork into the meatloaf and broke off a bite-sized piece, then shoved it into his smug mouth. The intimidation in his unblinking eyes and wickedness in his voice dried Adah's throat. "Well, this sure is a strange development, ain't it? We give you a home, despite us being pretty sure you're the best damn liar in the county and a killer to boot, and you wanna leave here with Daisy?"

Adah hated being reminded that she was kept. And now caught. Thoughts flailing, she said, "When I talked to Daisy about living in our old house, I was talking about the past. She's confused."

Buck guffawed, leaning forward in his chair as he chewed and then spoke out of the corner of his mouth. "The only person confused here is you if you think you can cross us and get away with it. Not after what you already done. You wanna leave here, go on ahead. Go on and git lost. Take off for Californy, like so many other idiots have done, like they're going to be starting over fresh. Or drown yourself in the river, that's what should've happened anyways. Or turn yourself back into a fortune-telling witch. Fine by us. But don't you go getting any ideas about that girl there."

"How dare you?" said Mabel, who was now clenching her hands together down in her lap. "I didn't think it could get any worse!"

Buck rocked forward in the chair and pointed his fork at Adah. "Lookee here. You gone and upset the missus, the lady of this house. And you done made me mad. You done made another big mistake." The skin over his eyes lowered in a scowl. "So listen up and listen good. From now on, you ain't taking that girl anywhere, not even to town." He pushed back his plate. "Come to think of it, you don't have no business in town, neither. You can conduct your laundering business on foot around here. You walk around and knock on the doors of these here country homes. You hear me?"

Adah nodded. She had hoped for something better, but now it was exactly as she had once foreseen.

"You got all that?" Jesse asked.

Adah nodded once again, fighting the urge to shoot off a retort, her angst growing and pressing against her ribs.

Buck addressed Mabel now. "Manfred Drucker is back in town." Adah breathed out a sigh of relief. At least Buck was changing the subject.

Mabel's eyebrows rose. "That so?"

"Yep," Buck said. "I ran into him in town and filled him in. He's gonna be coming by here real soon. Then me and him is gonna have us a nice little chat." Now he stared at Adah. "Yep, Manfred Drucker is a big shot in the sheriff's department and an old friend of mine. His father died over there in some home in Louisville, and he was out of town when they done found Lester. But now he's back, and he and I have some talking to do."

Adah worked hard to remain devoid of expression, as a creeping sensation claimed her. She might still be discovered somehow, some way, especially if Buck had a buddy in law enforcement, most likely a corrupt one, too.

"What's for dessert?" Buck asked Mabel, but his eyes never left Adah. His nose sprouted tiny red veins.

"Chess pie," she answered. "I'll go fetch it."

"Not yet. You just stay over there for a spell, resting in your chair," said Buck to Mabel, looking at Adah like a cat ready to pounce. "I done lost my appetite . . . for pie."

And so began Adah's true imprisonment. Even with Jesse tailing her earlier today, she should have taken her chances and headed out of town. Once she'd spotted him, she might have been able to lose him. At least then she and Daisy would've had a chance.

Chapter Eleven

Within three weeks, Adah had managed to secure four customers—the large family, elderly couple, and bachelor, whom Florence had mentioned, and another family, one of freckled redheads who lived off the main road on a small farm. The matriarch of the redheaded family had taken sick and couldn't do either her laundry or her household chores. Adah didn't tell the Branches that she did that household's laundry for free. She couldn't bring herself to charge those who were down on their luck, and often she did a little cleaning and cooking for that family, too.

Now her days were filled with hard work. It took most of a day to do one family's laundry, and she took over the duty for the Branch family as well so they could save the money they'd been spending on their washerwoman. Electric washing machines had become popular, but the family hadn't purchased one yet, so Adah did the work using three galvanized tin tubs: one for scrubbing the clothes on the rub board and the other two for rinsing. She boiled the whites in a cast-iron pot set up in the backyard on bricks with a fire under it. She starched the shirts. When the washing was completed, she hung everything on the line and ironed the previous day's laundry, folded it, and prepared it for return to her customers. Mabel often watched out the window.

It was honest, pure labor that pumped her heart, opened her lungs, and strengthened her arms and shoulders. She took pleasure in making soiled things clean, hanging clothes on the line with the sun on her back, and folding the scent of fresh air into the items she carefully placed in baskets to return to her customers. Wearing her wraparound housedress, apron, and oxfords, she walked the roads, shifting the basket from one hip to the other to better tolerate the weight. At night, she let a satisfied sense of exhaustion take her away into sleep, blocking the worries that she often was too tired to contemplate.

Of all her customers, Adah most enjoyed visiting the older couple and often sat with them for a spell on their front porch, watching birds flit about and squirrels climb their large dogwood tree. The old man still wore his overalls every day, and the woman wore a dress and old pumps with square heels. They told her about their grown children, who were providing support, and their grandchildren, who came to visit every Sunday. Sitting side by side in rocking chairs on the porch, the couple still held hands and gazed at each other lovingly.

Foremost in Adah's mind were always her thoughts of keeping Daisy close and wondering what Buck had told Manfred Drucker. What were they planning? It wasn't long before the gears in Adah's head started to crank out an idea of her own. Now that she had been banned from going to town, she would have to find an intermediary to go see an attorney for her. She couldn't send a letter—she didn't know the exact addresses of any attorneys, and even if she did, no one could have written her back at the Branch farm. Mabel checked the mail every day and wouldn't hesitate to open anything that came for Adah, especially if it came from an attorney.

Thinking through her options, Adah realized she couldn't do anything to disturb the peace of the loving couple she had grown to care about. Her next thought was to ask Florence Wainwright, but she daren't ask someone who had already confessed to being fearful of getting on the Branches' bad side. She couldn't implicate the two families, either. She wouldn't have been able to forgive herself if she were ever found out and the Branches learned who had helped her.

Thus her thoughts fell on the bachelor, name of Jack Darby. He was a strong, silent, and solid type who rarely spoke to her when she either picked up his laundry or returned it. His hands revealed him to be a man who worked his own farm without much help, and they'd seen a lot of sunlight. He held them steady and still at his sides as if he bore no pretense. She'd never heard much about him and guessed him to be something of a recluse.

So why would he stick out his neck to help her? Her sense was that maybe he would. When she'd first introduced herself to him, his jaw tightened just ever so slightly when she said her name was Adah *Branch*. And one day when she'd been walking away, down the gravel drive that led to his farmhouse—a small single-story house, painted white with black shutters and with the obligatory front porch—his basket of dirty laundry on her hip, she'd looked over her shoulder to find him standing on his porch, watching her as she walked away.

The day after her decision had been made, she walked to his farm—a forty-five-minute stroll through powdery sunshine that poured warmth on her shoulders. With no laundry to return to him that day, her goal was to befriend the man.

His truck was gone, and so she sat on his porch steps and waited. Soon she began to lose heart as she lingered alone, a desperate woman seeking an accomplice. The sun had crossed the sky and hung well into the west, spilling bright beams of light.

And then he pulled up and stepped out of his Huckster truck cab. For a moment, he held there in silhouette, but then he removed his hat, which was made of soft felt, sweat stained, and curled around the edges, and he came straight up to her.

"Mrs. Branch?" he said.

She had guessed his age to be about forty, as there were fanlike folds at the corners of his eyes. He had china-blue eyes set in a face bronzed by the sun and topped by dense waves of windblown caramel hair, and a hard-set jaw. A crescent-shaped scar arched over his left eyebrow, and the scent of wood smoke and horsehair bled from his clothes and skin. His nose was just slightly off to one side, as if at one point in his life he'd been in a fistfight.

She stood and said "Mr. Darby. How are you?" as she looked at him in a new light.

There was a change in his perusal of her in return, and it seemed to slow his movements, as if something about her presence today was unsettling.

He nodded and said, "I'm well."

Adah asked if she could sit and talk to him for a while, and he made a sweeping gesture, indicating two old wicker rocking chairs sitting on the front porch. He eased into one chair and moved his hands between his knees, holding the hat down between his shins. She hadn't expected him to be uncomfortable or that she would need to lead the conversation. But that was quickly made clear.

She said, "I hope I'm not bothering you."

"Not at all," he answered.

She sat in the other chair, which creaked as though no one had put weight on it for some time, and groped for something to say. "I've been wondering: How long have you been in these parts, Mr. Darby?"

He paused before answering. "About six years. Makes me rather new here, like you, Mrs. Branch."

"Please call me Adah."

He sat still, waiting.

She continued: "Well . . . where did you come from, and why here?"

He set the hat in his lap, moved his hands to the top of his thighs, and said, "I was a tugboat pilot for twenty years. Went up and down that river over yonder so many times I lost count. I saved up some money so when I got tired of living on the water, I could find some solid ground. This place seemed as good as any."

Adah gathered her words as his eyes fell heavily on her. There was something disquieting about him, and over the course of a long awkward silence, she feared she'd made a mistake coming here.

And then his stare changed to something almost kind. "How can I help you today?"

A bit anxious, Adah decided to spare the man her false and clumsy attempt at friendship and get right to the point. "I need someone to do a favor for me."

He straightened as if his interest had been piqued. "What kind of favor?"

"Before I get into that, may I ask you a question?"

He looked almost amused. "Shoot."

"When I first met you and told you my name, you flinched when I said Branch. I take it you're not friends with my in-laws."

He sat up even straighter. "You got that right."

"What happened between you?"

"I once sold them a horse, and we agreed on the price. They paid me some when I brought the horse over to them, but they never got around to paying the rest of what they promised. I went to see the old man about it, and he denied ever agreeing to the price. All of them's liars and cheats."

Adah let the information sink in. This was better than she'd hoped for. Not only did Jack Darby dislike the Branches, he'd had some personal conflict with them. Maybe here was someone who would help her.

Jack was studying her reaction. "What about this favor?"

Adah said, "It's a simple one, really. I need to talk with an attorney in town; however, I have no means to get there, and I'd like to keep the rest of the Branch family out of it. What I need is for someone to take messages to one of the lawyers. I have money to pay for it and for your time as well . . ." Her voice trailed off, and she had to stare at her hands. She should've rehearsed what to say in advance; she became inexplicably tongue tied. How to explain it better while also giving nothing too dangerous away? Even though she now knew that Jack Darby was no fan of the Branches, she was still taking a chance. Would he stay quiet, or would he run to the Branches with everything she said, hoping they'd reward him by finally paying him what they owed? Thoughts hung inside her head like the cobwebs that shrouded her secrets. How many lies would a person tell over a lifetime?

She looked up to watch how he absorbed this information. There was no change in his body's posture or movements, but his breathing had slowed, and the folds about his eyes had creased down a little more. There was a slight squint as he stared at her. He spoke slowly and carefully. "You want to get help from an attorney in secret."

He was watching her every breath, and she saw something in his eyes like horse sense. She felt quite transparent before him and found it unnerving. This meeting was not going as expected. She studied his hands, large compared to Lester's, thick skinned and brown. He held them perfectly still on his thighs.

She let her eyes travel to his face. "Yes. I don't aim to make any trouble for anyone. I just need to get some information."

He seemed to survey her again, gathering information from *her*, but she didn't feel viewed in a harsh light. "Then why don't you want the Branch folks to know about it? Is something wrong?"

"No. Nothing like that."

He ignored her answer. "If something's wrong, it could be a matter for the police, not an attorney."

Her face caught fire. "It's not a police matter."

His eyes never left her face as he just sat.

"I know it's a strange request, but the situation is a bit unusual."

"How so?"

"It's family business, and I don't aim to air out our dirty laundry for others to see. It's nothing all that important, really, just something I'd like to know, to learn about."

"If it's not important, then why are you looking for help from a perfect stranger?"

Adah blinked hard. "I don't know very many people around here. Almost everyone is a perfect stranger to me."

"Why do you need to see an attorney?"

Adah couldn't pull words out of her brain.

Then Jack Darby waited for a few more moments and finally said, "This makes no sense, Mrs. Branch. Sorry if I offend, but this makes no sense."

The day had been long, and the lengthy walk back loomed like a sudden heavy burden. She was tired and had no need to be drilled with questions. His gaze was beginning to annoy, and she was getting nowhere.

She said softly, "Maybe it only has to make sense to me."

He continued to study her.

She tried to appear confident, not like her entire plan was about to fall apart. "I'll pay you for your time. I'll pay you for every bit of information you pass along."

"I think I know what's going on here."

At first, she couldn't believe her ears. Did he know of her plight? There was a surreal, almost dreamlike quality about the way he'd made this simple statement. Was he the kind of person who simply knew things? Was he someone like Florence Wainwright, who might understand her predicament? Relief fell over her like a net, but there was a barb of fear in that net, too.

Her gaze met his: open, candid, dauntless.

She had but one moment to gain his confidence. The only card she could play now was honesty. "I need help," she said.

He gave one nod of his head.

Adah found herself breathing deeply. "Will you help me? Will you, please? I'd be so grateful, you have no idea."

"Why? What's been happening to you?"

A horrible urge to tell him everything struck her through the heart. The need for release was overwhelming, but not enough to break down her barriers. She could confide in no one, trust no one, not ever. Not completely. The Branches might still have friends, despite it all. She said, "Nothing. I simply need some legal information."

He looked away, as if searching for the right words in the air. Adah could almost feel the machinations going on in his head. She had a strong sense that he knew more than he was telling her. She could feel the intensity of what he held inside, and she could see it in his stillness. And he knew there was more to her story, too. It was as if they both sat perched on the edge of a cliff, waiting for the other to jump first.

Finally he leaned closer, and his tone was respectful, although there was a hint of challenge in his searching gaze. "It's going to be rough passing messages between two people and making sure no one else knows about it."

She tried smiling. "It's what I want to do, what I need to do. Or if it's easier for you, I could probably mail a letter from home in secret and ask for replies to be sent back here to you. Have you ever in your life needed legal advice?"

His gaze was unwavering, unflinching. Ignoring her question, he said, "Messing with the Branches, it's not a job for a woman."

A tiny flare of anger burst inside her. She remembered living on the streets, camping out with Henry and Chester, thriving without anyone's help, even though she had been told that doing so would be the death of her. This was no different. "I'm not a typical woman."

He leaned back a notch and appraised her anew. "Why would you trust me? Out of all the complete strangers 'round here, why did you pick me?"

She grasped her hands together in her lap. "I just did. No reason. Call me crazy; it might be true."

He smiled. Then his smile faded, and he waited for a few moments and said slowly but surely, "I need to know what's going on."

Gulping, Adah let a few moments of silence expand the space between them. "As I already said, I don't believe in airing dirty laundry—"

"So you came here acting like you want to be my friend, but you won't tell me what the problem is."

More long, heavy moments ensued, and Adah didn't know if she was being dismissed or was welcome to stay and sit awhile longer. She hoped that the more time she spent, the more he would warm to her and help her.

"Could I ask you something?" he said.

Not more questions, she thought, but she nodded.

"When you first came out here, what were you looking for?"

His question took her by surprise, and her heart stuttered. "When I first came?" Adah shrugged in as casual a way as she could manage. "I came to get married."

"Beyond that. Everyone is looking for something."

"At the moment, I'm looking for an attorney."

He glanced down and then back up to study her more. "Should you have come here?"

Adah wasn't sure why he was interrogating her, what he wanted from her. It was clear she was going to have to bare some of her soul in order to obtain Jack Darby's assistance. Ignoring warning stabs in her stomach, she said, "Living here has changed me."

"That so?" he said.

"I used to look for meaning in everything. Now I see that little of that matters. Things come about or they don't."

His face softened, and he appeared to be sorry for her, sorry he'd asked her anything. "Mrs. Branch, I think you're wrong about that. We're here to make things come about."

Adah remembered nights lying awake by the campfire, dreaming of a different life, a new life, of love, of happiness. What an odd conversation this had turned out to be. "You want me to bare my soul, while you refuse to even call me by my first name."

"Like I said, this isn't going to be easy. I need to know who I'm helping and why. You're asking me for a favor, but you're leaving me in the dark."

Neither spoke for long minutes.

She held his eyes until he finally said, "I can't do it."

Stunned into silence, Adah sat still while tears gathered behind her eyelids. She had been so close, and she couldn't fathom this sharp turn, this blunt denial. She nearly choked on her disbelief and anger. "Please tell me why."

He twitched once. "I just can't do it."

She drew in a ragged breath. "I'm disappointed. I've been looking for someone to help me for some time now. You have a sense of my quandary—I can tell—and yet . . ." Her bottom lip quivered, and she bit it. "If you aren't interested, maybe you know someone else who'd be willing to help me quietly and earn some money in the process."

"No one else will help you."

Adah wanted to scream. She wanted to shout, *Why not?* She wished she could tear off this armor and tell him how much this meant to her and Daisy.

But she couldn't form the words.

Instead she gathered her composure. Grappling, she said, "Why won't anyone help me? Why?"

"I think you know why. The Branches have a long history, not only with the Ku Klux Klan, but with using people, cheating people in general. I heard that if you hurt them, even in business, they'll hurt you back double. Isn't that why you don't want them to know you're going to an attorney?"

"I'll pay more."

He said, "You insult me by offering me money."

She blinked hard again. "How do I insult you? I'm offering you a fair business deal."

His eyebrows, which were heavy and set in a straight line, shifted, but there was no other change in his face.

"This isn't just about business, is it?" He sighed. "It's much more than that."

All the way back home, she admonished herself. She should have left Jack Darby alone. She wished she could take it all back. If only she hadn't gone. Her steps thumped the dirt road to the same beat that a cacophony built in her head, till she was nearly running and crossed a rare intersection of roads only to realize that she had lurched in front of an oncoming Plymouth pickup truck. She didn't know the family inside.

"Excuse me," she mouthed to their astonished faces.

Chapter Twelve

Jack Darby's dismissal had hit her hard. She tangled with the sheets at night as she tried to think of someone else to ask for help. To whom could she turn next? She had thought Mr. Darby would pave the way, but he had inexplicably shut down that path. How he'd said *No one else will help you* was another blow.

And now, every day, she watched the Branches anew. It was late March, and the men were mixing the minute tobacco seeds with ash, hand-sowing the seedbeds, and raking and walking the seeds in. Adah helped the men with the final step for the seedbeds, staking and then sheltering them with linen. At the end of the day, Buck and Jesse sometimes disappeared into the old log curing barn, loading crates from it into the truck bed after nightfall and then heading off to God only knew where. There was another secret out there, she knew it.

One night Adah, trying to make her voice as neutral as possible, asked Mabel, "Where are the men off to?"

Adah had just handed over her laundry earnings for the week, keeping a few coins for herself and Daisy, and Mabel had put the money in her pocket as usual without thanking Adah. "They got business in town."

"This late?"

Mabel froze for a moment, then turned to face the icebox as if about to open the door. "What's it to you?" she said over her shoulder.

Adah replied to Mabel's back, "Just curious."

Mabel finally turned around, never having opened the icebox. She was having trouble meeting Adah's eyes. "I stay out of their business. You best do the same thing."

"Alright," Adah said and relished a tiny victory. Her question had unnerved Mabel, who was gazing away wistfully, and Adah thought she saw something sorrowful and maybe a bit regretful in the woman's eyes.

"I was wondering," Adah began, "if I could take Daisy with me when I return the laundry the next time I visit that family with all the redheaded kids. Since it's getting warm, I think Daisy would benefit from some fresh air."

Mabel's face hardened as she stared at Adah. "Daisy can get fresh air right here."

"I know, but the walk might do her some good. And I don't get to play with her much anymore since I'm working most of the day. She could play with some other children for a short while. I just thought she'd like it."

Through her stern mouth, Mabel spat, "That girl is just fine. And you know Buck don't want you to take her anywheres off this property. So why are you asking me?"

Adah shrugged. "I know you love your granddaughter, Mabel, and I was only thinking of her. What harm could come from it?"

Mabel looked doubtful but also the tiniest bit sympathetic, the tiniest bit vulnerable. What was going through her head? Could Mabel ever relent? Could she ever allow a crack to open in the wall between them?

"Maybe you could ask Buck about it."

Mabel visibly bristled. "I don't have to ask my husband's permission for decisions I can make on my own. Now that you done said such a foolhardy thing, you made up my mind. You ain't taking Daisy anywhere, not now, not ever."

The next day, the hum of a car's engine grew louder as it came up the drive. Adah had just started down the steps, holding on her hip Jack Darby's laundry basket full of clean and ironed clothing and sheets. She was planning to go return his things, although she dreaded seeing him.

The sheriff's department car came all the way to the house, bringing with it a more desperate shade of dread.

A man of about Buck's age stepped out from the car. He was more white haired, taller, and thinner than Buck, but he had the same commanding manner about him, one that said he was fierce and would always get his way. His step was heavy, and his eyes were sharper than Buck's, too, with an eaglelike intensity.

"Adah Branch," he said in a calm, smooth tone that spoke of endless confidence.

"Yes, I'm Adah Branch."

He strode up to her. "Manfred Drucker here." He hadn't needed to tell her; she already knew. Immediately she noticed his large-knuckled, big-boned hands and nails cut to the quick as if he'd groomed himself with a blade. If hands could be cruel, they would look like his. He asked, "How are you this sunny day?"

"Fine."

"Good, good. So . . . what do you say let's you and me sit down and talk for a spell."

Adah fought for composure. Showing any signs of guilt would be devastating around this man. "Sure thing." She gestured with her free hand toward the house. "Would you like to sit on the porch?"

"Now that'd be right nice," Drucker said with a sly smile.

Adah led the way, and on the porch she set down the laundry basket, and they sat on the rocking chairs. Drucker turned his chair to face her more directly.

"What brings you here today?" Adah asked when it became obvious he was still studying her, trying to make her squirm.

Drucker sat back, stilled the chair, and, with his elbows on the armrests, steepled his hands in front of him. Steady as a stone. "You know, me and Buck go back a long ways," he said while keeping his eyes fixed on her.

"I heard about that."

A tiny hint of a smile curled one side of his lips. "You heard right. Me and him grew up together. Yep, sure did, and over the years we done some favors for each other." He blinked once. "Too bad I wasn't here when they done found Lester's body."

"Yes," Adah said and gulped. "My husband."

"Yep, I would've liked to been around so I could help out with the police for my old friend."

Adah simply waited, trying to keep her expression as open and unguarded as possible.

"But since I come back, old Buck here, he done come around and told me some interesting stories and proposed some interesting theories."

Adah never even shifted in her seat. She'd known something like this was coming, but Drucker's scrutiny was worse than she'd imagined. And still she remained blank on the outside.

"He's plumb convinced you had something to do with his son's death."

Adah allowed herself to exhale slowly. "Yes, I know. I think it's very difficult for Buck to believe that something so random and cruel could've happened to his son. He can't accept it, he needs someone to blame."

One of Drucker's eyebrows lowered. "That so? That your theory?"

"Yes."

Now he sat forward and let his hands fall. "Buck says when he saw Lester's body, it looked like his head had been bashed in."

"Yes, I know that, too. But the police saw nothing of concern. Although I'm sure Buck and Jesse tried to change their minds."

Drucker made a fist out of his right hand and gently bumped it against his thigh. Once, twice. "But I weren't there to see for myself."

He waited, and Adah had nothing to say to that at first. But then she picked up a thought. "The coroner was there."

Drucker allowed a smile, as if enjoying this game. "Funny thing you mention that. I had me a talk with the coroner, and the way he sees it, Lester got struck in the head while he was caught up in the river before he drowned. He also had some broken ribs and a broken leg. He got pretty roughed up. You know about all that?"

Adah shook her head. "I didn't want to know the details."

"Oh, but the devil is in the details, honey." He smirked. "The devil is in the details. What he said didn't rule out what Buck suspects. The coroner done guessed it happened in the water, those injuries, but he don't know that for sure. That's the way I see it."

Adah fought the urge to grasp her hands together, instead keeping them still in her lap. "I don't think anyone else on the police force or in the sheriff's department agrees with you."

He laughed, a loud, menacing bark. "They don't yet." He scooted his chair closer and leaned in farther. "Let me tell you something, sweetheart. There was a rush to get Lester into the ground, condition he was. There was no autopsy done. They should've done it, but they didn't. But his body can still be exhumed. There can still be an autopsy." He paused. "That's the only way to know for sure how he died."

Her mind scrambled, but she kept control over her voice, hard as it was. "The river was full of debris—big things, like logs and doors and tanks. I was in it, too. I know."

"Yep, I know about that. But like I said, there's only one way to find out for sure the cause of death. You're the man's widow, so I figured you'd want to know how he died."

"I already know how he died."

He smiled again, as if he might have admired her spunk for a passing moment. "According to you, yes. And if you got nothing to hide, I reckon you wouldn't have no objection to getting that body back out of the ground and doing some work on it, now, would you?"

Adah shrugged. "I think it's desecration of a body that's already been put to rest, but if you're asking if I'd put up a fight . . . probably not."

"Good to know," he said, nodding. "Good to know."

Adah kept still. The idea of an autopsy was terrifying. She knew little of forensics but had the impression it was known for accuracy. But could an autopsy be accurate enough to determine if Lester had died from a blow before he went into the water? Could the past come back in such a powerful way? Could she still be found guilty of murder?

Drucker fished a small notepad out from his jacket's inside pocket. "Why don't you tell me the events of that night, blow by blow." He threw her a menacing stare. "Blow by blow, so to speak."

Adah didn't crumble but instead relayed her now tired, worn story, including how she and Lester had gone for the milk cow, being careful not to add anything or leave anything out.

After he listened while observing her with a skeptical eye, he made a few notes, then abruptly closed the notepad and seemed to be working himself up to leave.

"Is there anything else I can do for you?" Adah asked.

He smiled ruefully. "I think we done enough for one day." He stood, and Adah followed him to the porch steps.

Adah said to his back, "I have a question." Then sucked in a tight breath as Drucker turned to face her. She had to let Drucker know she was no easy target. "If I may be so bold as to ask."

He swept his right hand in front of himself. "Go on ahead."

"Why did you come out here to question me?" Adah figured Drucker didn't have enough cause to bring her to the station for a more formal interrogation, and she hoped she was correct. "Why didn't you take me to your headquarters if you suspect me of something? Why not bring me in?"

He seemed a bit startled. Then quickly recovered. "You want me to do that? Believe me, sweetheart, I can bring you in at any time."

Adah shrugged. "No, thank you."

He laughed again, and the sound grated against Adah's skin. "You want me to put you in handcuffs, too?"

"No, thank you," Adah said again.

He was openly studying her. Then he finally said, "You can be sure I aim to keep in touch, Adah Branch. And you best know this, too: I'll be quietly working behind the scenes to get to the bottom of this matter. It takes a while to get a body exhumed, but you better believe I'm going to keep at it till it's done."

"Feel free," Adah said and then regretted her tone. She lowered her voice. "For your information, I don't have anything to hide. Do what you think you have to do. I hate the idea of my husband's battered body being brought out of peaceful slumber and getting cut into pieces, but do what you have to do if that's what Buck and Mabel want. In fact, it will prove my innocence, once and for all."

Drucker took the steps down two at a time, then turned and set his heavy gaze back on her. With a sinister grin he said, "We'll see about that."

The rest of the day, Adah was close to useless, thoughts braiding together into a complex web. How much influence did Manfred Drucker have at the sheriff's department or with the police? What could he really do? She didn't even know his rank. She didn't know if it was the police department or the sheriff's department that had jurisdiction. But the image of Drucker followed her now, a shadowy form that could not be shaken off. His words as menacing as Buck's had been. *We'll see about that.* She had no one to consult, no one to turn to. She had the money from Lester's cash box, but for the moment it was useless to her. What good was money to a prisoner?

She still had to return Jack Darby's laundry, and Adah hoped he would be gone. Since her disastrous request and his denial, she'd had no want of making any small talk with the man. But as his farm came into view, she saw his truck. Not seeing him anywhere about, however, she moved quietly, aiming to place his basket on the front porch and then turn around and leave.

Instead he opened the door and came outside as soon as she reached the bottom step, as though he had been watching her approach. His mysterious appearance and the way he held her gaze made Adah feel uncomfortable. She waited for him to speak; time was suspended. Expectancy dangled in the air.

He never said hello or greeted her. Instead he spoke slowly. "You've made me curious, Mrs. Branch."

She had no idea what he was telling her or how to respond.

"If you still want my help, I'm now offering it."

She gulped as she looked into his face. Hatless today, he appeared older, wiser. His forehead was shades lighter than the rest of his face and tracked with deep horizontal lines.

Taken aback, she was eventually able to answer, "Of course I still want your help."

"Then you have it."

His change of heart touched her. She wasn't as alone now. And with Manfred Drucker on her trail, she was even more in need of help, and a friend. "Thank you, Mr. Darby," she managed to say.

He gave one nod of his head.

She finally breathed in. "What made you change your mind?"

"Nothing made me," he said a little tersely. But the kindness in his eyes came back just as quickly. "I couldn't get it off my mind. Figured the only way to do that was to tackle this thing."

"I'm sorry if I've been a . . ." Adah searched for the right words. Obviously her situation had been disconcerting to him, but she was thrilled it had worked in her favor. "A bother."

"I didn't say it was a bother. I just had to work it through a bit. I'll take your letter to an attorney in town, if you really want that. No need to use the mail."

Adah placed the basket down, took a step back, and stared down at her feet. The concern in his gaze had embarrassed her. "Well," she said, "I thank you. Thank you so much. More than you know. I don't have any money on me now."

"I won't take any money."

Adah looked up. "But you do need some money to give to the attorney, right? Do you have someone in mind to talk to?"

"Yes," he said simply. "And I don't think he'll be asking for money just yet. When he does, I'll let you know."

"Do you have some paper and a pen, so I can write a letter?"

He nodded and ushered her into the house.

Inside was a center hallway flanked on either side by a high-ceilinged dining room and living room. The white walls and wood floors were unadorned, and the furniture was simple and functional. Everything looked tidy and clean, but there was a fine drift of dust in the air. Plaid drapes on the windows had been opened, letting in bright wedges of light. All in all, it was a tight ship of a house.

He motioned her into the living room and pointed to a writing desk facing the two front windows.

She sat at the desk, took the stationery and pen he offered, then wrote a letter identifying herself and asking for information about a possible insurance policy, her rights to the land, and rights to Daisy.

Jack handed her an envelope, but she shook her head. "You might as well read it. You were right. I was a fool to ask for help and also not confide in the person I'm asking."

She stood up. Adah was having a hard time meeting his firm, studious gaze. This was a crazy thing to do, to place her trust in a man she knew almost nothing about, and one who had already changed from refusing her to now wanting to help in only a few days' time. But she couldn't dismiss the feeling that a broad door was opening for her.

He read the letter and then handed it back ever so slowly. He looked disturbed. And yet there was something like sure knowledge emanating from this man. He knew things he would not say. What was in his eyes? Pity or promise or both?

"Leave it there on the desk, Mrs. Branch. I'll take it to town tomorrow."

Obviously he wasn't going to give up on formalities and call her Adah, as she'd once asked. He walked her back outside, and she squinted up to the sky, where a single shaft of sunlight was searching its way through the firmament like a god leaning in with his luminescent arm.

He stood in front of her on the porch, and she thought he had something else to say, that he wasn't quite through with her yet. She glanced at his face. The scar over his left eyebrow had turned from white to pink. Now that they had plans together, a sense of hope came to her. She made no move to leave or to hide.

He shook her hand, and the silence between them was filled by the wail of a distant train whistle.

With his right eyebrow lowering, he said, "Are you sure you want to do this?"

She thought for a moment; his question was, in a way, a warning. But he didn't know how driven she was to succeed. "Yes."

His gaze never left her face. "How much do you know about the Branches?"

The question took her by surprise. "I know a great deal. I'm living with them." She shifted her weight from one leg to the other. "Is there something I *should* know?"

"You best sit down," he said, gesturing to the chairs.

She did as he asked and then stared at the front lawn as he began to talk.

"Most of the time I make it a point to mind my own business, but I can't help overhearing what people have been saying in town."

Adah tried for patience. "You're going to have to be more specific."

"Do you know anything about how your husband's first wife died?"

Adah's head jerked in Jack's direction as her breath halted. She'd anticipated that this talk would be about Lester's death or, if she was lucky, something about the Branches in general. This, *this* had never entered her mind. "Betsy?"

"Yes, Betsy Branch. I remember her. I remember when she died."

"Why . . . yes. She fell off a horse."

Jack locked his hands together in between his knees and leaned forward. "That was the story. But I don't believe it."

"Why not?" she gasped.

"Just sit and listen for a spell."

Adah sucked in a deep breath.

"Thing is, supposedly it happened on the very farm you're now living on. Story is, she and Les went for a ride. Betsy was on their pretty chestnut mare with the white socks, and that horse went wild and tore through the woods, knocking Betsy around and then throwing her and killing her."

"Yes? That's what I was told, too."

"Trouble is, I saw Lester go by in the truck that day. He was heading for his folks' house alright, but there weren't anyone in the truck with him. He was driving crazy, kicking up a cloud of dust—that's why I looked up. He was alone, or maybe he had the baby with him in his lap. But if Betsy had been in the truck that day, she was lying down . . . or already dead."

Adah gazed back at a pastoral view suddenly turned dismal and full of confusing green dips and swells. "What are you saying?" she urged out.

She became aware that he'd lit a cigarette, and then he said, through the smoke he exhaled, "That wife of his was all banged up. Talk is, she looked like she'd been beaten to death, but with three eye witnesses—your husband, Buck, and Mabel—telling the same story, that made for no investigation. But I know that horse. That's the one I sold to the Branches and never got fully paid for. That horse wouldn't hurt an ant on the ground."

"I-I'm not following . . ."

"What I think and what lots of folks think is that Lester Branch killed his wife on his farm, and then in a panic brought her body down yonder to his folks' place, where the three of them concocted a story to tell the police."

Adah's vision went hazy. The world slowed to a crawl, and her heart clenched in her chest like a fist. "Are you saying . . . ?"

"Yes," he said just above a whisper, gently, as if he knew what the information he was imparting could mean to her, how it could scare her out of her mind. "I hate to be the one to tell you this, but the way I see it, your husband was a cold-blooded murderer. And the people you're living with made up a story with him to cover up the crime."

Chapter Thirteen

The air froze around her, and the ground vaporized beneath her feet. For a moment, she felt like she was floating. But she could not escape this, and she breathed in the cool air in silent gulps and worked her way back to what was real.

Of course. It made perfect sense. Lester had killed his first wife, and his family had helped him hide the truth. Now she knew the nefarious secret that Lester had held on to the entire time they were married, and now she knew the Branches', too. And these were secrets blacker and bleaker than she could have ever conjured up, even during her most imaginative moments.

The silence was deafening, screaming in her ears, and yet she forced herself to take in the impact of what she'd just realized. She could not turn away from the truth. And then she thought of Daisy. How had such a sweet little girl been born into such a family? How could she have come from such wretched people, and now they had her in their grasp? Everything about it seemed at such odds with her innocence and purity. Adah almost couldn't believe it.

Adah said, "My stepdaughter," and then her voice failed her again. She gazed away and wiped her nose with the dusty bandanna she retrieved from her pocket. "Maybe I was better off not knowing."

Jack waited for a moment. "I'm sorry, but I disagree. You're much better off knowing."

She laughed pitifully. "So . . . what else is there?"

He leaned back. "They never did put down that horse they say killed Betsy. Do you know of her?"

Jack Darby was a rather attractive man, but she hated the sight of his face just then, and this was beginning to feel like foreign soil, some kind of weird dreamscape.

Adah's voice cracked as she answered, "Yes, she's Mabel's prized possession, although she rarely rides her. A beautiful chestnut with white socks. Mabel calls her Miss Socks."

"Now . . . just think about it for a minute." Sympathy evident in his expression, Jack went on, "Don't you think if that horse had killed Betsy, they'd have put her down or at the least gotten rid of her?"

Adah glanced about furtively. She said, "Okay, I agree you have a good point. So what did you do about it? Did you go to the police with your suspicions?"

"Sure I did. But they had questioned the three Branches who told of the accident, talked to them separately, and they all had a story and they stuck to it. They were so slick they gave the police nothing. Seems to me some of the police suspect what might have happened, but it would've been near impossible to prove in a court of law. There was no evidence. The police who arrived first on the scene found that Lester had already carried his dead wife back to the house after he supposedly found her, and they never did go look in the woods for where she had, according to the Branches, gotten all beat up by trees, and they never checked the horse's hooves for mud or anything like that. Guess it just didn't occur to them. Police around here aren't used to investigating murders. They botched the case real bad."

"And the Branches have at least one good friend in the sheriff's department."

"No doubt."

"So they got away with it."

"Seems to me."

Adah gulped and looked at the sun-washed land before her, so at odds with the blackness permeating her from within. "Now what am I supposed to do with this information?"

"That's up to you, but about that letter . . . I wouldn't send me to town with it." He leaned closer. "Hear me out, I really want to help you. I don't know what lawyers to trust; even the one I have in mind is a stranger—just a hunch as to who to approach—and if word got back to Jesse and Buck what you're up to, no telling what they'd do."

"Kill me, too?"

"I wouldn't put it past them. And besides, I know a little bit about the law. If your husband died without a will, then the case goes to probate court. You'll probably get a percentage of the farm, about 25 percent is what I heard widows usually get, and the court won't give you custody of Daisy unless you had adopted her or the blood family doesn't want her. The way I see it, that letter isn't going to do you a bit of good and might cause you more trouble. You go ahead, and you might be throwing a rope over the barn rafter and preparing your own noose."

Adah stared blankly ahead. "I never adopted Daisy."

"That's what I figured. And so you'd have to prove the Branches aren't fit to take care of her and you're better for her. One of the first things they'd ask is if you have a home for her, if you have a job to support her, if you have something to show that the Branches aren't good to her—all things I'm willing to bet you don't have."

"How do you know all of this?"

"I spent more than two decades on the river and on the docks. You learn all sorts of things. Everyone has a story to tell. I just listened and soaked it all in."

She took a hard look at Jack Darby then. Yes, she could see he was the kind of man who desired knowledge the way that others yearned for success and money. And he was clearly on her side now. She gulped. "So . . . you tell me this horrible information and then expect me to do nothing with it."

"I didn't say do nothing."

"What do you think I should do?"

"Get the hell away from there."

"Right."

"I mean it. Walk away and never look back."

Of course that's what he would say. It was what anyone would say. But no one else loved Daisy the way Adah did. It was an impossible situation, and now she had Jack Darby to deal with on top of everything else. She had somehow sought out the help of the one man who had seen Lester that fateful day his wife died and could tell her this story. How strange and fragile were the connections that bound people together. The tendons in her neck tightened, and she hauled in a ragged breath. "Funny you tell me about Betsy's death only after you'd read my letter and knew what I wanted."

At first, Jack didn't respond. Finally he said, "I didn't know you. Now I think I do."

"I see."

"I'm worried about you." He paused, then said, "But it's still up to you to make this decision. Your call. I just wanted you to have all the information at hand. So . . . what do you want me to do?"

Blood drained from her cheeks as she realized she still had a decision to make. One that was hers and hers alone. Something that could have huge ramifications. "I don't know. I just don't know."

"I'm sure this has come as a shock." Jack looked at her as if he wished he could take it all away. He was like a geode, hard and scrabbly on the outside, but now she was beginning to see some lovely particles inside. "Did you have any idea?"

She sat statue still as a slow dawning settled over her. "No," she answered, realizing how ignorant she had been. "People sometimes get thrown from horses. Sometimes people die that way. I had no reason to doubt the story, which was relayed to me briefly and only once, soon after I met Lester. I never mentioned it again, not wanting to bring back sad old memories."

Jack looked up at her cautiously, and Adah could see the question on his lips. He wanted to ask if Lester had ever hurt her, too. A shiver coursed through her, one so powerful she feared it would show, the way sometimes a horse's shiver rippled down its flank.

She said, "I have to think about this. Then I'll come back. Tomorrow," and she stood up and bounded down the steps.

As she walked away she had to mentally pull herself back into the present day despite carrying a knot of new and terrifying knowledge that had formed in her head and a fiercer and even more terrifying fear in her gut. Over her shoulder she said a quiet "Thank you," but she was almost sure Jack Darby didn't hear.

She took one look back just before she turned from the driveway onto the road, and Jack was standing there, as still as the air around him, watching her with wide-open concern as she left his place and went back to hell, alone.

After returning to the farm, she sat on the back stoop with Daisy, staring into the night as if it could give her some answers. A late-afternoon thunderstorm had passed over quickly, during which Adah had had to quickly rescue sheets and clothing on the wash line, but now it was gone, leaving the air so still she could hear Mabel clanking dishes in the kitchen and running water in the sink, snippets of Buck and Jesse's conversation floating out of open windows—they were discussing tobacco prices and the farm's ledger—and the building song of grasshoppers. Sounds of ordinary domestic life seemed so far from the story she'd heard today, and Adah doubted herself for a moment. Could Jack Darby's theory be true?

"Where were you today, Mama?" Daisy asked as she held her doll in her lap and scooted closer to Adah.

"I went to see one of my customers."

Daisy rubbed her eyes, which looked tired and sad. It was almost bedtime. "I don't like it when you're gone. I wanna go, too."

Adah hugged the girl. "I know, honey. Maybe someday."

"When you're gone, all I do is wait for you to come back."

Adah had to fight tears now climbing from her heart into her eyes. She couldn't remember one instance of Mabel sitting down to play with her granddaughter or even letting Daisy watch her in the kitchen. Instead Mabel usually shooed Daisy away, saying, "Go play." The girl would spend time around Adah while she did laundry, terrifying Adah that she would get too close to the boiling clothes or the strong lye soap. Often Adah had to shoo her away, too, having to ignore her wide-eyed pleading and curiosity about everything, her frequent questions.

Lately Daisy's favorite word had been *why*. She wanted to know why the sun went away at night, why Miss Socks had white feet, why her grandparents made her eat things she didn't like, and why they wouldn't let her play on the parlor furniture.

During meals, she was required to sit and eat without speaking except to say her prayers and thank God and Mabel for the food. She had few toys, and so when Adah had found an old broken wagon beside the road one day, she'd taken it home in hopes of repairing it and painting it, but as of yet, she'd not had the time.

Once she'd asked Jesse if he would help her, but he had responded, "Hell no. I cain't believe you carted that trash back to this house."

She and Daisy were alone. No one knew what they were going through, as if they were marooned on an island. Linked by an invisible bond that no one else might understand. But as years passed with the Branches, would their bond break? Would pain and helplessness drive them apart? Would Daisy end up believing that no one cared or wanted to help her? What was Adah waiting for? Some benevolent spirit to swoop down and save them? She had to keep the peace, get help, get some more money or a home away from the farm, and she had to get custody of Daisy.

Now Daisy began to whimper.

"What is it?" Adah asked.

Daisy wiped her perfect button nose, now reddening, with the hem of her play dress. "My bottom hurts."

"What?"

"I got a spanking today."

A sudden rage snapped to life inside Adah. "Why? Let me see." Adah helped Daisy stand, then lifted her dress and bore witness to red swollen swaths across the girl's upper thighs.

Daisy said, "I was bringing in the eggs from the coop, and I dropped them. All but one of them broke."

"Who did this?"

"Grandma."

Adah's first urge was to march into the house and demand an explanation from Mabel. Spanking was one thing, and most people believed in it, but to leave marks amounted to a beating. Surely everyone in this family had been raised with regular beatings, and it had made them into the cruel people they were today. Adah couldn't allow it for Daisy. If hatred alone could kill, then Adah's would still Mabel's callous old heart with her thoughts. Blistering, seething words gathered in her mind and begged to be spoken. But then again, what could she do? Any confrontation could result in her being kicked out of the house, and where would that leave Daisy? Alone with the monsters. As Jack had said, she had to be careful she didn't string up her own noose. If she did, she'd never get her share of the farm or anything else.

"It was an accident," Daisy whispered, her sweet little voice breaking through Adah's fog of fury.

Adah worked hard to catch her breath. "I know, honey. I know."

That night Daisy fell asleep while Adah stared out the window, and the bald moon rose and lit the land with silver light that made even the shadows of branches and leaves stand out in sharp relief. There was no wind that night, and the bare fields looked how she imagined the moon would—stark and serene, calm and quiet. Shadows were absolutely black in that brightness, and now Adah knew that the ghost of a woman beaten to death walked this land along with the shadows. Her daughter abused now, too. Probably Betsy would haunt this place forever.

Beyond the moon, there were millions of twinkling stars in the sky. Adah sighed and closed her eyes. What had happened between Daisy and her was as insignificant as one tiny star in the vastness of all space, but it was, like each one of those shining lights, beautiful and special. A gift had fallen into her lap in the form of Daisy, and she had to be ever so careful what she did with it. She was the girl's only hope.

When the house was silent, Adah reached under the bed for the wooden box of letters she'd found in the attic. She had never read the letters from Doris McNeil. But now . . . even though she was invading a dead woman's privacy and could be opening a Pandora's box, it was time.

The letters were housed in ocher-colored envelopes and written in black ink, with the latest on top. Each was folded in half, and Adah handled the pages as if they were some kind of holy parchment. If she stood by the window, the moonlight was bright enough for her to read by, and what she found there did not exactly provide credibility for Jack Darby's theory, but it certainly didn't disprove it, either.

In the last letter Betsy Branch had received from its author, who did indeed turn out to be her mother, Doris had written, *Dearest daughter, if you need a rest, please come.* Other letters referred to injuries due to vague accidents that her daughter was healing from. But the rest was about family happenings, church, friends, special occasions. There was nothing here that Adah could take to the police. And according to Lester, Betsy's mother had died soon after her daughter did, so there was no way to glean any further information from her. Daisy had her father's family and no other living relatives.

Adah read through the stack and then put each letter back exactly the way she'd found them.

It appeared as if Betsy had been enduring the kind of treatment that Adah had, that she hadn't confided completely in anyone—people rarely talked about mistreatment or unhappiness—and Adah hadn't, either. But if Lester had been abusive to Adah, why not toward his first wife, too? Why wouldn't his fists have made contact with more than one woman's flesh? But had he become so enraged he had actually killed her?

Her mind was a labyrinth of questions.

Then Adah remembered back to the night of the flood, something she rarely did now, and her ribs ached as she relived Lester's hitting her in the face and kicking her sides. How long might the assault have gone on? She couldn't say. It had always taken Les a long time to simmer down. And then it dawned clear. Yes, Lester had been capable of killing her: he'd killed his first wife.

So did that let her off the hook? An eye for an eye? A life for a life? Was she less a murderer because Lester had been one? Was it less a killing because he might have killed Adah, too?

She wasn't sure, but she was suddenly able to breathe again, to pull life into her body again in a way she hadn't done since the night of the flood. This new information about Betsy Branch, while both terrifying and horrifying, was also a gift, one delivered by the most unlikely of messengers, an unusual man named Jack Darby.

Adah eased off her tight-fitting wedding band, a thin gold circle. Not once had she removed it since the flood. It had survived along with her, and it would've seemed odd to others if she had already stopped wearing her dead husband's ring. *But now . . .* The ring warmed in her hand, and she set it on the bedside table.

During the first year of her marriage to Lester, Adah had missed her period and after a few weeks had told Les she thought she was expecting. Her husband had slapped his hand on the table, not in anger but in happiness, and said, "It'll be a boy this time." He'd been thrilled for a few brief days, but when Adah began to bleed heavily and concluded that she'd miscarried, his mood had transformed. He'd hit her hard the first time a few days later, and a pattern had started to develop. Anything that disappointed Lester ended in his curled fist. The last thing she had wanted was a baby in the mix.

Once, she'd overheard Jessamine, who had been an expert in herbs, tell a woman how to make a homespun spermicide to prevent pregnancy. Adah had remembered the recipe and followed that advice for the remainder of the marriage, even though her apparent barrenness had angered Lester further and driven an even bigger wedge between her and all the Branches.

Her wedding ring seemed to glare at her now with one knowing eye. She would have to wear it around others for appearance's sake. But no way would she ever again wear that ring to bed.

Chapter Fourteen

The following day, Adah returned to Jack Darby's house on the way back from delivering clean laundry to one customer and picking up a load of dirty laundry from another. She set her laundry basket on his porch, went in search of him, and found him grooming a horse in the barn, where two stables flanked the front section.

He looked up at her, surprise on his face, and stopped what he had been doing.

"Don't take the letter," she said, standing in the broad, open sunlit doorway. Adah had thought about suggesting Jack take the letter to a lawyer in another city, but she'd decided it would be asking too much.

He gazed at her with one eyebrow lowered, and she had the feeling she always had around him, that she was transparent. With the prismed sunlight and soft hum of the land, they were on their own. But frankness was foreign to her, so it took her a while to form her words.

"I'm giving up," she finally said as explanation, "at least for now. I'll never give up entirely, but I don't have a way out at the moment."

And then the most profound sense of failure came over her. Over the course of the night, she'd decided she had no choice but to stay put and look after Daisy, protecting her as much as possible from the Branches until she was old enough to leave on her own. Even though she knew with some certainty that the family was capable of covering up a murder, she also felt something of relief about her safety. The Branches weren't stupid enough to think that another accidental death on their farm would not be looked at with suspicion.

Adah was safe, or at least safer. She could stay on for Daisy. At least her purpose was clear. The events of recent months had revealed a grand picture of the enormity of nature and human life. Yet also how any one life was so small and short and ultimately . . . meaningless in the larger view of things. But even one small life could mean something over the course of its existence—a tiny breath in time. Adah had ended one life, but maybe she could save another. The idea that she had to stay with the Branches was dreadful, but it was the truth.

Jack registered what came over her, and he simply watched her for another long moment, but she found she didn't mind his scrutiny. She had put her faith in this man with her letter; he knew what she wanted, and if he saw through her even more so now, she did not care.

He turned back to face the horse. "Does that mean you're staying on?"

"Yes," she answered. "I have Daisy to think about."

She watched his smooth movements from behind and could see by the way Jack ran his hands over the mare that he loved these animals. His touch was easy but sure, and the way he handled the mare was like one would caress a child.

She bit her lip to keep from gnawing on a nail. "I'm not giving up on someday getting custody of her, but for now . . . I don't want you to take the letter. You were right; it could backfire."

He darted a glance over his shoulder. "What about you?"

"That doesn't matter now. It's all about my stepdaughter."

He brushed the horse slowly, calmly. "Like I said, you should get away from there."

"I can't leave her," Adah barely managed to say, her voice trailing off.

"They're the most bloodthirsty people in these parts."

"I can handle myself."

He stopped brushing and simply laid his hand on the horse's neck. "The way I figure it, justice was done when that river swept your husband away. No matter how it happened, he got what he deserved."

No matter how it happened? Adah's spine stiffened. What did he mean by that? What did he know or suspect?

He turned again to face her. "Go for a ride with me."

His mood shifts were rather startling, and she could hardly believe his words. "A ride? I can't. I have to get back home."

"What's your hurry?"

Adah didn't answer.

"They're watching you, aren't they?"

She blinked. "I'm practically a captive."

"What are you afraid they'd do if you came back late?"

She gazed up at him and met that gaze again. His eyes were open and candid like a door to his soul while also communicating to her, *I'm safe.* "I don't know. I'm worried every day about what they'll do to Daisy."

"Hurt her?"

Adah nodded once. She paused and waited for better words to come. "If not by beating her, then by killing her on the inside."

"You want something on the Branches?"

Baffled, Adah finally nodded again.

He said, "Go snooping around. There's other rumors about what the Branch clan is up to. I'm not sure how you can use the information, but you never know . . ."

She shuddered. "I'm sorry, but you're going to have to spell it out for me."

"Rumor is they're making moonshine and have been since Prohibition days."

The old log curing barn, of course. She said a slow "O-kay." Here was another thing that made perfect sense. Even with tobacco farmers faring somewhat better than others, the Branches seemed to positively *prosper* during these times, and the selling of illegal moonshine to supplement their income had to be the reason.

"So when's the last time you did something nice and easy?" he asked. On his face was a lovely expression of hope and expectancy.

Adah gulped. He was standing before her so honestly vulnerable, and he had been so helpful. He had told her the truth, a truth they now shared. There seemed little reason not to let down her guard a bit.

"You're not afraid of a little nice and easy, are you?"

"Should I be?"

He laughed, and it was the first time she'd heard him laugh, an amused low-pitched chuckle. "Come on. Come with me. We won't be gone long, I promise."

Adah stood by silently, unable to summon a protest, as he saddled a chestnut mare for his mount. Another horse, a gray gelding, would be Adah's for this ride, and she moved forward to saddle him herself, showing Jack that she knew what she was doing. She had learned how to handle a horse and ride with Chester and Henry's family before leaving them in Virginia.

Adah was wearing a faded calf-length print dress that was too big for her and old brown oxfords, not exactly riding attire. But she gathered the skirt up to her knees and swung into the saddle. They rode to the back of his farm and soon left behind all signs of human life as they entered a wood. Jack took the lead, and she followed. The horses were sure and sound animals, and her gelding had a nice gait that she soon fell into.

Jack was following what looked like old wildlife trails. This land, lusher and dimmer than the farm, was marked by streams down every small green gully. They passed an undersized herd of deer that regarded them, flicked their ears, and then bounced away as if propelled by springs. Occasionally Jack stole a glance at her over his shoulder, and she could tell he was sizing up her skills, making sure she knew how to handle a horse.

Why was she doing this? Why had she agreed to take this time with Jack when the most important thing right now was getting back to Daisy as soon as possible? Why did she trust Jack? She couldn't say why, but she simply understood, as if by instinct, that he would not betray her. She might have been a bit intrigued by him, too. It was more than his rugged attractiveness. He held something inside, something she wanted, even needed.

The wind rushed in through the trees and moved her hair, the sun was still and warm through the branches, and the land was damp and sprouting new life. She had a momentary sensation of frozen time, as though her light and spirit were a permanent part of the landscape. So many moments went unnoticed, and suddenly, for this brief one, she was thankful for everything that had brought her to this place and this second and this sensation—an awareness of her unique life. However imperfect, it was hers alone. And if personal sacrifices were a part of it, so be it.

They stopped in the dappled shade of a stand of maples, Adah reining in her horse next to his. She looked up to the sun through the lacing of tree leaves, then closed her eyes and felt the warmth on her face. As a bird *crr-reek*-ed in the branches over them, Jack asked her where she was from originally.

"Nowhere," she answered and then changed her tone. Jack had been nothing but kind to her, and yet she still disliked revisiting her past. "Back East, originally."

"What did you do before you married Lester Branch?"

"I was a reader. Of the tarot cards."

His eyebrows lifted. "Interesting." He paused. "Do you still do it?"

"No. After I got married, Lester disapproved and took away my cards."

He paused, digesting that information. "Interesting," he said again.

The woods seemed to release something in Jack; he wanted to tell her about himself. He said he was born in Galveston, Texas, just before the infamous 1900 storm virtually washed that city away. His father, an oysterman, had been aboard a boat and had never been found.

"I'm so sorry," Adah said.

He shrugged as if it were something long gone and no longer felt, but she could see the leftovers of that old pain in his eyes. "Not your fault."

"Do you remember the storm?"

"Barely even remember the sea. My mother left those parts right after it for Lubbock, where she remarried a man who worked at a bank."

"Was he a good stepfather?"

He laughed dryly. "Hardly know. By that time, I was already running crazy wild, getting into trouble, then getting into rodeo. That's where I fell in love with horses. I didn't go back home until tuberculosis took my mother."

"I'm sorry."

"I wanted to fight in the Great War, but they wouldn't take me on account I'm color blind."

"Really?"

"I can see some colors, but not all of them." He glanced at her. "But I see that your eyes have some green in them."

She looked away, tucking an errant strand of hair behind her ear, more questions falling into her mind, and a sense of something unspoken, something unknown, tilting her off guard. "That problem, the color blindness, it might have saved your life."

He said, "Maybe."

She glanced at him. "How did you end up on the river?"

He gave off a shrug and a half smile. "When I was making my way around the country, I made a buddy who got me on a boat, then I worked my way up."

She could almost see him now, the younger Jack Darby—cocky, confident, tackling the world on his own two feet, much as she had been at one time. The things that mattered to independent, self-reliant people like Jack and her had to be as real as the light that shone on them now and the earth beneath their feet.

"The river saved me in more ways than one."

Adah was puzzled. "How so?"

"I'd finally found something I wanted, and so I gained focus. Learned. Became good at something besides being a reckless young man and . . ."

"Catting around?" Adah asked and watched his face fall a bit. "Don't worry. You don't have to mince words around me."

"I fell in love with the woman a river is, complete with curves and changes of mood, and always in motion."

"How else did it save you?"

"It's confining, made sure I stayed within proper bounds. Sure, I moved up- and downriver, but I couldn't ever stray very far from the water's edge. I couldn't leave my woman." He winked.

Adah blinked up at the sky. Jack was far more complex than she'd first thought him to be. More confounding. She found herself wanting to know more. "So why now, a farm?"

"Why not?"

Adah shrugged.

"I started out near the sea, then spent most of my life on the river. Figured I'd find my own little piece of land and put down roots for the first time in my life. You probably noticed I don't grow tobacco—too much work. Just some corn, and I've bred some horses, including that chestnut with socks they claim killed Betsy."

"So . . . you've found a real home."

"Something I'm guessing you've never done."

She made the corners of her mouth lift upward as she lowered her gaze from the sky to the woods. A clearly half-hearted smile. "I guess you're right about that. For a moment, I thought we were alike, but even though I want it, I don't imagine I'll ever find a home."

Jack pulled in a deep breath, as if inhaling the moment with her. "It's a good feeling, having a place of your own. I was once like you—full of doubts. But this place has been good for me. It takes all my thinking and keeps me from drifting."

She turned to face him. "Why do you need that? What are you afraid of?"

"Now?" He glanced away quickly and didn't answer. Adah realized Jack wasn't scared of much, but perhaps the possibility of being alone for the rest of his life kept him up at night. What was his secret? She had the urge to ask him if the land was his woman now, but she hesitated. She didn't know him well enough yet.

Instead she said, "So you're here now, but you've led an interesting life. You haven't stayed in one place. And I bet you have stories. Many good stories. Maybe some secrets, too."

"I bet you do, too."

She trembled against the image of Lester sprawled on the ground after she'd killed him. For a moment, she struggled for air. "Not so much."

He persisted. "I bet you do."

His skin was flushed, and a sad, heated look flooded his face. Jack's gaze fell over her in a way that spoke of kindness, maybe even loneliness. She sensed that he might be starting to care about her. What had she done? And yet his openness nudged at her heart. Such honesty was rare.

Quickly she said "I need to go back now," which broke the spell that had fallen over them.

Upon their return to the barn, Adah unsaddled her mount, and as she was saying goodbye to the horse, Jack's presence closed in behind her. His proximity brought on a chill, or was it a tingle? He was close enough behind her that she could hear him inhale sharply and feel the air he exhaled on her shoulder. His breath smelled of the earth.

"Your hair is chocolate," he said.

She froze. Then spun around.

His lips were still, his brows bisected his face in a straight line, and his eyes asked for a response. It was the first time she could remember having absolutely nothing to say.

Your hair is chocolate. His words swooped around in her head, silencing all else, and his stare paralyzed her body. The grip of his eyes held her fast. Deep down, there was a quiver, a finger tapping at a door she thought she had closed for good.

The power of his steady, intense attention pulled her into his face. He was a mix of a cowboy and a king, and he drew her inside the open doors of his insistent eyes.

The world came to a stop, and in that tiny wink of time, nothing existed but the two of them. He held her gaze with a steady stare, as if he was absolutely sure of himself, as if he had read that deep down she needed adoration and he was the only one who could give her what she craved.

Finally she said, "Excuse me," and managed to walk away, leaving him standing in the barn, staring after her once again.

After midnight Adah silently left the house through the back door and crossed the broad, open patch of land between the house and the old log curing barn; her body and shadow were distinct and sharply outlined like ink on the moonlit lawn.

The image of Jack standing there looking at her had not left her mind. Had she wanted him to come after her? Should she have gone back?

Both of the dogs rushed up to greet her, and one of them looked anxious. It was out of the ordinary for someone from the house to be outside in the middle of the night.

She reached down to rub the dog's head. *Please don't bark.*

With the dogs on her heels, she tried the doors of the curing barn and found them chained and held together by a padlock. Funny, she'd never noticed that the Branch men kept the door barred. Nothing else on the farm was so fortified, meaning that what lay inside had to be of importance.

After picturing the hook on the hall tree where Buck always hung his keys, Adah crept back to the house and located the keys, gently took them down, and then retraced her steps toward the back of the house.

A sound of creaking wood on the stairs. Adah's heart catapulted and she swung the keys behind her.

"Mama," said Daisy, standing about halfway down the stairs and rubbing her eyes. "I woke up and you were gone."

"Shhh," Adah whispered. "Everything's alright. I'll be there in just a few minutes."

"Are you coming back? I want to hear a story."

"Of course. Wait for me in bed. I'll tuck you in. Give me just a few minutes, okay?"

Daisy turned a moment later and seemed to float up the stairs, a small sleepy princess returning to her bed of flower petals. Adah waited a few minutes to make sure that no one else was up; then she resumed her quest, nearly running across the lawn to the curing barn again, fumbling through the keys until she located the right one, inserting it into the padlock, and turning it until she heard the click and the lock popped open.

After slipping the chain off and laying it on the ground, Adah opened one of the double doors. Inside, the black obscurity was broken only by slivers of moonlight leaking in between the logs where the chinking needed repair. Not enough light for her to see. She took a few tentative steps while reaching forward with outstretched hands.

She bumped against something and ran her hands over it. A table of sorts stacked with objects covered by a tarp. Carefully she pulled back the tarp, and her hands landed on what felt like quart-sized mason jars. Some were lightweight, as if empty, but others were filled and heavy with liquid, and she thought she smelled alcohol. To be sure,

Adah grasped one of the full ones, unscrewed the lid, and breathed in the scent. Definitely moonshine. Adah replaced the lid and put it back where she'd found it, then fumbled around long enough to determine that there were stacks of similar jars on several tarp-covered tables. When her foot brushed up against something on the floor, she crouched down and explored, finding what seemed to be bags of sugar, enough for several families to bake pies and cakes for years to come.

Obviously the old log curing barn was used to store and perhaps age the moonshine, and the still was probably located somewhere back in the woods near the creek. She didn't even need to find the still; the amount of liquor in the log barn surpassed what would be considered appropriate for personal use. The Branches were indeed breaking the law, making and selling white lightning.

Quickly she felt her way back through the doors, then looped the chain to hold the doors closed. Somehow the chain slipped out of her cold hands and landed coiled on the ground, metal against metal, making a loud clinking sound.

She stopped breathing and instinctively fell to her knees as one of the dogs let out a confused, muted, growling type of bark. How had she let the chain fall from her hands? How could she have been so careless? Now she would be found out, and what excuse would she have for having gone snooping?

Someone must have heard; she was sure of it. Curling inward, she scooted up against the barn door, hoping to hide in the shadows, even though it would do no good. At any moment, she would see a light go on in the house or hear the back door flung open.

Her chest rose and fell with rapid breaths as she waited to be discovered. And waited.

But nothing happened. Perhaps in her excited, anxious state, Adah had imagined the sounds of the chain and the dog's half bark to be much louder than they were. The house remained silent while Adah gradually regained her composure, gazed in gratitude up at the sky, and eased to a standing position again, barely breathing.

Still half expecting to be met somewhere along the way with a gun aimed at her head, slowly but surely she retraced her steps back to her room.

She was tired. Suddenly so tired. Daisy had fallen back to sleep, and Adah crept slowly into the room, then lowered herself onto the bed, lifted her legs, and lay down on her side, hugging her pillow. She gazed out beyond the window, where the moon was sinking and new leaves flitted in the branches just outside.

The view brought back memories of her childhood before her parents died. She blinked and wished for the impossible. It wasn't long before she had been forced to face the reality of being an orphan. Then reality after reality. And now the newest ones: The Branches were capable of hiding a murder. And they were making moonshine. Her mind was awash now in new questions, the main one being, *How can I use this to my advantage?*

Chapter Fifteen

After church on Sunday, Mabel seemed to be going to extra trouble for supper that night. She had pulled out her best Crooksville china, baked fresh bread, and was making an extra pie for dessert—one made with strawberries, the other custard. Adah then noticed that none of the Branches had changed out of their church attire. *A guest or guests must be coming,* Adah concluded. Building up courage, Adah offered once again to help Mabel in the kitchen.

"No, thanks," Mabel replied as she pulled a pork roast out of the oven and started to baste it, not making eye contact with Adah.

The "thanks" part was new, and Mabel was moving around excitedly, as if anticipating something special.

"Are we having guests for supper?" Adah asked.

Mabel looked up at her warily. "You could say that."

"Who's coming?"

"You'll find out soon enough," Mabel snapped. Then, changing her tone somewhat, she said, "Keep Daisy in her church dress, and don't go letting her get dirty. We want her looking her best."

Looking her best? Daisy? What did this guest or guests have to do with Daisy? As Adah had feared, so far there had been no lifting of her restrictions. She had not been allowed to take Daisy with her on her laundry rounds, not even to see the family with children Daisy could've played with. She and Daisy were like prisoners here, barely seen by others. So why did Daisy need to look good today? Instead of clarity, Adah had gained nothing but new questions. Who was the mystery guest? And what scheme was Mabel launching?

"I don't want no trouble outa you today, you hear? Both you and the girl need to be on your best behavior," Mabel said as she continued to flutter about the kitchen.

The thought of food curdled Adah's stomach. She had to inhale deeply and let out her air slowly. Hoping to calm herself, she turned away and left, knowing she would receive no answers from Mabel.

Soon after, Jesse drove away in the sedan and returned about half an hour later. From an upstairs window, Adah watched him pull up, get out of the car, and go around to open the passenger-side door.

A woman stepped out. A tall woman who looked to be in her early thirties, wearing a severe dark-brown suit without jewelry or adornments, but having a stately and noble appearance. A memory of the woman suddenly floated to the surface of Adah's mind. Esther Heiser, a former teacher and now the principal of the town's elementary school. She was the district's staff advisor and the only woman on the school board. She had visited the Branches' church a time or two.

Adah couldn't imagine why she was here. Daisy wasn't old enough to start school.

Adah watched as Jesse led Esther to the front steps. She walked as upright as a flagpole, and Adah remembered her impression of the woman, that she seemed as allergic to smiling as the Branches did. She had a plain appearance with small birdlike eyes, a stern face, and her dull hair pulled back taut with combs. Adah was intimidated by a woman who was so well educated, who functioned on the same level as men, and whose astute eyes searched with the calm sharpness of someone who knew a lot about people. Both her striking demeanor and position in the community had inspired in Adah a rather wary admiration.

So what was Esther Heiser doing as a supper guest of the Branches?

As Esther climbed the front-porch steps, Jesse placed his hand at the small of her back. Adah blinked a few times. Was it even remotely possible that Jesse Branch and Esther Heiser were dating? How could a woman who didn't need a man, who had a career and a life of her own, possibly be interested in Jesse Branch? A woman like Esther Heiser would be too smart for that.

And then a surge of excitement. Tonight there would be conversation at the table. The Branches would be putting on their happy-family act. Adah was still nervous about Mabel's mention of Daisy's attire and what it meant, but at least this would amount to a different afternoon and evening.

Adah headed downstairs with Daisy in tow and found Jesse, Buck, Mabel, and Esther standing in the living room sipping on iced teas that Mabel had already passed out. Immediately Adah noticed that Jesse was wearing heady aftershave. After cursory introductions were made, Adah couldn't wait to speak to Esther.

"Do you recognize me?" she asked Esther and stepped up to greet her. Esther's face was unreadable as she stared down at Adah. But now Adah could get a better look at the woman's hands—square and sturdy and large as a man's, but also smooth and nicely manicured. Hands that had seen very little labor during their lives, not even household work. She could also see that Esther's skin was almost translucent, and her eyebrows had been plucked into two barely arched narrow lines.

Esther's voice was strong but cool. "I think so."

Adah said, "I've seen you at church."

Esther's gaze was of solemn appraisal. Not warm, but not distant, either. Just plain *there*. She had probably learned a great deal of self-composure and restraint from working around teachers, parents, and powerful men. Esther stood rock still as she spoke. "Yes, I've seen you several times."

Adah pushed back her hair. The afternoon was warm, and that, combined with her bafflement over Esther, was making perspiration bead on Adah's forehead. "I had no idea you were coming over."

"I had no idea you would be here."

Adah tried smiling. "I live here."

Jesse said, "We've given Lester's widow a place to stay until she can get back on her feet."

Well, that was about the nicest thing Adah had heard since coming back from the river to the Branch house. Maybe they were softening toward her in ways she had yet to see.

"I see."

Adah stared; she couldn't help herself. "Welcome. It's so nice to have you here."

The Branches were watching this interaction with fierce attention, but they made no interference. Mabel's eyes were sharp points.

Esther said, "Thank you."

"Congratulations on the school board."

"Hardly," said Esther with a tiny smirk. "It's a battle."

"But you're so accomplished," Adah objected.

Esther leaned in closer. "I'm accomplished on the job."

Adah blinked hard. She couldn't get a grasp on Esther Heiser. Something in the other woman's eyes remained untamed, even though her words were so direct and sensible. Despite the contradiction, Adah was happy to have another woman to talk to.

"So why do you do it? I mean, bother with the board, since you're already an accomplished teacher and principal?"

"Oh, I don't know. To do my part in a bigger way. To help more than just my students and teachers. To get out of my house when I need to." Adah could see Esther swallow. "I live alone."

Adah's words seemed to come of their own bidding. If the Branches liked Esther, perhaps they wouldn't mind Adah keeping company with her. They wouldn't want to have to explain that Adah was a virtual prisoner here. "Do you want to go to a movie or lunch someday . . . ?" Her mouth dried. Why was she asking this?

Esther seemed equally confused. "Why?"

Adah said, "Why not?"

Esther's look had changed. Her tone was lower and somewhat indignant now. "Okay, I understand. How obvious you are. You must know."

A tap on Adah's shoulder could've knocked her over. What in the world was Esther talking about? "Know? Know what?"

"Oh, come on. You're kind of obvious, you know."

Taken aback, Adah managed to sputter, "I have no idea what you're talking about."

"Let's not behave like children. Someone must have told you about Lester and me."

Adah's knees turned to mush. "What?"

"Someone must have told you that I dated your husband at one time."

A full shock sweat broke out. If she had been near a chair, she would've fallen into it. "N-no . . . no one did."

Now Esther's face was pliable, and there was a new curiosity in her eyes. "I'm sorry. I don't think anyone could fake the reaction you're having right before my eyes. I've shocked you. I can see now that you really didn't know."

Adah had wrapped her arms around herself and her hands were shaking. Other than Betsy, Lester had never mentioned anyone from his past, and the idea of him with *any* woman was now unsettling. Esther probably had no idea that she had dodged a bullet. "I didn't know."

What followed was a confusing supper, during which Adah had a hard time reading anyone's hands or anything else about them. The talk was about flood reparations—Congress had been petitioned by the city for a levee, a seawall of sorts around the city, and the estimated cost was over five million dollars. They also discussed conflicts among school-board members, some town gossip, and radio programs.

Throughout it all, Adah read no sparks of romance between Jesse Branch and Esther Heiser. Adah kept quiet, and Daisy, too, remained silent during the entire tedious meal, showing no interest in their guest whatsoever.

Later, after supper had finally ended, Esther took Adah's arm and steered her onto the front porch, where the daylight was drifting away. Then she stood facing her. "Look, it was before he met you, just after his wife died. We went out a few times. Nothing serious. No harm done."

Then what was that pain Adah saw in Esther's eyes?

"He ended it when I told him I was falling for him. Now *that* was a mistake. I've picked up too much of an aggressive style from managing teachers and parents all day. As soon as I spoke of the future and my feelings, he jumped ship. Les said he wanted no 'entanglements,' and that was that. But we remained friends. I'm sorry to hear what happened to him, God rest his soul."

Still gathering herself, Adah said, "I had no idea that Les was friends with . . . really anyone. So you've known this family for a long time?"

"Almost my entire life. I went to school with the boys."

Adah could detect no ill feelings about the Branches coming from Esther. How was that? If Jack Darby had heard the gossip, why not this strong woman?

"I-I'm surprised."

Esther seemed a little offended. "That we would stick together in these parts?"

Adah shook her head adamantly. "No." But she was. Why would a fine woman like Esther Heiser be friends with the Branches? A horrible urge. Could she tamp it down? "I have to ask you something: What are you doing here with Jesse?"

A hard stare now. "Just as I thought. You judge, like everyone else."

"I don't. It's just that you're here, and then the shock that you might be dating him . . ."

Esther shifted her weight, and now she crossed her arms. "Why wouldn't I date him?"

Groping for the right words, Adah said, "You just seem so much . . . more sophisticated."

"I'm almost thirty-three years old, and I've never been proposed to. You're younger than I am and have already been married. You have no idea how it feels. I've been stuck in the same place for my entire life, waiting for something to happen. I've left it to the Lord for many years, and now it's time to take matters into my own hands."

Adah frowned, more questions cramming her mind. "So it was your idea to date Jesse?"

Esther's bristling was only barely discernible. "At Lester's funeral, Mabel and I spoke for the first time in a long time. Really spoke."

Adah mulled over this information. She had not noticed Esther at the funeral service or the graveyard. "Oh, so it was Mabel's idea?"

"She had just lost one son. You bet she wants the best for her only remaining one. And she knows what I want. Let's just say it was a meeting of the minds."

Realization sinking into her, Adah started to see Mabel as the quiet manipulator, the master planner, the real force behind the family. On the surface Buck was in charge and had the more commanding presence, but on a personal level Mabel orchestrated everything. She had coordinated the romance between Jesse and Esther with the fervor of a thief planning his next heist.

Having a woman like Esther Heiser marry into the Branch family would be a definite triumph and would lift their position in the community decidedly higher. "It sounds like a business transaction, rather than a romance."

Esther Heiser silently and only scarcely shook her head, as if she had been hurt. "Again, you judge. What would you know of my feelings? Or of Jesse's?"

Regret flooded Adah. She couldn't imagine Jesse Branch turning into anything but a less awful version of his father, but Esther had set her sights, and Adah doubted anything would deter her. "Nothing, I guess. I'm sorry. I shouldn't have said anything."

"You're right. You probably shouldn't have."

"I owe you an apology."

"You owe me nothing."

Adah gulped. She watched as Esther, too, swallowed hard. Adah could not get a read on the woman.

But any new presence in her life was good news. At the very least, Esther offered some contact with the outside world.

Esther extended her hand. "I'm not one to hold a grudge." Her countenance changed faster than any other person Adah had ever known. "No hard feelings?"

Adah took Esther's hand. "I think maybe you're a kind person."

"Not at all. I simply know what you're going through."

Adah had no idea what Esther meant. Did she mean losing her husband, being a widow, living with the Branches, taking care of Daisy? Or something else? "And . . . ?"

"You're all alone now, aren't you?"

Chapter Sixteen

All alone, indeed, and without any plans to get Daisy away, Adah was shocked that time continued to tick on. Each day of her continued confinement was marked by moments of hopelessness as no ideas came to her. But May ushered in the warm weather Adah had been craving, and Daisy could spend more time outside playing rather than inside surrounded by the Branches' toxicity.

By midmonth it was time to transplant the tobacco seedlings from the seedbeds to the main fields. These were hard, long days of labor, during which extra workers had to be brought in, and Adah joined in if for nothing else than activity and a break from the despair she held inside. Buck always took on the most desperate of men and paid them as little as he could; at least in her own small way, she was helping them.

When four colored men arrived one day in a wagon and pulled up before the house, Buck made them get down and undergo something of an inspection, and it reminded Adah of what it must have been like when slaves were put up on the auction block.

"You're pretty scrawny, ain't you?" Buck said to the men; then he circled them, looking them up and down. Buck's cheeks were aflame, his posture straight. Despite his age, he appeared tough enough to jump into a boxing ring and throw punches whenever he chose to, making it clear he was always in charge.

One of the youngest in the group allowed his mouth to fall open; his nostrils flared and his chest heaved, but he spoke not a word. Just tolerated it.

Scrawny was an understatement, Adah observed, swallowing back a warm flood of compassion. These men were withering away, shrinking into themselves, as if even the marrow of their bones had been leached. Tall and lean, their faces gaunt, though still young, hair twisted in knots, their clothes threadbare and hanging loosely, they seemed muddled as to what to say. Their faces were stoic, but their eyes remained bright.

Another of the men finally twitched under Buck's perusal. Buck stood still for a moment and stared at the man, as if daring him to twitch again, taking pleasure in their discomfort.

"You always this jumpy?" Buck asked with a sly smile.

"No, sir," the man answered.

The one who looked the oldest shifted his weight from one foot to the other and said, "We's right hard workers, sir."

Buck took another look over them and rubbed his chin. "That's still to be determined, now, ain't it? I bet you ain't ate a full meal in a month, so I don't figure any of you's capable of giving me a full day's work. I'll offer you seventy-five cents a day."

The four men glanced at each other with stunned expressions, and the oldest, still focused on his role as leader, cleared his throat before saying, "We was hoping to get at least a dollar."

Buck held a twig in his hand and proceeded to pick at his teeth. "I'll go up to eighty cents. Take it or leave it."

The leader held still, his eyes awash with a pleading desperation. "But sir, most of these spreads around here is paying a dollar."

Buck flung the twig to the ground and hitched up his pants, held by suspenders. "Then why aren't you working one of those spreads? There has to be some reason you ain't been hired on elsewhere. Probably because you look weak as women."

"Mr. Branch, I gives you my word. We's gonna do good work for you."

A cruel grin spread across Buck's face, as if he knew he'd won. He spat on the ground. "Eighty-five cents, and that's my final offer."

Again, the men glanced at each other, and Adah could read defeat in the set of their shoulders. The oldest, wearing a sorrowful but resigned expression on his face, eventually said, "Alright, sir."

Buck lifted his arm. "Well, hop to it now. What you standing there for? You got work to do."

Appalled, Adah sighed with dismay and turned away. Life could be brutal even during the best of times, but for men like those four, every day probably amounted to facing another shameful humiliation and degradation. The Depression had weakened almost everyone, and 1937 had been a year of setbacks, but even those who weren't directly hurting were usually kind. Many people were trying to help their fellow man. But not Buck Branch. Scruples meant nothing more to him than the gravel in the driveway he kicked as he walked away.

Later, when she overheard him tell Jesse he'd hired the men for only eighty-five cents a day, he laughed. The mad rumbling sound like thunder announcing a coming storm, combined with Jesse's snortlike laughter, sent a trail of sweat down the center of Adah's back.

The tractor was hitched to the tobacco planter, and one man drove while two others sat on the back of the planter and set the seedlings eighteen to twenty inches apart, then watered them while a fourth man followed on foot. Adah helped from time to time after doing laundry and trying to do some fun things with Daisy.

But the downside of the warmer weather was doing the laundry in the heat and over a fire. On occasion Adah found herself overcome by the smoke that set off coughing and gulps for fresh air. Often her back was drenched in sweat, and her cotton dress clung to her body like a second set of skin. Sometimes she had to walk away for a while and stretch her back, look to the horizon, and breathe deeply, reminding herself to take care of her health for Daisy's sake.

After the tobacco plants were in the ground, and after each rain, Buck and Jesse spent all day running harrows down the rows in the fields to turn under weeds and keep them at bay. If the two men weren't in the fields, they were inside the old log curing barn, or they disappeared into the woods for hours, obviously making more moonshine as the weather warmed. With dirt-cheap labor doing most of the field-work, they could give time to their other enterprise. Most of the days, only Adah, Daisy, and Mabel kept to the house, the silence between the two women as loud as a blaring horn.

The conversation with Esther ran through Adah's mind, in particular Esther's comment about judgment. Esther had indicated she was interested in Jesse and wanted a proposal, and that could mean that Esther would be moving into the Branch house. Or if they married, would Jesse finally leave home and get a place of his own? Adah thought that unlikely—Jesse was to inherit—so it was altogether possible that Adah and Esther would end up living under the same roof someday.

Their first meeting hadn't gone well, but it hadn't been a disaster, either. Adah pledged to herself that she would do better next time. If there was a next time. She also kept thinking that a smart woman such as Esther Heiser would soon come to her senses and lose all interest in Jesse Branch.

As she gazed about, her eyes landed on the livestock barn, and an idea hit her.

She found Mabel in the kitchen cutting a chicken carcass into pieces she would flour and fry later. Adah said to her mother-in-law, "It's such a nice day, I thought about taking Daisy for a ride around the farm on Miss Socks. What do you think?" She had learned to ask permission for everything, especially if it had to do with Daisy.

"Fine by me," Mabel answered.

Something hooklike lodged in Adah's windpipe, but she cocked her head and her words slipped out as if they had minds of their own. "Isn't Miss Socks the horse Lester's first wife was riding when she was killed?"

Mabel's face registered shock. The skin was hanging off her cheekbones, and her pupils became pinpoints as she blanched. "I can't remember." She wiped her hands on her apron, and Adah noticed a slight tremor in her fingers. She appeared to have to force herself to meet Adah's eyes. "Who told you that?"

"Someone at church mentioned it." Funny, Adah thought, how these days she could walk in and out of the truth as though through an open door. "Said she was surprised you'd have kept a horse that killed someone."

Mabel fixed a pained but angry stare on Adah. "Like I said, I don't remember."

"How many horses did you have back then?"

"We had several."

"But still . . ."

"What are you saying?" Mabel demanded as she shifted her weight from one foot to the other.

Adah's gaze never fell. "Only that it seems strange you'd let your granddaughter ride a horse that killed someone—her mother, in fact."

Visibly shaken, Mabel darted her eyes away, and a line etched between her brows. "I changed my mind," she said fiercely, her hands clasping her apron. "I don't want Daisy on no horse."

Adah smiled; she couldn't help it. Then she spun around and walked calmly to the back of the house and out the back door, filled with satisfaction at being able to challenge any of the Branches, especially Mabel or Buck. But Buck was too terrifying to face head-on, and he was sure to hear anything Adah said to Mabel anyway.

On the heels of her satisfaction, pure dread. Why was she making things harder for herself? She hadn't been thinking straight. Why hadn't she kept her mouth shut? She remembered one of the first things she'd learned while out on the streets of New York City. If you spot some-one's weakness, avoid touching upon it at all costs, unless you want a confrontation.

Adah was running late that day, and by the time she returned home from making her laundry rounds, supper was over. But Mabel, Jesse, and Buck were still sitting around the dining table, apparently in rapt conversation that stopped as soon as Adah entered. Buck was spinning quarters on the tabletop.

"Mama," Daisy cried and ran to Adah, wrapping her arms around Adah's legs. "You were gone so long."

"Not long enough," Mabel said.

Buck shushed her. His nostrils visibly flared, and he gave Adah a look that felt like the tips of a hundred sharp knives were pressing into her flesh. He caught the quarter he'd been spinning and slammed it on the tabletop, his eyes still boring through her.

She supposed they had been discussing the earlier talk of Miss Socks and Betsy, and she figured they were none too happy about it.

So why were they keeping her around? Did they still want her part of Lester's farm? Or was there more? Were they planning to rid them-selves of her, too, just to make it easier? Even though Adah had once believed the Branches wouldn't dare stage another accidental death on their property, that night she told herself to be extra careful around farm machinery and make sure that the Branches kept their distance when she was around fire or in any other vulnerable situations. She decided to always prepare her own plate of food and pour her own coffee.

One never knew.

Chapter Seventeen

On the day Ben Harper came to retrieve the tractor that had been heavily used for tilling and planting, his face had been transformed from one full of energy, optimism, and enthusiasm to one that looked as though it had experienced a grave disappointment for the first time. He wore casual slacks and a plaid shirt, and together with his trailer driver, they loaded the dirt-encrusted tractor onto the flatbed without saying a word, their faces blank. Buck and Jesse hadn't even washed it.

After the trailer started lumbering off the farm, Adah ran to catch up.

The driver must have seen her in the mirror and stopped. Ben Harper looked out of the window at her and then stepped out of the truck as she approached; he was wearing a curious but wary expression.

When she reached him, she was heaving dry breaths. "I'm sorry if I startled you. I just had to . . . to ask . . . are you going to be okay?"

First, he seemed to pass through the surprise that she had come after him; then he plastered on a smile and forced a carefree tone of voice. "Of course. Why do you ask?"

Adah caught her breath. "I know you paid for the tractor and expected Buck to pay you back."

His face fell. She could see how much his innocence had suffered, how many years he had aged over this affair. He asked, "Who else knows about this?"

Adah shrugged. "Don't worry. As far as I know, only this family."

He regarded her warily, but finally asked in a low voice, "Do me a favor, then. Don't tell anyone."

"I won't. I'm so sorry." She tried unsuccessfully to stifle her questions. "How are you going to handle this?"

Ben Harper laughed. "Why would I tell you?"

She supposed she deserved that. Ben Harper knew nothing about her. Hands on her hips, she shook her head. "I hate what they did to you."

He studied her, and his eyes showed that he hadn't given up hope in humanity yet. There was an almost imperceptible hint of brightness on his face, and his expression slid from distrust to something more open. "Yes," he said slowly. "I see that now." He recovered himself and stared ahead wistfully. "I told my father. Only person I told, not even my wife."

So Buck's plan had worked to perfection. He'd managed to hurt the father, too.

Ben turned to Adah. "He's going to loan me the money I lost. I borrowed from the bank to buy the tractor in the first place, so at least I can make my payments. And I'll sell this tractor used and get at least some of the money back. I'm sure hoping word of this never gets back to my boss."

"Don't worry," Adah breathed out. "Buck and Jesse will brag about it to themselves, but Mabel doesn't want anyone to know. She'll make sure it's kept a secret."

Ben's face slid into a wary smile. "Hard to imagine they'd take orders from a woman."

"Mabel Branch is no ordinary woman."

He flinched. "Don't know much about Mabel, but it's no secret that Buck and Jesse will do anything to save money, even if it means cheating people."

"Why, then . . . ?" Adah whispered, dry mouthed. "Why, then, do people never confront them?"

Guilelessly he peered at her then. "Years of knowing 'bout them and the things they do has left people scared."

"Why did you trust Buck, then? Why did you make this deal?"

Deflated, he laughed again, pitifully. "That's the same thing my father asked. Can't say he's exactly proud of me right now. He told me the biggest lessons in life are learned the hard way, but I'm not to make the same mistake again."

"I'm so glad he's helping you."

"Yes," he said pensively.

She glanced behind her. Ben Harper was going to survive the Branches' scheme because his father was going to help him. Perhaps he'd see that helping her would ease his own pain. The Harper family probably hated the Branches as much as Buck hated the Harpers. Now they were most likely enemies for life. And the Harpers were powerful people and had more influence than Jack. Seeing no one in sight and not even knowing for sure what she could gain from him, she took a chance. "Would you ever consider helping me?"

"Helping you?" He seemed genuinely surprised. "What's going on here?"

Adah gulped. What exactly was she asking? Aware of her desperation, she said, "I need to get custody of . . . Daisy."

Ben Harper leaned back. "The girl?" His eyes lurched away. "I can't help you, I'm sorry. I can't do anything against the Branches. I couldn't risk it. My wife's expecting, my house is in shambles, and they've done enough harm to me and my family already."

"I understand."

And she did, although in that moment, she became acutely aware that a weight on her chest had been sitting immovable for some time. It had first formed when Jack Darby dismissed her, when her plans with him fell apart, and had gained shape and heft as Adah looked about her and saw no other paths to follow.

She had been slipping food to the four farmworkers Buck had hired, although their pay was without board, and she had briefly entertained the idea of asking for their help. She'd quickly discarded the idea, however. What could they possibly do? She couldn't put any extra risk on people who were barely surviving as it was. Everyone around her had a difficult lot, and life could simply blink its eyes or shrug its shoulders and make each and every one of them sink into the silt.

The anvil in her chest took on extra weight as another possible avenue closed with Ben Harper. She had left herself utterly exposed. She resisted the urge to bury her head in her hands and weep.

He tipped his hat. "You have my sympathies, however."

That night, when Mabel set an extra plate on the supper table, Adah expected the guest would be Esther Heiser again. Instead it was Manfred Drucker, who entertained the family with stories about townsfolk who had tangled with the police or the sheriff's department, and every so often he glanced at Adah as if making sure she knew he hadn't forgotten about her.

She had to endure his leering glances and outright stares that brought a chill to her skin; all the while she pretended to be unaffected and continued to force her food down. Nothing was mentioned about the exhumation of Lester's body. Nothing was mentioned about Lester or his death at all. And yet the threat was explicit. All it had taken was Drucker's presence to remind Adah that he was probably slowly but surely closing in. Gathering information and perhaps uncovering the truth that would seal her fate. Could her arrest come any day now?

Before he left, Adah was heading toward the stairs to ready Daisy for bed, but he stopped her, saying, "Adah Branch."

She turned to face him.

With a face full of smug satisfaction, he said, "I'll be seeing you real soon."

What did that mean? Sleep that night was a place Adah would not visit. What could she do? She had no one, save a little girl who needed help even more than Adah did.

She had been avoiding going to Jack Darby's place, even though she was a day late in picking up his laundry. One evening as the sun was sinking low in the sky, she donned an old straw hat and started trudging down the driveway. She also had to go see two of her other customers. She saved Jack for last as she had no idea what to expect from a man who had never failed to surprise her.

The dirt roads were dry, and by the time her rounds were nearly complete, she was bathed in a layer of fine dust, her skin gritty and her hair hanging. She had dropped off a basket of clean laundry for one family and had picked up a dirty one from another, which she had then dropped off at home. Now, back out and exhausted, as she turned from the road up to his drive, she saw him sitting on the front porch as if he was waiting for her.

At first, he didn't move as she approached, but then he stood as she came nearer, his eyes lighting up at the sight of her. Jack was becoming handsomer the longer she knew him; each time she laid eyes on him, she found more to like and explore. Lester, on the other hand, had over time become ugly in her eyes.

Jack said, "I was hoping to see you today."

Adah stopped at the bottom of his porch steps. "Yes, I'm sorry. I should've been here yesterday."

He squinted. "Are you avoiding me?"

Adah removed her hat and let the air touch her forehead, closing her eyes for a moment, remembering: *Your hair is chocolate.* "I'm avoiding the heat."

He gazed out to the sky and the burning yellow hole of hazy sun. "We are having quite the early heat spell, aren't we?"

Adah opened her eyes and looked at him. "Do you have a basket for me?"

Jack nodded once and went inside through the screen door, then came back out carrying the basket of laundry. He set it down and reached into his chest pocket, retrieving something. "I got these for you." He opened his hand and revealed a set of worn tarot cards held together with a rubber band.

The breath caught in Adah's chest, and her eyes flicked upward to his face. "Where did you get them?"

"Bought 'em off a trinket trader passing through. Thought you might like them."

Adah took the deck and ran her fingers across the back of the top card as she gazed at the filigreed design. How many hands had touched these cards? How many fortunes had been read using them? How many lies had they told? How many truths had they revealed?

"Will you read for me?" Jack asked.

Adah's head jerked up. Then she shook it fervently.

"Why not?"

"Have you ever taken a reading?"

"No."

"Then you don't want to."

He eyed her curiously. "Tell me why not."

She sighed and replaced the hat on her head. "It's nothing. It's everything. Most often the cards say nothing of importance and are simply a means to predict something that may or may not happen. Other times I've found them to be accurate, often when it's the most important thing. But there's no way to know if something mystical has intervened or if it's just gibberish. Once you've had a reading, however, you'll always wonder."

"You say sometimes the reading is valid?"

Her arms remained at her sides as she lifted one shoulder. "Yes."

"Then I'm willing to take my chances."

Fatigue began to seep out of Adah's marrow. Why did people want to hear about the future, even when the odds were against knowing anything? Blood draining from her face, she turned and sank down onto the lowest porch step, removed her hat again, put her elbows on her knees, and rested her forehead in her open palms.

Jack's voice had changed into a sweet murmur. "I'm sorry. I thought you'd like the cards. I figured a present might do you some good." She heard him laugh in an ironic way. "Guess I'm not much adept at wooing a woman. Guess it weren't such a good idea after all."

Eyes still closed, she barely breathed as she realized that she had hurt his feelings. A radiance emanated from Jack now, and it was all too evident that she had been wrong about him in the beginning. He'd been wary of her just as she'd been wary of him, both of them wrapped in a protective shield that was slowly peeling away. Every little layer that fell from Jack revealed something unexpectedly sweet.

"It was very thoughtful, Jack. Thank you." Jack didn't make any sounds of movement or say a word, and when Adah lifted her head, she breathed out, "I found evidence of moonshining because of what you said. Thank you for that, too."

"I see," he said slowly, as if forcing himself to change the subject along with her. "What will you do about it?"

Now Adah was the one having to stick to the new subject at hand. The sound of his voice was like a salve, a healing salve. For the first time in a long time, someone cared about what she thought and felt, and the result was like a sip of Kentucky bourbon—a velvety warmth in her chest. "I don't know yet. I could go to the police, but I figure Buck and Jesse must have at least a few friends on the force."

Jack nodded. "Most likely they've paid off a couple of them to be left alone. And if you happened to be unlucky and ended up speaking to one who's in on the action—"

"It would do me more harm than good. Again," Adah finished for him.

"I'd be willing to bet most of the police are on the up-and-up, but you'd never know."

"So what use is it to know they're making moonshine?"

"It's always best to know as much as possible. Just wait and watch. Something might come up."

She was so tired now. How had she made her way here? And how would she ever escape from the Branches? She glanced up to see a tiny bit of trembling at the corner of Jack's mouth. Kindness intensified all that she'd been feeling, and a silent sob seeped from her mouth. She swallowed against a thickening sensation at the back of her throat. Something hot and urgent prickled under her eyelids. And then she did something she'd never imagined she'd do, not while sitting on a quiet porch, especially not in front of another person, and never with such great heaving movements racking her body. Whether she cried for herself or for Daisy, it didn't matter; it was all the same.

He sat still, and she was aware that he did nothing but watch her silently, that he waited for her to pour it all out, until her self-awareness slowly returned, and she occupied her head again.

She heard the screen door open and close, then open and close again a few minutes later. Jack set a porcelain basin full of water on the step beside her.

"Here," said Jack and came around in front of her, rinsing a cloth in the basin. He sat low on his haunches in front of her and gently but with assurance washed her eyes, her nose and forehead, her cheeks and lips, then her neck, as though she were a child, and then he came around behind her and gently raked his dampened fingers through her hair, pulling it back and away from her face, combing it smooth with his fingertips, and lastly forming it into something of a loose knot at the back of her head. Gratitude pooled in her body as she submitted to his touch and tears formed again. Somehow he knew what she needed: the comfort of human hands.

He said in the softest and most sultry voice she'd ever heard, "You want to know what I think . . ."

Adah simply waited.

". . . about you?" he finished.

Adah didn't know if she wanted to hear this, but she was powerless when he spoke to her.

"Most of the women I've known were nothing like you. They were mechanical, always saying the proper thing, moving the proper way, like machines, like everything were greased and set to run just so, never giving a glimpse inside. But I knew you weren't like them others the first time I saw you on this porch step, your hair as rich as chocolate, your shoulders held square, and your eyes in search of something that mattered to you. And when we first talked, I knew the burden you carried, the weight of thoughts that couldn't be said."

Adah closed her eyes. His voice sounded like the earth, as if it had been born from riverbeds and bedrock and then had slowly worked its way out of the soil and into the air. It still held that inner-earth warmth inside. Jack had turned out to be a tender heart. Inadvertently she had uncovered his secret. Jack Darby was lonely and in need of love.

He placed his hand on her shoulder, and she could feel his breath flowing over her. "Your neck is a slice of white cake."

She blinked and then searched the lawn before her as if expecting something to pop up and tell her what to do. She couldn't encourage this attraction. "Why must you say such eccentric things?"

"Maybe I'm eccentric."

"It's not something most people aspire to."

"I'm not most people."

"Yes . . ." She paused and waited for better words to come. "I see that now."

The tone of his voice changed, becoming sure and level and direct. "Leave that horrible house. Get away from there. I'll help you. I'll do whatever I can. If you need money . . ."

Night was settling over the land now like a blanket, and something baffling was drifting down over her. Still not facing him, she said, "I can't go. I'd be leaving a helpless little girl with people who'll ruin her or turn her into a monster like they are."

"Couldn't you stay in touch?"

She reined in her voice. "They might not let me see her. I'd be completely at their mercy."

She heard him breathe out slowly. "Aren't you at their mercy now?"

She answered yes and was surprised she was being so candid. She turned, gazed up at him, and met that stare again. His eyes demanding attention and telling her, *I'm safe.* She explained to him about the crazy accusation of murder leveled against her by the Branches and now by Manfred Drucker, and Jack listened intently.

"It won't be easy to exhume the body," he said. "Takes a court order and lots of just cause, I think. It won't be easy, but it's not impossible, either."

"That's what I figured."

She heard him breathe in and out again, and there was a sea change in the atmosphere, as if a coiled shell were opening up. "Adah, listen to me. There's something I have to say to you." He pulled in a ragged but determined breath. "You've woken me up. I've spent most of my life doing things that weren't, in the end, all that important. I let those things pull me away from what I really wanted and needed. Now I know what I need, and it's because of you. You've awakened me to the fact that my life is probably more than half over, and I haven't done the most precious thing—loved a woman. I know you care for the girl, but now you have other things to think about, don't you? You want to be loved, you need love, don't you?"

Making an effort to speak, Adah said, "Love has never worked out for me."

"That can change."

"I trusted someone once. My husband . . ." Adah nearly choked on the word *husband*. Had Lester ever really been a husband? More like an enemy.

"Is there something you want to tell me?" he said, soft as a lullaby.

With her scalp prickling, the words slipped out. "Something happened to me, over and over with Les, by his hand."

"Oh, Adah . . . I figured."

It was the first time he'd called her by her first name. She turned away again, more thoughts falling into her mind. "I can't let anything like that happen to Daisy."

"She's their flesh and blood. Don't you think that makes a difference?"

"I don't know. I can't say for sure."

"Once you got away, maybe you could forget about all of this and what happened back at your old house." Now he touched her neck. "Seems to me forgetting is the only way to get past the bad things in life."

How could she forget? The worst thing had been Lester, and he in turn had led to so many more bad things. What had she missed before marrying him? What signs had there been? But she found that trying to remember was like trying to recall the fleeting thoughts that cross the mind while drifting to sleep. There—and then gone. And if she hadn't married Lester, what would've become of Daisy? No, she couldn't imagine Daisy ever slipping away.

Sniffling, she said, "I won't forget her. Ever. And I'll never leave her there."

She had to go back, right now. Jack's words, his touch, and his kindness had reminded her of the things missing in her life. Just as she had shown him what was missing in his. But she had to bury any longings he brought out in her. She stood, thanked him, and began walking away.

"Adah," he said, and she stilled at the sound of her name on his lips again. "You forgot something."

Yes, she'd forgotten to take him in her arms, tuck her face into his neck, then look upward and find his mouth.

She turned and witnessed the aching pain on his face. He opened his hand.

It was the deck of tarot cards.

Chapter Eighteen

As summer settled over the land, Esther Heiser seemed to be settling in as a future member of the Branch clan. She visited every Sunday for church and then had supper at the house and often spent additional evenings sitting in the parlor with Jesse, Buck, and Mabel. Once in a while she and Jesse took a drive or a walk alone. Whenever they were together Adah observed them carefully—they now seemed to share some genuine affection, which shocked her. She hadn't thought either of them capable of caring for another person. But maybe the needs and desires of the human heart were universal, even among the Esther Heisers of the world.

As Jesse and Esther's relationship appeared to be budding, Esther's relationship with Mabel was absolutely blossoming. Mabel allowed Esther to help her in the kitchen, where the two women could be heard laughing and gossiping over the sounds of the teakettle whistling, grease sizzling, and utensils clinking against pans as they prepared luscious summer meals. They baked a lattice-crusted apricot pie and soft white bread.

Ever since the conversation about Miss Socks, Mabel had put up even more of a wall between Adah and herself, rarely making eye contact and speaking only when it was absolutely necessary. Jesse and Buck acted much the same, choosing to ignore the subject of Miss Socks she had broached but making it ever so evident they hadn't forgotten about it, either.

Jesse was obviously still trying to impress. He had shed some weight from his massive frame and now asked for his shirts to be smartly starched. He loosened his tie but stayed in his church clothes all Sunday, at least while Esther was around.

On several occasions the women invited Daisy to join them in the kitchen, and it soon became apparent they were preparing for the day when Adah would be gone and Esther could take over as a substitute mother. Adah squeezed her eyes shut at the mere thought of that happening. She tried to see any signs of affection from Esther aimed in Daisy's direction, but there were none. In fact, Adah often saw a heartlessness in Esther's small joyless eyes as she gazed at the little girl, and Adah had to battle the urge to place her body between Esther's and Daisy's, as a bear would protect her cub.

Once, after a windy day and a long church service, Esther led Daisy into the parlor by the hand and sat next to her on the sofa, complaining that the girl's hair was "a mess" and pulling out a comb from her handbag. She then proceeded to rake the comb through Daisy's hair a little too roughly. And Daisy had always been so tender headed. When the girl protested and whined, Esther unstiffened her touch a bit but told Daisy to stop complaining.

Adah observed the interaction with silent astonishment. How could someone who worked with children all day long be so coldhearted?

As Esther continued to rake the hair back and off Daisy's face, she said, "You should always pull your hair up to your crown and hold it up with combs. You have big features, so you need to get the hair away from your face. You'll look prettier that way."

Daisy frowned and then hung her head and bit her lip. Already she had learned to keep silent, even in the face of the Branches' hurtful treatment and now Esther's backhanded compliment. Adah's skin crawled as she realized that the Branches were succeeding in breaking Daisy. Could these effects ever be undone? Or was it already too late?

One thing, however, soon became all too clear: Esther didn't like Daisy any more than Mabel, Buck, and Jesse did. Maybe she disliked all children. But she was committed to seeing her romance with Jesse through to its end, or so it appeared. Her attention to her appearance, regular visits, and growing camaraderie with Mabel made that richly clear.

Adah longed for a private conversation with Esther, although she didn't know why. She was clueless as to what she hoped to accomplish but couldn't help clinging to the hope that Esther could, even in some small way, help her. Opportunities for them to be alone, however, were almost nonexistent.

One day Adah decided to charge forward, so she asked Esther if she'd like to take a turn around the lawn. It was the hottest hour, or near to it, on a warm, sunny day, so they both donned straw hats following Esther's hesitant agreement to the stroll. Today Esther wore a dress Adah could tell was factory made of green rayon crepe and featured padded shoulders, a belted waist, and large yoke. Perhaps Esther was building up her trousseau.

After Adah reluctantly left Daisy alone with Mabel, she and Esther headed out. Beyond earshot, Adah darted little looks at Esther, still trying to size her up.

"What is it you want?" Esther snapped after she had returned the darted glances.

Adah's spine stiffened, but she made herself take quiet, solid steps. "Just to talk."

Esther slipped her hands into the small front pockets on her dress. "About what?"

"Well . . . for one thing, I wanted to say this: you're getting along here very well."

Esther didn't respond, instead simply fixed her gaze straight ahead.

Adah sighed. "I meant that as a compliment. That's what you wanted, wasn't it? To get along with everyone?"

Esther took one hand out of her pocket and fanned herself with it. "Frankly, yes. Not that it's any business of yours."

Adah pressed her lips together. "Obviously they've poisoned you against me," she said flatly.

Esther faltered in her step, and her face became even more somber.

Adah continued. "With all due respect, I'm not your enemy."

Esther shot her a guarded look, but her voice was steady, solemn, and strong. "I don't see you as an enemy. There's no threat. For you to be an enemy, you'd have to pose a threat."

Adah grimaced. "Go ahead and shoot me now. What have they said about me?"

"Are you dull? You should know already."

"I know they hate my past. I know they have some strange notion that I played a hand in Lester's death."

Esther said, "I know all that, too. Even the last part. Jesse let it slip one night, but Buck and Mabel haven't said a word. For some reason Mabel wants me to believe you all are one big happy family."

Adah walked a few more steps and then breathed out, "But you see through it, don't you, Esther? They want me gone, don't they?"

Esther shot a peek behind them as if she was afraid they were being followed. Her voice lowered as a line ran down the middle of her forehead. "So help me God, if you ever breathe a word of this, I'll deny I ever spoke to you in this way. But I'll say this much alright: they figure that given time, you'll give up on getting your old place back and then move on."

Adah could feel heat staining her cheeks, even though this was not unexpected news. They had to know that her only hope of salvaging anything from the marriage was winning some ownership of the farm, or at least getting some money from the farm. "Hmmm. That's about what I figured. They want all of the farm. They're waiting me out until they get it. But I won't give up easily."

Esther said nothing, again retreating into silence.

Not willing to give up on the conversation and her thin slice of hope, Adah asked, "So why did you tell me this? You certainly didn't have to."

Esther sighed. "Because I'm not so crazy about the idea of you leaving."

Something tripped in Adah's chest, but she simply waited for Esther to explain herself.

"I think it would be better if you stayed here." Esther wrapped her arms around herself even though the day was hot. "You see, I'm not so keen on the idea of playing mother to an orphan."

Adah almost gasped. "You mean Daisy."

Esther nodded. "Between you and me, I've waited a long time to have my own child, and I'd prefer to focus on nothing else."

Adah couldn't quite conceal the surprise in her voice. "You want children?"

Esther stopped walking and turned to face Adah. "You think I'm too harsh, but it comes from having to deal with other people's problem kids all the time. I want one shot, one baby, and one chance to do it right."

Adah heaved in a gulp of hot air. Esther had revealed her secret. Would she, could she go further? "Esther, I have to ask you something. Have you ever heard anything . . . suspicious about how Betsy died?"

Esther's eyes sprang open. "No." Then a more determined stare, but one that held wariness inside it. "And I don't want to know. I leave such things to the Lord."

Adah had the feeling that Esther knew about the rumors but wasn't breathing a word about it. Adah had already gone much further than she'd anticipated going during this conversation and pulled back now. "So Daisy doesn't exactly fit into your plans, does she?"

"No," Esther said through an exhaled breath. Her eyes were awash in resignation when she said, "But things rarely unfold perfectly. I guess I'll have to get used to the idea of being a step-aunt who has to act the mother."

Adah looked away for a moment and carefully considered her words. Turning back to Esther and placing a firm, open gaze on her, she said, "If Daisy wasn't here, you could have Jesse all to yourself, your future child or children to yourself."

Esther's face paled, and every muscle appeared tense. "I can't believe you said that. You must not be right in the head." She wagged a finger in the direction of the house. "I could march back into that house and tell Mabel or Jesse what you've said, and they would turn you out in the very next moment. You have no claim on the girl. There's nothing you can do about it."

"I know that. Why do you think I'm still here?"

"Really? You just said you're staying because of the farm."

"The farm, yes, is part of it, but there are some things more important than land and money."

"You've been staying because of the girl? They know you're attached to her, but they think you're staying on until Les's estate goes to probate."

"They'll fight me tooth and nail?"

She nodded brusquely. "Jesse is thinking of building us a new house there, up on higher land, farther from the river."

"But he's going to inherit this farm, the much better farm."

"Believe it or not, he wants to live on his own—I mean with me— away from his parents for a while. He can take care of your old place over there and help out here, too."

"So he has proposed."

"Yes."

Adah's temples throbbed with conflicting emotions. If Esther married Jesse and moved into the Branch house, at least Adah would gain the possibility of a faint friendship or a comrade, even a suspicious one. On the other hand, the situation practically shouted that Adah's replacement was already in the works. "My best wishes," she said dryly.

"Oh, cut it out. Lack of sincerity doesn't suit you."

"I was trying to be . . . polite."

"You and I don't have to be polite to one another."

Adah saw a chance, but she nearly choked on her words. This could backfire, and yet she pushed on because desperation was in the driver's seat now. She put a hand to her heart. "So . . . don't you see? It's so clear to me now. In many ways, you and I want the same thing . . ."

Esther bristled and then thrust out her chest. "Maybe . . . maybe we want the same thing in the end, but don't go thinking that I'd do something about it. If you get nothing and have to stay, it works well for me, too. You'll always be Daisy's mother."

"Unless they send me away. Then you'll get the job. A job you don't want."

"I'd never help you leave with her, if that's what you're thinking. And you're lucky I won't say anything about your idea."

"What idea, Esther? I'm simply pointing out that we might benefit from each other. You must sense this. Otherwise why would you protect me?"

"Like I said, as long as you're here, Daisy thinks of *you* as her mother."

Adah's lungs emptied. "It lets you off the hook."

"Maybe," Esther said again slowly, her expression closing up. "But I have to grant you one thing: if they get sick of you and send you off, Daisy becomes my responsibility. Mabel says she's too old to take care of her. But don't go getting any ideas. Whatever happens, happens. I'm not a part of it. As far as I'm concerned, this conversation never took place."

While the so-called family sat down for supper and dug into the pork chops, scalloped potatoes, and canned butter beans, a storm swept in—one that brought fierce wailing winds, a dark-green sky, and much cooler air, as if some soulless spirit had descended from a place frozen in ice and time.

Was it Lester's spirit? Adah shivered as she ate in silence and listened to mundane comments about the storm and the food.

When thunder roared out of the blurry skies and joggled the house, Daisy whimpered, hopped down from her chair, and went to Adah. As Adah was lifting the girl onto her lap, Buck said, "Oh no, you don't." Today Buck's eyes were rheumy and heavily lidded. Probably he'd been sampling his moonshine. His eyebrows fell down over his eyes like a pair of hairy worms, and his cheeks were russet.

Daisy stopped still. But she looked up at Adah with pleading eyes, and Adah's confidence died. Fixed on them now, he said through one side of his mouth, the other side, as usual, full of partially chewed food, "You're too big to be sitting in somebody's lap. You go on and git yourself back in your own chair, young lady. We don't have no crybabies 'round here."

Daisy did as she was told, and Adah bit down so hard on her lip she thought she might draw blood. It hadn't taken long for Daisy to submit almost entirely to the whims and wishes of the other adult Branches. Fear and recrimination would do that to a person, especially a child.

For the rest of the evening, the storm punished the land, and rain fell like so many hard little stones, then soaked into the earth, turning the ground into mush. Later it was decided that the roads would be too slick and maybe even impassable over creeks, and it was too risky for Jesse to drive Esther home. Mabel told Adah to make herself a pallet and give up her room and bed to Esther.

As the rain continued to hammer down and darkness encroached, Adah donned a sweater and helped Daisy into hers; then they took blankets and pillows out to the covered back porch. There, they watched the rain. The thunder and lightning seemed to have passed, and Daisy was no longer afraid. Adah reread *The Cat Who Went to Heaven*, and Daisy barely made it through. She fell asleep under Adah's watchful eye, Adah's hand placed on the girl's back. But sleep eluded Adah. She gazed out into the rain and soon could see the pale glow of the moon as it fought its way up the sky through fog and clouds.

Esther was a confusing woman, not what Adah would consider to be a nice person, but for some reason she had confided in Adah. And the two women were in agreement on one thing: Adah was the right mother for Daisy.

How could the two of them, set up to be enemies, find a way to accomplish what both of them wanted? And how could they do it without the Branches knowing?

An hour or so later, the rain stopped, and the skies began to clear as if now some much kinder and gentler spirit in the heavens were breathing out fresh, warmer air. The moon appeared as a near-full silver disk in the sky, marred only by one hazy edge. One day away from being a full moon.

Adah's thoughts drifted beyond the farm and to all the others who might be watching this moon emerge out of a storm like peace after war. Was Jack watching it, too? Adah closed her eyes and remembered his touch on her shoulder, then her neck.

Your neck is a slice of white cake.

The idea of escape came to her the next day as the ground began to dry, as she helped the men inspect the new tobacco plants for insects and worms, as she laundered a large load of clothes for the redheaded family and hung them on the line.

In the fields, the rows of plants transformed into roads that led away from here, and the sheets on the line became sails that floated vessels in the faraway seas. When Adah gazed at the truck, she saw only its wheels in imagined movement. In the silent sky she saw scudding clouds and observed how they could cross the sky and then disappear off the visible ether. When the full moon rose the next night, its face was a honed and bright map that could lead her away. The thought of leaving infused her lungs with morning-fresh air cleansed by the rains, her mind coming alive with images of bright, open spaces.

Lately she and Daisy had spent many nights on the back porch. After Daisy fell asleep, Adah sent her gaze into the yard, where the moths were beginning to come out, and fireflies blinked against the oncoming dusk. Freedom called during so many nights out there alone, the stars as her ceiling and the night air as her blanket.

Now, her hands reddened by the lye soap she regularly used for washing, her back aching from leaning over in the fields and carrying heavy laundry baskets, and her mind a tangle of troubled thoughts and new fears, one thing haunted any happy moments: Manfred Drucker was probably closing in, working to get Lester's body exhumed. And what would be learned from an autopsy? It was too scary to stick around and find out. It wasn't even worth getting her part of the farm if she was to be arrested. As she'd said to Esther, some things were more important than land and money. Perhaps she had been too hasty and naive when she'd thought Esther might help her; Esther might just as easily become an enemy, and there was no way to know.

Adah's only option was to give up on the farm and the money it could provide. She had to give up on finding a legal way to keep Daisy, too. There wasn't enough time.

She had to escape as soon as possible and take Daisy with her.

Chapter Nineteen

The next time she saw him, Adah found Jack in his cornfield, standing tall in the growing stalks like a lighthouse overlooking a sea of green. His was a beautiful farm with towering trees in the distance, straight rows in the cornfield—not a weed in sight—and another field cultivated in meandering rows up a low slope. Around it all, fresh air sweetened of earth and oak and sun.

"Why are you here?" he asked in a harsher tone than she had expected. His gaze was measured, too. Obviously Adah's disappearing acts were not sitting well with Jack, and Adah looked down, disappointed in herself for what she had done. Jack suddenly looked as though he regretted his tone.

She looked down at her feet, squarely set in the furrow where they stood. Then she took off her hat and squinted up at him. "I have to leave here. You were right."

She couldn't be sure, but she thought she saw a pained expression sprint across his face, even though it was shaded by a hat.

"That so?" he asked. "What set you off?"

Adah bit her bottom lip. "It's too long a story, but . . . I have to go."

"Go where?"

She lifted her hands and then let them fall. "I don't know yet. You don't know me well, but I lived on the streets on my own for a long time."

"Don't you have some family somewhere?"

Adah shook her head. "Only Daisy." It took her a moment to gather the words that she had only ever spoken in her mind. Somehow putting the words out there would make it even more real. And now she was trusting Jack . . . perhaps with her life.

"Go on. But you don't have to ask. You know I'll help you, even though it means I'll lose you."

His words broke open her core. She'd never expected to receive such kindness, such caring. She made herself meet his gaze, which was soft and sincere. "That's not it, Jack. I know you'll help me. But . . . when I say I have to leave here, I don't mean that I'll leave alone. I'm going to disappear and take Daisy with me."

Looking rather taken aback, he studied her for a moment. "You mean you're going to run away with the girl . . . ?"

She held his gaze firmly now. "I can't think of anything else."

He looked askance, removed his hat, and let the fresh air bathe his forehead, then slowly replaced the hat and stared her in the eyes again. "Do you realize that's kidnapping?"

"Yes." Adah's voice cracked, but she was determined to show Jack how serious she was about this. "I have to do something or get something on them that would make them hesitate to come after me or even report what I'd done."

He leaned back a notch as if some ghost or spirit had just given him a shove. "You think you can beat the Branches at what they do best? Intimidate people? They're the masters. No one beats them at that game."

"I have to try." She gulped. "I haven't seen Manfred Drucker lately, but I know he's out there working against me, working for Buck. And Jesse has been bringing a woman around, name of Esther Heiser. At first, I thought she'd make things better . . ."

"And now . . . ?"

"It's baffling. She's by all outward appearances a successful and independent woman, and yet she wants to marry into the Branch family. She's almost desperate to get married."

"What scares you about her?"

"Did I say I was scared?"

"I can see it; it's written all over you."

Adah lowered her voice, even though no other soul was in sight. "She doesn't like Daisy, and if they ever decide to kick me out, Esther will become her mother. She'll take over."

"So . . . what's your plan?"

She shrugged. "I don't have one yet."

He reached across the space between them and touched her cheek softly, like a kitten brushing by. Adah's breath stalled. His voice changed yet again. "Come with me. I want to show you something."

"I don't have time."

"Sure you do."

Jack turned and headed down the corn row until it ended where it almost met the woods. Then he headed down a nearly overgrown path into the trees, and Adah, unable to resist, followed on his heels. The woods were hot with pollen-filled air and no breeze.

When they came to a barbed-wire fence, Jack spread the wires for Adah to slip through.

She shot him an admonishing glare. "Private property, I presume?"

He nodded. "I have no idea who owns it. But I've come out here for years. No one has ever bothered me."

Adah said, "There's a first time for everything. If we start taking bullets from some outraged landowner, you'll protect me?"

He snickered. "With my life."

Adah gestured beyond the fence. "What's over there?"

"Patience, please."

Adah ducked through the fence, and Jack followed her through. He took the lead again, and in only a few minutes, the trees opened up to the broad and gleaming sight of a small lake more richly blue than the sky above and so still a breath could have sent it rippling.

Jack said, "We have this all to ourselves."

Adah stared at the pristine sight before her. "How did you ever find it?"

"Just by wandering."

Jack then started stripping down to his underclothes, totally unself-conscious, and Adah didn't know what to do. She found a patch of willows, where she kicked off her shoes, unbuttoned herself out of her shirt, shimmied out of her skirt, and hung her clothes over reeds, then emerged self-consciously to see that Jack was already in the water. She hoped he wouldn't notice that her body was as white as chicken skin and that her bra and underwear were old and tattered.

"Over here," he said, his voice ringing in the cloudless silence, and she saw the white dome of his head out in the center of the lake. She stood for a moment in silence, breathing deeply, mesmerized. There was nothing except him and the lake's mossy smell, the sheen off the water, a line of black trees in the distance, and blinding light.

She touched the water with her toe. It was colder than she'd expected. A shiver lifted the hair on her arms, but she hugged herself and took a few steps down into water that was clearer than she had expected, too. It must have been a spring-fed lake.

Up to her thighs in water, she plunged in headfirst, immediately engulfed by the sweet water. Sounds were muffled as she pushed back up and broke the surface.

After swimming in his direction, she began treading in the blue-green water, whose surface under the sunlight appeared as if strewn with rhinestones. Adah had never been a strong swimmer, but Jack seemed completely at ease. In fact, he'd never looked more luminous. His wet hair was like dark whiskey now, and the squinting about his eyes lifted his cheeks and beamed back the brightness.

He was treading water, sweeping his arms through it, and he had droplets in his eyelashes and on his face like pearls she wanted to take into her mouth. He drifted closer and she could hear each breath. He took her wrist in his hand and drew her nearer. Her body charged with something unreasonable and joyous, but fear fell into her chest, too. Once they had done this, there could be no turning it back. Did love always come joined with a certain amount of trepidation? Along with the good feelings, was there always dread that something wouldn't go right or that love could be lost? Love and fear seemed twined like stalks of a grapevine—so close they couldn't be separated.

Aware of her helplessness, she glided onward. She was in his arms before she knew it, his body like oiled velvet against hers.

He ran his hands all over her goose-pimpled flesh, across her back, and down her bottom. And then his mouth—silky, tobacco rich, open, and luring. It was everything. Nothing sealed away, nothing suppressed. A line of poetry came to her so strongly she almost said it aloud. *Come live with me and be my love.*

From the sensible chambers of her mind, a calming voice told her to *stop this, don't do it, you'll regret it.* But another voice, one that came from a more primal place, said, *I want him, he wants me, this is so right.* She might have done anything he asked, but he surprised her by stopping at kissing and stroking her body. She could feel him swallowing back desire. Then he simply held her entwined while keeping them both afloat with one strong arm and his legs.

They swam side by side back to the shore, and when Adah emerged, the fresh air on her chilled skin felt as if an icebox door had been left open. She wrapped her arms around herself and aimed for her clothes.

Jack said, "You're cold. Wait until you dry off."

She became aware of his near nakedness, his chest of sculpted ivory with a scattering of brown hair that shimmered in the sunlight, his arms hefty, his body as big and warm looking as a cabin. He led her to a clear spot at the edge of the water, out in the open sun, and they sat.

Jack stretched out his legs in front of him and leaned back on his elbows. His thighs were like urns, but they tapered beautifully to almost-slender ankles. "Lie back and get some sun on you," he said and then whispered seriously, "I promise not to touch."

Adah did as he said; all the while her mind scuttled. She wanted him to touch her. She was ready for something like this, for a moment of reprieve. She wanted to live, really live, as she hadn't before. *Just make love to me, just love me,* her mind pleaded.

But he was the one who had resisted. She searched the sky above for answers to the spiderweb of mysteries surrounding Jack. He did crazy things, such as taking her here, but then behaved cautiously. He was enamored of her, but he was a gentleman. On the grass and under the late-afternoon sky, the moon was visible and she could've sworn the ground was trembling. She had to place her hands flat at her sides. But it wasn't the earth, only the hammering of her heart that shook the world around her. Desire clustered around Jack and her much too readily, and the longer they didn't act on it, the stronger it became. Like an adrenaline surge when suffering a fright, it struck Adah at the mere sight of him now.

She said, barely above a whisper, "You must have a strong willpower."

He rolled toward her and tenderly moved the wet strands of hair away from her forehead, his eyes melting over her. He let out a breath that sounded different than before—huskier, deeper, but soft as a petal. His gaze trained on her; it was brimming with something that looked like love. "Only because I have to. You just told me you're leaving these parts. I've waited my entire life for you, but you're telling me that it doesn't matter. I can't have you."

An endless beat in time held her still.

Then he whispered, "Your lips are a drink of red wine."

She'd never heard such things before, had never read them in a novel or listened to them on a radio program. And she'd never imagined being the recipient of such ardor. It was unknotting all of her tangles.

Later she would not even remember how it happened, but then they were kissing again, kissing deeply, exploring each other's mouths as if exploring their minds. He moved down to her neck and breathed into it. "And do you remember when I said your neck was a slice of white cake?"

By then it was too difficult to gather words.

But after moments of passion, Jack pulled back. Again. She should've taken it as the ultimate sign of respect, but instead rejection landed in the pit of her stomach.

Jack seemed tormented, looking away into nothing. "What you're thinking of doing, taking Daisy away. It's dangerous."

She had to work to find her voice, and she was surprised how weak she sounded. "Life is dangerous."

Jack looked as if the gears in his brain were working overtime. He jerked his stare back to her face. "I'm going to get you a gun."

The mood shifted as quickly as a gray cloud can block out the sun. An appalled snort exploded out of her. "Surely not."

"It's obvious you're going to do battle with the Branches. They'll stop at nothing to stop you. They've killed before and covered it up. And they've got Drucker on your back, too. A bad cop is more dangerous than anything. I want you to have a means of protecting yourself—"

"I don't know anything about guns. I wouldn't even know how to fire one. And I doubt I could ever shoot a person with a gun."

"I'm talking about a small gun, a .32 caliber, small enough to fit in your purse or an apron pocket. You should be prepared for anything and everything. Drucker's always got a gun on him, and you best be aware the Branches probably have plenty of guns."

"There's a rifle cabinet."

"And they probably also have a pistol or two. They have a lot to guard over at that place."

Each new argument Jack presented added a new fear and drained a few more drops of life from her body. "I can't see myself going around carrying a gun."

"It's always a good idea to carry a gun."

She glanced around, checking that she was really here, having this conversation. *How could this be happening?* "You've been listening to too much *Green Hornet*."

"No. I don't need to listen to fiction. Real dangers exist in the real world. You just said so yourself."

She closed her eyes against the sun. "I don't think I can do it."

"Then give up on your idea."

Jack was paying a price for this situation, too. She was going to hurt him, and she couldn't put him at even more risk by involving him too much in her escape. Whether she got away or not, the Branches would seek revenge on anyone who had helped her. She had to end this, for Jack's sake. "I think we've said enough." Adah turned her face away.

He lightly took her in his arms again, his eyes now aglow, his gaze penetrating, his voice near desperate. He pulled her closer, his words an urgent plea. "Marry me. Stay here and marry me. You'll be near the girl, and as she gets older . . . she'll be able to seek you out on her own."

His proposal rang in her ears like the echo from a shotgun. Then finally landing in her heart, ripping a hole wide open. "That's years away" was all she managed to say.

He whispered, "If something happened to you . . ." He blinked. "I'd never forgive myself."

A thunderstorm was rolling in rapidly; the sky was hazy and low, like smudged glass. "You honor me, Jack. I wish it were simple and I could stay here and perhaps marry you. But I have to finish this. I have to get Daisy away from them . . . now."

"You don't."

How could he not see how vital this was? How could he not understand? "I do. I'm sorry." As if the sky had read her mind, it thundered a protest and then let loose a spray of rain pellets. She and Jack jumped up, grabbed their clothing, and took shelter under the canopy of a large spreading sycamore while they watched it pour. They stood side by side in silence.

The rain started to let up, the clouds burning off, the sky always in motion, never stagnant. Hopelessly and desperately she had let another month pass by, and absolutely nothing good had happened.

Through a long sigh she said, "Jack, rest assured, the next time I see you, I'll have a plan."

Chapter Twenty

As she toiled in the heat of July, days filled with backbreaking work, Adah's mind was muddled with ideas and plans that had yet to come to fruition. There were many days of warm sunshine and afternoon thunderstorms that approached as a curtain of gray mists and slant rain, and often there were rainbows. Adah leaned against the doorjamb and watched the wind push the rain in whatever direction it willed. Kentucky farmlands were lovely, but Adah's dream of keeping part of Lester's farm or selling it for needed money was slipping away just as surely as summer would slide into fall. She had to give it up. And no matter how tired she was, she had to stay alert and attentive. She had to come up with an escape plan.

On a steaming afternoon, when heat rose like wavering spirits out of the fields and roads, the roar of a car engine made Adah freeze. The crunching of tires on the gravelly road and the heat of a motor assaulted her senses as dust enveloped her from behind. Adah had been going to deliver a basket of clean laundry to the redheaded family, and now the dirt from the road was settling on the top of the stack. She spun around. The front bumper of a sheriff's department patrol car was only a foot or so away, and Manfred Drucker sat at the wheel.

He could've so easily mowed her down, and the devilish smile on his face, which she could see through the windshield, made it clear that was the exact message he meant to deliver.

He stepped out. "Get in," he ordered. His face was red and his forehead greasy. Big half-moon-shaped sweat spots festered on his shirt underneath his armpits. Even on the still air, Adah could smell his skunklike body odor.

She set down the basket, rubbed dirt from her eyes, and fixed her gaze on him. "Am I being arrested?"

"In good time, sweetheart. In good time," he said as he hoisted up his belted slacks, pistol in the holster. "For now, I just need a moment with you." He swaggered over to the passenger door and opened it.

Adah held her ground. "Don't you need a warrant?"

He grinned. "I'm not arresting you, doll face, not yet." He pointed at her. "And let me give you a piece of advice: if you don't cooperate, then I will arrest you. Disrespecting a sheriff's officer is not taken lightly in this county."

She did as Drucker said.

Inside the car, the smell was overwhelming. Cold fear falling into the pit of her stomach, Adah sat still and faced forward.

"So," he said after he slid in behind the wheel and turned his body in her direction, his right arm draped over the top of her seat. "I've been doing me some investigating on you, sweetheart, and you sure do have what people 'round here call a checkered past. I know all about it, about how you was orphaned and no one wanted you, how you was turned out on the streets of New York City. And I know you hopped trains for a while and set up camp with gypsies and hobos, tricking people into paying you for fortune-telling."

Adah resisted the urge to say, *So what?*

Drucker breathed out, and his mouth odor was as bad as his body's. "Any other tricks you turned out there?"

Adah glanced at him, finally, and he winked. A shiver ran up her arms. There was no one else on the road. She hadn't missed the predatory innuendo of his comment or the vulturine look on his face. "No. Never."

He smiled. "We'll see about that."

Then he seemed to be waiting for something. He clearly enjoyed every moment of making her squirm.

"Besides, the Branches know all about my past. I've never kept anything from them. Everything you've just said you could've learned from Buck or Mabel."

"Yep," Drucker said. "I did hear about it from Buck and Mabel, but now I'm finding some records, too. Some facts, not just hearsay."

Adah doubted that but held her tongue.

"Records are much more convincing than people's accounts of things that done transpired. They provide much more cause, if you know what I mean."

"I think you're going to have to explain. I'm not used to being threatened."

He laughed. "You think this is being threatened? Oh, darling, you have no idea." His face grew serious again. "Once a judge done seen how you lived before you caught yourself a land-owning husband, it sure does give credence to motive for killing him. You must've been thinking you'd come out like the poor widow, only with a lot more money than you ever had in your life."

"How does a person's past provide motive? Seems to me the past is just that—the past."

"That ain't the way most people 'round here think. No, sweetheart, the good people here think it speaks of character. Why, pray tell, did no one take you in when you was just a youngster?"

"Everyone died."

"Not likely. Must be there was something wrong with you from day one, and everybody knew it, and nobody saw fit to help."

His words burned, but she had to remain composed. "That's not true."

He leaned back. "Well, I just wanted you to know I'll be presenting my case for exhumation to a judge pretty soon, and I wondered if you might wanna save us all the trouble and just go ahead and tell me now what you done. You could save yourself a lot of sleepless nights, and confession now might make for a lighter sentence once you're convicted of murder."

"I'll take my chances," Adah said and then added, "since I'm innocent."

"Suit yourself," Drucker said. "You want to do this the hard way, then that's just peachy keen with me."

Adah put her hand on the door handle. She couldn't remain in control much longer. "Are we done here?"

He smiled. "We're done when I say we're done." Adah held still for a few more tortured moments; then Drucker said, "Go on now. We'll be seeing each other again real soon. You can mark my word on that."

After opening the door, she walked away back toward the laundry basket, in complete awareness that all Drucker had to do was run her down, and the Branches' revenge would be enacted. He could say anything, that she'd resisted arrest, that she'd mouthed off, anything. So when he whipped the car around her and left her in the dust again, she was surprised to find herself still standing, still alive.

But now she was vulnerable in another, newer, and more vicious way.

From then on, she started picking up and delivering laundry at different hours of the day, sometimes early, sometimes late, in order to avoid another confrontation with Drucker. And she rarely stuck around to talk with her customers, instead returning as soon as she could and making herself helpful on the farm. But even though she managed to evade Drucker on the road, he ran around unbidden in her mind. She felt him closing in, running a spherical course that was getting smaller, tighter. She had no idea if he was doing what he told her he was doing—still working toward exhuming Lester's body—or if he was doing something else.

One thing was certain, however—he was doing something. And she had to come up with an escape plan before he pounced. Every day she concocted scenarios that she then had to discard because there was too much risk, too high a chance of failure. Soon it became clear that there was no easy solution, and whatever she came up with could end in disaster. She was being watched closely; she had no easy way out.

At night, she dreamed of finding herself in the morgue with Lester's body, now more decomposed, on the table in front of her. Then Manfred Drucker, dressed in surgeon's attire, grinned at her from beneath his mask and, holding a scalpel, cut into Lester's body, straight down the center of his right temple. Blood and brains. Cold metal handcuffs clamping down on her wrists, feeling herself shrinking, becoming smaller and smaller as Daisy's voice was becoming fainter and fainter as it called "Mama" until it faded away altogether. She awakened, bolting upright in bed, clenching her hand against her sternum, barely stifling a scream.

Her time was limited; this she knew even as she foundered helplessly with no clear plan. But she had to go on feigning innocence and acting as though there was nothing to fear. She had to go on living and breathing and keeping her head for Daisy's sake. Time, her enemy now, seemed to be racing forward. The summer was heating up, the crops were growing, and each day felt like a lost opportunity.

Late in July, the tobacco plants were shoulder height, and the flowers had to be broken off by hand in order to focus the plant's energy on its leaves and produce a better crop. Adah had been taking Daisy into the fields when she could manage a break from her laundry work, and there she showed the girl how to snap the flowers.

Daisy wanted to collect the flowers, and Adah fashioned together something of a bouquet for her, tucking a few blossoms into her hair. There was time for a few moments to play hide-and-seek among the rows, but otherwise it was endless work under the relentless summer sun. Over exhausting suppers, Adah's mind drifted in strange directions. Any road sound outside reminded her of Manfred Drucker's engine and that he could come out in his patrol car at any moment to arrest her. And when Buck cut into his pork chop one night with a steak knife, Adah saw a scalpel in his hands and heard a jail-cell door slamming shut, the freezing metal sound of her future confinement.

One night, after a particularly grueling day, Buck and Jesse brought out the bourbon from a cabinet in the living room and poured themselves shots before dinner. Adah watched as Buck drank and drank without showing any change, while Jesse became a sloppy drunk. His eyes were ribboned with tiny red veins, and he was unsteady on his feet.

When Mabel called everyone for dinner, Buck strode out of the living room into the kitchen without even the littlest waver, whereas Jesse excused himself and lunged for the front door. Adah peeked out of a slit in the curtains and saw Jesse retching into the front flowerbeds. She had to smile. Obviously Jesse couldn't keep up with his father.

The door flung open again, and Jesse walked back into the house with a halting gait. His eyes met Adah's. "What're you staring at?"

Adah shrugged. "Nothing."

Jesse harrumphed and nearly fell to the side. Still sloshed even after throwing up. "Funny you said 'nothin'.' You think you're somethin', but one day you're going to be nothin', girlie. Nothin'."

Adah's back went rigid. Jesse's threats had never before felt so ominous. His eyes had never before looked so acidic. Something new was in the works; Adah knew it, but she had no clue what it was.

There was no choice except to push forward, pretending to be calm.

The family finally took a breather from the demanding farmwork one Sunday to herald the upcoming wedding at the summer church picnic. There, the engagement of Jesse Branch and Esther Heiser would be announced. Turnout for the event was expected to be large, even though it was a busy time on local tobacco farms. The weather was perfect that day, and everyone looked forward to a chance to gather after church, talk, taste others' dishes, and watch children at play, a reprieve from grueling farmwork.

Mabel and Esther prepared side dishes, dusted off jars of home-made preserves, and dressed in their Sunday best, as did the men. Jesse had bought Esther a ring with three small diamonds set on a filigreed band, which she proudly wore on her left hand. Before they left for the church, Mabel told Adah, "This is a celebration, and we're all happy about it. Got that?"

Adah nodded, having absolutely no intention of shattering their public façade. Humiliating them would do her no good.

The picnic was held on church grounds, with tables and chairs set under spreading oaks and maples and grass underfoot as soft and green as forest moss. The scents of hay and strong coffee floated on the air, which was alive with the sounds of bees, cows, and birds. There were so many casseroles and cakes covering the tops of picnic tables, it reminded Adah of the offerings of the New York delicatessen where she used to peer in, hungry as hell.

She couldn't help glancing around and noticing how large the crowd was getting to be. If only she had a means of transportation! She might have been able to slip away with Daisy while the Branches were otherwise engaged. Instead she and Daisy were never far from their eyes, and there was no way out.

Daisy had the rare opportunity to play with other children, and she and another girl were somehow managing to play house among the thick ropes of some gnarled tree roots. With a white pinafore over her dress, Daisy reminded Adah of a fairy. The little girl she played with,

Rebecca, was much like her—a sprite with sparkling blue eyes and thick, wavy hair that could only be held in check by a ponytail.

As she did whenever they attended public events, Adah observed the wary but polite distance others typically maintained from the Branch family, even as they paid their respects and offered their congratulations about the upcoming nuptials. Watching carefully, Adah took note of the coolness with which Esther Heiser was treated as well. It was baffling. What did people have against Esther? Was it her power and position? Had it always been this way? Or was the coolness in anticipation of her soon becoming one of the Branches?

Crazy as it was, Adah's sympathy went out to Esther. No matter how strange, she wasn't an evil woman, and Adah couldn't help but be concerned for her. The wedding was planned for October, and Jesse and Esther had let it be known that Esther would not be returning to her position within the school district come fall.

What would happen to Esther once her life became more and more isolated within the Branches' stronghold? Did she really know what she was doing? Were marriage and possible children worth the price she apparently was willing to pay? Adah couldn't get the alarms to stop ringing in her head. She spotted a single pure-white feather on the ground, picked it up carefully, and slipped it into her pocket.

The picnic crowd began to filter away, but Daisy still played contentedly. Adah helped Esther clear away dishes, utensils, and tablecloths and take them into the church communal room, where the walls had been decorated with cross-stitched Bible verses set in wooden frames and there was a sink for washing, some dusty cupboards, and old tables and chairs.

"What's on your mind?" Esther said as she set down a stack of plates and turned to face Adah.

Today Esther's hair wasn't pulled back as tightly as it usually was. There had been moments during the picnic when she'd actually seemed happy, when a smile had ridden over her face like a ripple crossing a pond. Perhaps she was truly in love with Jesse Branch, as unlikely as that seemed. That or the hope of having her own child was beginning to transform Esther. But her gaze was full of trepidation when she looked at Adah. Her caginess didn't deter Adah; Esther was one of her only contacts with the outside world, and they knew things about each other that no one else did.

"You've been following me around."

Adah's chest tightened, but she had to seize this opportunity. "I'm not following you . . . but . . ."

Esther crossed her arms over her chest. "What is it this time?"

Adah focused on the softness of Esther's cheeks, which today had been lightly powdered, and then gazed upward toward her eyes. "I'm worried about you."

Esther scoffed. "Worry about yourself."

Adah almost laughed. Esther was one blunt woman. "What does that mean?"

Esther shrugged.

Knowing their time alone was limited, Adah pulled in a breath, hoping it would make her feel braver, and, letting it out, finally said, "Okay, I don't know how much time we'll have, and I want to ask you something important. About those rumors about how Betsy Branch died . . ."

Esther blanched, but her hands remained steady as she donned an apron and tied it about her waist. "I don't listen to rumors."

"But you admit there *are* rumors."

"People gossip, that's all I know for certain."

"Did you know Betsy?"

Esther took one small step back. "Yes."

"Tell me about her."

Esther batted her eyelashes in a way that made her appear both sadder and younger as she gazed away, a far-off look on her face. Then she peered back at Adah. "You'll find this odd. Believe it or not, she was a lot like you. She went to school with Lester and me. But she stuck to herself, she was kind of mysterious, also like you."

"So you weren't friends?"

"No. She was quiet, almost always serious. She was a good student, but she never went out on dates or came to parties. She had one good friend, who's also a friend of mine. Kate was able to get close to Betsy, but none of the rest of us could. I tried once or twice. Betsy was a pretty girl and could've been popular, but she was a closed book."

Adah absorbed this information, trying to fathom why a woman so described would've married Lester Branch. Why had someone so cautious fallen for him? But then again, Adah had, too. "Do you have any idea why she was 'closed'?"

Esther shrugged again. "Her father disappeared when she was younger, when we all were still back in school. Ran off with another woman, they say, and her mother was left always working hard, trying to make ends meet. I don't think Betsy ever got over her father taking off like that and her mother having to sacrifice so much."

"Did she have anyone else?" Adah asked this even though Lester once told her that Daisy had no living relatives on her mother's side.

"No, it was just the two of them, Betsy and her mother. After Betsy and Lester got married, her mother had to move to Louisville for work. I heard she got a job on the bottling line at Brown-Forman. I think that nearly killed Betsy. I heard from Kate she missed her mother something fierce, and she wrote her letters every few days."

Adah nodded, remembering the letters from the attic.

Esther shrugged. "It's odd, though. After a while, she started sending and receiving letters to and from her mother at Kate's house."

All sounds disappeared from the room, and Adah's flesh rose in goose bumps. She barely remembered to breathe while the sickest feeling overcame her. Something like a vision from the past clawed through Adah's body. She looked outside and saw an image of Betsy Branch fighting for her life, like a bird with a broken wing, struggling on the hard ground, never to fly again. "She wrote her mother through a third party? Why do you think she did that?"

"Funny thing. My friend Kate thought it was strange, too, but she never questioned it, just did the favor for her friend. Like I said, Betsy kept to herself." Esther paused for a long moment and then set a firm, flat gaze on Adah's face. "I think I know what you're going after."

Esther was having the same thoughts; Adah knew it. A simple understanding ran between them now, back and forth during the hush between their spoken words. It didn't need to be said. Esther wanted Adah and Daisy gone badly enough that she was willing to pass on information that might help.

If Betsy had been communicating with her mother in secret, not wanting Lester to know about it, there had to be a reason. Perhaps there were letters that followed the ones Adah had found in the attic, and maybe they would reveal what had transpired between Betsy and Lester before her death. What had happened to make Betsy Branch correspond with her mother in secret? Was she scared? Had her spirit been destroyed before her body was? Had every tiny bone in her bird body been crushed one by one?

Adah's voice surprised her when she spoke. She somehow managed to sound as if she was carrying on a typical conversation, while inside she was roiling in utter turmoil. "Will you help me?"

"Of course not," Esther barked. Then her voice calmed. "I can never *help* you, you understand. But . . . I won't interfere, either."

"Do you think Kate would talk to me?"

"I have no idea. What excuse could you possibly have to talk to her?"

Adah searched for a reason. "I have some of Betsy's letters from her mother. I found them in the attic. Her mother is now dead, is that right?"

Esther nodded. "I think she died soon after Betsy did."

"All the more reason for me to keep her letters for Daisy. You could find out if Kate has any other letters and tell her I'm keeping them for when Daisy is old enough to read them. After all, that's all she has left of her mother and grandmother."

"I can't talk to Kate for you."

Adah gulped. "Then I'll talk to her myself."

"What are you looking for in those letters?"

Adah fought the urge to gnaw on her nails. She skimmed through the thoughts now pounding in her mind while trying to hide that she was trembling. She was walking a precipice with steep drop-offs on either side. But she had few options; there was no choice but to trust this strange woman and tell her the truth. They were, in some ways, allies. "Something that could help us both."

"That's what I thought. But what about your part of Lester's farm?"

"I have to give up on that. I don't have time to wait it out."

"So you're really going to leave?"

Adah held her breath. "I'm not sure. But it's what you want, isn't it?"

"I never said that."

Exhaling now, Adah said, "I know."

"Go ahead and do what you want, then. I just don't want to know anything about it."

"You don't want to know if Lester had anything to do with his first wife's death? You're marrying into that family, and you don't want to know the truth? You'll simply ignore it, put it out of your mind?"

"I don't care what Lester did."

"What if the other Branches helped cover it up?"

"Jesse wasn't there that day. He was in Louisville on business."

"I wasn't aware of that," Adah said, then remembered that Jack had told her three people gave the police the same story of Betsy's death: Buck, Mabel, and Les. "But . . . he could still know what happened."

"He doesn't know anything. Jesse's a good man."

Adah paled, her eyes welling with tears she would never let fall. "Love truly is blind," she finally said.

Esther smiled sadly. "Maybe so."

"How can I talk to Kate?"

Esther blinked hard, once. "Kate Johnson. She lives in town. On Langstaff Avenue. In a pretty white house with black shutters, redone since the flood. There's a wishing well out front. You can't miss it."

"Thank you, Esther."

"Don't thank me."

"Why not?"

"Because I'm not having anything to do with this. I'll never admit that we even talked."

"I know that, Esther."

"I'm just waiting on the sidelines, watching and waiting. You might be digging a hole that you'll never get yourself out of. And believe me, there won't be anyone willing to give you a hand up."

Adah thought of Jack Darby. Esther was wrong. Or at least she hoped Esther was wrong. She had received vital information from two of the most unlikely sources, and today's news was the most valuable so far. She didn't know why, but unexpected help was coming her way. Some from a man who was enamored of her and didn't want her to escape; some from a woman who wanted nothing more than Daisy and her gone.

Something of a road map was beginning to unroll in front of her. Would the information she'd gleaned from Jack and Esther pave a way forward? Or would one or both of them betray her? Would her trust in them be destroyed?

"Thank you anyway," she said to Esther, who simply nodded.

Adah caught her breath. She felt winded, as if she'd been chased.

Outside, a small group of adults had gathered around the spot where Daisy and the other little girl had been playing among the tree roots. Adah rushed forward to find that Daisy and Rebecca had argued, and Daisy had pushed the other girl down. Now Mabel had hold of Daisy's arm and was forcing her to apologize, while Rebecca whimpered into her mother's skirts.

Mabel was saying to Daisy, "You go on and say you're sorry again."

Daisy's eyes were red rimmed, and her little chin trembled. She said, "Sorry."

"Again, and louder this time," Mabel said, then glanced at Adah as if making sure she was registering the seriousness of what had happened.

Daisy whimpered. "Sorry."

Mabel jerked Daisy's arm and said to the other girl's mother, "You can be sure she'll get her real punishment later."

Rebecca's mother's face changed, as if something had just dawned on her. Mabel stood her ground, obviously not the least bit aware of the effect she had on others. Rebecca's mother said definitively but softly, "No real harm done. They're just children."

Mabel insisted, "Daisy knows better than to behave like that. The Branches know not to act that way, and we don't raise our young 'uns to act that way." She shot a pointed glance at Adah.

Daisy rubbed her nose and then looked at Adah and whispered, "Mama . . ." A sound that threatened to pull a moan out of Adah's chest, and yet she had to stand frozen in place.

Rebecca's mother said, "Kids make mistakes, and Rebecca isn't hurt. All kids push from time to time . . . and Daisy has apologized." She leaned down and spoke to her daughter. "You and Daisy are still friends, aren't you?"

Rebecca had stopped crying and simply nodded. Then asked her mother, "Can we play now?"

Mabel was quick to say, "Daisy will not be allowed to play again today. In fact, I think it's time we go home."

If Adah had been surprised by the ferocity with which Mabel doled out punishment and shame earlier in the day, she was shocked by what happened later that evening. After supper, Mabel announced that Daisy would spend the night out in the barn as penance for her actions at the picnic. Daisy sat like a deflated balloon, but Adah found it impossible to hold back her thoughts against such extreme punishment.

"No child should be forced to sleep outside by herself."

Mabel's face reflected a moment of regret, but she seemed to push it away as easily as swatting at a fly and retorted quickly, "She won't be outside. She'll be in the barn."

"The barn at night is no place for a little girl." All sorts of awful visions of Daisy later that night swirling in her head, Adah asked, "What if she gets scared? Has a nightmare? Gets cold?"

Mabel had to look away for a moment, but she soon turned back, determined as ever. "Then she'll think twice before she bullies a friend again. No, sirree."

This from a family of bullies. Adah had to hold on to her stomach with both hands. "Mabel, please don't do this. It's too harsh. Please. Let her sleep with me, and we can keep her indoors tomorrow as punishment. Or anything else."

Mabel leveled a hard stare at Adah. "You best stay out of this. This ain't any of your business."

"Mabel, please. She thinks of me as her mother. Let me deal with this."

"The way you'll deal with it is to do nothing. You ain't like us; we been bred a different way than you was. Daisy's getting out of control under your hand, and let me remind you that both of you are eating and sleeping and living here under my good graces. That's the only reason you're still under my roof."

Buck, who had been observing this interaction, said, "And under our rules." He grabbed an old tin can and spat in it.

After dusk Mabel led a weeping Daisy out to the barn, allowing her to take a blanket and pillow with her and admonishing Adah to stay out of it. And so Adah went to bed that night after listening to Daisy call out for her—"Mama, Mama!"—for an hour and sob in between her calls.

Sleep was impossible. Instead she battled the sheets for hours, the air in the room suffocating her. Alone in her bed, she went from hugging pillows to hugging herself. She got up and opened the window. Beyond, only an empty farm, night birds crying out, the rumble of a faraway truck, the smell of summer and grass filtering in through the screen.

This was the landscape of her misery, and the night was playing out over a hundred hours. She tried to imagine how a four-year-old girl, who was probably terrified, would get through such a night. She closed her eyes and wondered if she could send love across a distance. Could feelings be conveyed on air currents? Adah clenched her eyes shut, trying to let Daisy know that she loved her and that even if she wasn't able to protect her right now, someday she would protect her from everything.

When the house became silent, Adah slipped out of bed and, wearing a robe and a pair of shoes, left the house and went straight to the barn. She found Daisy curled up in an empty straw-covered stall, fast asleep, her head on the pillow, her arm clutching the blanket against her chest, her breathing deep and regular. It seemed that crying had finally led to exhaustion.

One of the dogs lay beside Daisy, his back to hers. The other dog was up and sniffing Adah's hands, begging for attention, but he had probably been lying with Daisy, too. She had to stifle the urge to gather Daisy into her arms and make a dash for it into the woods. But what then? With no transportation, no one waiting for her, and not even the money she had hidden back in the house? She wouldn't get far.

Heart fractured, Adah stared at the girl for a long time, and then decided it best to leave her be until morning. At least Daisy had the company of the dogs, and bringing her indoors might've gotten her upset again, and it certainly wouldn't have boded well for either of them with Mabel and Buck.

Adah headed back to the house, and the sensation of being watched hit her long before she reached the porch. It raised the hairs on her arms and the back of her neck. Her eyes caught sight of a shadow in one of the windows; it shifted and then pulled back. The dark shape of someone who hadn't wanted to be seen.

Adah never paused, just kept walking, putting one foot in front of the other, showing no reaction. There was no doubt in her mind, however. One of the Branches had been watching her every move.

Chapter Twenty-One

The next day, Adah, jittery with anticipation, walked the roads to deliver laundry to a customer. The sun had already reached its apex and was sliding down the sky. After she dropped off the laundry basket, she hitched a ride into town, and the old farmer driving his pickup truck never asked about her business. They made the short journey in silence. She was taking a chance going to town after being warned not to, but it was a chance she was now willing to take.

Once there, Adah removed her apron, folded it, and brushed the dust off her clothes, then walked swiftly to Langstaff Avenue and found the cottagelike house with a wishing well in front. After only a moment's hesitation, Adah walked to the front door and knocked. If Kate Johnson still had any letters . . .

A blonde woman wearing a housedress and old T-bar shoes and carrying a baby on her hip answered and looked at her curiously through the screen door. Her hair was mussed, her face flushed, and she seemed slightly winded, as if Adah had caught her cleaning or cooking.

"Hello," Adah said. "I'm Adah Branch. Could I bother you for a moment of your time? I'm a friend of Esther Heiser's."

"Yes, I know who you are," Kate said after a short hesitation. She opened the screen door with her free hand as she hoisted the baby, who appeared to be nearly a year old, higher up on her hip. "Come in."

"Thank you. I'm so sorry to bother you during your busy day."

Adah followed the woman into a house strewn with toys and children's books, with laundry stacked on the sofa and the smell of food mixed with the odor of diapers.

"I hope you don't mind the mess. My three-year-old is taking a nap, so at least it's quiet. But I wasn't exactly expecting company," Kate said as she set the baby down in front of a set of blocks on the rug-covered floor.

Adah grasped her hands together as she glanced about and fought off the urge to beg the woman for help. She had to remain composed and focused. "I'm so sorry to intrude, but I didn't know of another way to contact you."

Kate nodded. "Let's sit for a spell."

She led Adah into a dining room that opened to one side off the living room, where she could still watch the baby. She shoved aside books and baby burp rags and a sleeping cat on the round oak tabletop. As she slumped into a ladder-back chair, she pushed back her hair, which was falling down into her face in coils that reminded Adah of question marks.

With serious but open, kind eyes, Kate asked, "What can I do for you?"

Adah didn't know of any other way around it except to begin. "This might seem an odd topic of conversation, but . . . I understand you were a friend of Betsy Branch's."

"Yes, that's correct."

"She was my husband's first wife."

Kate nodded. "I'm sorry about your loss, by the way. That flood was the devil's making."

"Yes. Thank you." Adah paused, then, not wanting to waste any of Kate's time, went straight to the point. "As you know, Esther is marrying into the family, and she and I have become . . . friends. Esther told me that Betsy corresponded with her mother through you and that you might still have some letters."

"I see," Kate said, then sat up straight in the chair. "Yes, I do have letters. I couldn't just toss them out once Betsy died, and I didn't want to pass them on to your . . . husband."

Adah, struck by how well things were going, cocked her head. Did Kate Johnson know something about Lester that no one else did? "Why do you think Betsy wanted to receive letters from her mother here instead of at home?"

Shrugging, Kate glanced into the living room, where the baby was still at play. She looked back pensively. "I don't know. I never asked. Betsy asked me for a favor, and I did it."

"You weren't curious?"

Kate shrugged again. "Sure I was, but Betsy became my friend mainly because I never pushed myself on her. She told me what she wanted to tell me, and that's all."

"What did she tell you?"

Kate's face fell. "Why all these questions? Why all of this sudden interest in Betsy and her mother?"

Adah had to refocus. "After our farmhouse flooded, I found a box of letters from Betsy's mother in the attic, and I'm saving them for Daisy. When I heard that you had others, I thought it would be nice if I could pass them all on to Daisy when she's older. After all, now the girl has lost both parents . . ."

"I see," Kate said. "Well . . . I find that a lovely sentiment." She looked as if in deep thought. "I do think Betsy would've liked that; however, I have no idea as to the content of those letters."

"What do you mean?"

After a long moment, Kate said, "Betsy wasn't happy; that was easy to see. I have no idea if it had to do with Lester. I never probed, and I believe she was getting letters here because her mother was sending her money. That's why she didn't want her husband—your husband—to know about it. She read her mother's letters here, then left them with me. I've held on to them, untouched."

"So even after Betsy died, you never read them?"

"No, I did not. Those letters are private—sacred, even. I wrote to Betsy's mother shortly after Betsy died, and my letter came back as not delivered. Later I learned that Doris died of a heart attack a day or so after hearing of her daughter's demise. It's a heartbreaking story, one I haven't been able to forget."

Adah observed Kate's still-obvious grief in her glistening eyes. "You must have cared a lot about Betsy."

Kate blinked. "I did."

"And I care a lot about her daughter. Now I'm the only parent she has."

"I see." Kate sat for a few moments more, then slowly rose and left the room while Adah suffered through even more anticipation. Was she soon to be in possession of ammunition she could use against the Branches?

Kate reentered the room and set a bundle of letters tied together with a white ribbon on the table in front of Adah. "I'll be glad to see these leave this house. They've haunted me, but I resisted the urge to read them. I have a feeling you won't."

Her eyes pooling with grateful tears, Adah looked up at the woman. "I will read them. I don't want to lie to you about that." Then Adah had to stick with her story, difficult as it was to lie to someone of Kate Johnson's character. "I will read them to make sure what's inside is suitable for Daisy to someday read."

"I understand."

Adah stood and wrapped the bundle of letters in her apron.

Walking away from Kate, Adah knew she had accomplished something significant. She hadn't been followed. No one seemed to be paying any attention to her as she walked back through town, looking upward at telephone and power lines that connected the buildings like the outstretched filaments of spiders, and she began walking toward Lone Oak.

She would stop at Jack Darby's house and read the letters. She daren't take them back to the house with her.

Even though Adah was able to catch a ride with another passing farmer, it was still nearly an hour before she could sit on Jack's front-porch steps and open the first letter, postmarked most recently. Trembling, Adah unfolded it and began quickly reading. Heart thumping up high in her throat, she saw that Betsy's mother had enclosed money for her daughter and granddaughter to move to Louisville. She had warned her daughter to be careful and come straight away, as fast as she could.

Adah sucked in a hot, shaky breath. The money was not there, so Betsy had taken it. And now it was evident: Betsy Branch had been in the process of leaving Lester when she was killed.

Adah skimmed through other letters and soon learned all that she needed to know. Doris had written such things as *A good man never strikes a woman*; *He could do some permanent damage, or he could kill you*; *That place in that man's house is no place for you and Daisy*; and *Don't think twice. Leave him. We'll make do here.*

There was no reason to read more just then. Adah slipped the last letter she'd skimmed back into its envelope and looked to Jack, who had come in from his cornfield and now stood before her.

She gazed up into his backlit silhouette, his face in shadow, and said, "I have it, Jack. I have something here."

As he came closer a strange euphoria fell over her. His shape, his movements, the anticipation of his close proximity made her giddy. Pushing those feelings aside, she stared out into the yard that was gathering the twilight. She watched the first firefly blink in the blue-gray air.

He sat beside her while she relayed securing Esther's help and then getting the letters from Kate, and he listened in silence, without even nodding his head.

He removed his hat and fanned himself with it. "There's no definite proof that Lester killed her. It certainly provides a motive, though. These show without a doubt she was packing up and giving up on him."

Adah nodded. "But I'm not going to the police or the sheriff with this."

He rubbed his chin, the beginnings of an evening stubble catching the sunlight.

"What I need is leverage, something to bargain with. When I make my escape, I want there to be something I can hang over them so they don't follow me or report Daisy as having been kidnapped. I can always threaten to expose them as moonshiners, but I'm not sure that's enough."

Jack said, "Yes, we've discussed this before. They probably have some of local law enforcement bribed off."

"I need more to hang over them. These letters could be that."

"But there's nothing in those letters that clashes with the Branches' cover-up story. The crime hadn't even happened yet."

"Yes, but do you think the Branches would want these letters to be made public? It would ruin their dead son's reputation and also question the way she died. Supposedly she died on the Branches' farm, and who would believe that 'accident' story after having read these letters? I'm talking about the court of public opinion."

Somber, Jack breathed out, "People are already wary of them, but I'm not sure the Branches are wise enough to recognize it. This would set them apart in a way that even they would be able to see. Yes, I understand what you mean."

"They don't love Daisy anyway. They're cruel to her. They just want to win. And if I can disappear and leave a note saying that the letters are in safekeeping but can be brought out at any time, I'm thinking the Branches wouldn't want to take a chance on coming after me and making the entire community suspect them."

His face was starting to darken. "It's risky. No telling what the Branches might do. And since people don't like them much anyway, maybe they won't care about those letters."

"The Branches will care. Mabel will care. They wouldn't want to be seen as *murderers*, and even if these letters don't provide definite proof of murder, they still make it clear that Betsy was being beaten and was planning to leave with Daisy. Most people will be able to put two and two together, and taken with what you could say about the day of Betsy's death, I think everyone in town will know what happened to Betsy. It could ruin Jesse's wedding plans; it could ruin everything for them."

Jack gazed down at his grasped hands between his knees. "I guess you're right. It's a real threat." He glanced up. "So what do you want me to do?"

"Will you keep these letters for me? When I escape I'll leave a note saying that someone in town has them and will give them to the police and the newspaper if they try to get me for kidnapping. It's my only card to play."

"You're making a lot of assumptions about what they'll do," Jack said, and then his voice lowered and eased, "but of course I'll do anything you ask." There was a sad sinking of the skin at the corners of his eyes.

Adah stared into the pollen-filled air before her. Making escape plans had helped her keep panic at bay. "I told you that when I next came back here, I'd have a plan . . . I don't know if I should tell you or not . . ."

"Tell me."

"I don't want the Branches to find out you had anything to do with my leaving. I don't want them to know you're the one holding the letters. If you have to use them, you can turn them over only with a promise of anonymity."

"I'm not afraid of the Branches for myself, only for you."

Adah breathed deeply. "Okay, I'll tell you. I could use some advice anyway." She paused. "So last night they made Daisy sleep in the barn, and I couldn't sleep at all. Then a plan came to me, Jack," she said and turned to face him. "I have to create a distraction, a big and unexpected distraction." She gulped.

"And . . . ?"

"I'm thinking . . . I can do something to the still. Maybe . . . blow it up."

Jack's eyebrows flew skyward.

"I know," Adah said. She'd even mouthed a few words of prayer, asking for divine guidance. She'd heard it said that everything was the will of God. Often when she was out in the fields, she laid her palms flat on the earth, feeling its lingering warmth, letting it seep into her. She had never before been in such need of help. But she'd received no answers to her prayers so far. "I know it's a crime, but I have to fight criminals with something as deep and dark as the crimes they commit. I'm thinking I'll slip away after supper one night and light the fire, then sabotage the still so that it explodes. If the sound's loud, as I expect it will be, people will come, and the Branches will be terrified of discovery. They'll hightail it to the still to get rid of any remaining evidence. Then I'll make my escape."

"What of Mabel?" Jack asked.

"That's the part I'm unclear on. I'm not sure she'll go outside to help. But I'm certain she'll do something. She might call on the telephone for help, but I don't know. If she does, people could find evidence of the still, and it would be difficult for the police to ignore it. But I don't have any idea how to explode a still."

"I've heard of stills exploding while they're being operated, but Jesse or Buck or both of them would be there if it's running. When they're away, you could try to start it up yourself and trigger an explosion, but you would have to know what you're doing, or you risk doing it wrong." He drew in a deep breath, brow furrowed. "Do you realize that someone could get hurt or even killed? Do you realize that it could cause a fire, and the fire could get out of hand and spread to the house and the woods and even to other farms? If you're caught, you could go to jail for the rest of your life. The Branches could say that you started the fire, and you would be wanted for arson even if they don't report you for kidnapping."

Adah tried to ignore her shame. It had been awful to admit to herself that she was capable of enacting such a plan, but it was another thing altogether to see the heartlessness of it revealed in Jack's eyes.

Jack stood up. "You can't do this, Adah," he said.

Adah sucked in a tight breath. "All of my life people have been telling me things I can't do, and yet I do them."

He took a few steps away, then turned. "You're being reckless, careless. I understand you're under pressure, but this is not the best plan."

"It's the only plan."

Jack hinged his hands on his hips as he continued to pace. "You could be killed."

"I'm very aware of that . . . although I think it's unlikely."

Jack finally stood still. He looked helpless and furious about his helplessness. "Don't do it."

"I have to."

A burst of anger entered his eyes as he stared at her. Then he reached down and picked up a small wayward tree branch off the ground.

Adah's breath halted.

But he flung the branch into the yard and then simply stood, breathing deeply. Jack would never hit a woman. He was no Branch man.

They remained that way, Jack standing and Adah sitting, through a long, suffering silence, and Adah had to pull her eyes away. But she finally pushed herself to face him. She feared a look of condemnation, but his anger had quickly been replaced by concern. Emanating from him was a sad combination of intelligence, awareness, and love, closing in on desperation.

"I know it's not an ideal plan, but it's all I have." Adah's hands were shaking so much she slipped them under her thighs and pressed them still. "I'll have to hope that my threat to turn over the letters is enough for them to let me get away with blowing up the still and taking Daisy. I can move around and live on my own. I've done it before. But I've never had the law on my tail. I know I'm taking huge chances, but there's no other way."

"They're two of the most heinous crimes: kidnapping and arson."

Adah was hoping for bravado, but her voice sounded hollow and weak. "I know. But I can blow up the still after we've had a hard rain and everything is damp. That'll lessen the chance that the fire spreads."

His voice barely above a whisper, he said, "There has to be another way. You have to come up with something safer. Don't fight the Branches."

Frustration stirring in her chest, Adah audibly exhaled. "We've been down this road before." She avoided his gaze.

Jack stood still, awash in worry, but the helpful part of him won over the worried part. "You don't know enough about a still to make it explode while it's operating. I'd say you need to use a stick of dynamite and simply blow it up."

Adah flinched. "Dynamite? How would I get that? And how would I get away before it blew me up?"

"I'm thinking," Jack said. Then sighed. "There has to be a woodpile at the still. You could light a fire on one side of it and place the stick on the other side. The fire will grow and eventually meet the dynamite. But you'd have to hope the dynamite doesn't go off before you've had a chance to get back to the house. How far away is the still?"

"I don't know."

"You haven't found it?"

"I haven't had a reason to."

"Well," Jack said, "you do now. Find it and hope it's far enough away to stay cut off if a fire gets out of hand, and definitely light the fire after a rain. Let's also hope the still is close enough so you can get back to the house before it blows."

"I'll do that. The only other thing I haven't figured out is how I'll get Daisy and me out of town. I'll have to clear out fast. I'll leave my bargaining chip on the table in the kitchen—a note telling them about Betsy's letters—and then we have to . . . vanish."

Jack's eyes were hazy with sadness when he said, "You can go to the docks. I'll meet you somewhere near the farm and drive you there. Then bribe your way onto a riverboat, any boat. There's always some boat put in there for the night. They'll hide you away even if they're not leaving until morning. You still have that money, right?"

Adah nodded. She and Daisy would assume new lives on the other side of the river. They would put the cold cage of the Branch family home and the snake of the Ohio behind them.

"For a price, they'll take you and drop you anywhere along their course."

Adah almost smiled but couldn't. Jack was giving her what she wanted even though it was the opposite of what he wanted. A form of illness was coming over her. This was not supposed to happen. She wanted to gaze upon him like this forever. How beautiful he was when his mind looked as open as it did now. What did he dream of? What ideas and memories lived in his mind?

"That's brilliant, Jack. I knew you would come up with something."

They sat in a silence that drew out.

He reached over, rubbed her arm, and looked at her with eyes as warm as a fawn's, his face as bright as moonbeams, and he spoke deeply from the back of his throat. "If the Branches catch you trying to destroy that still, they'll kill you. You're really playing with fire now. I've said it before and I'll say it again: you shouldn't try to beat the Branches at their own evil games."

Adah remained silent and let his warning sink in. She knew the stakes were high. More than anything at this very moment, she wanted to go into his arms.

"What if you don't hear an explosion, and you go back to start all over only to find out that the fire has finally reached the dynamite, and it's about to blow?"

"I have to take my chances."

Jack's gaze was firm and yet easy on her face. She closed her eyes, and it was just the two of them alone in the universe. No farms, no land, no other people, no kidnapping, no arson. If only they'd met under different circumstances. If only she'd met Jack instead of Lester. If only . . .

He tugged in a big breath. And then his voice, languid and lovely. "Your skin is vanilla."

Dazed by the beauty of his words, even so, she didn't turn to him. She couldn't give him false hope. Instead she whispered, "You have to stop this, Jack. Either I'm going to leave here, I'm going to jail, or I'm going to die."

"I know," Jack said. "You don't do anything halfway. That's why I love you." Jack spoke as if each word were his last dying wish. Slowly, ever so slowly, convincingly. Sure but sad. And then he said something that ripped away what little she had recovered of her composure. "You're the bravest woman—no—the bravest of anyone I've ever known."

But she'd never seen herself as brave. True she was a fighter, but not all fighters were brave. Brave people didn't end up in such a mess, layered in sheets of deceit.

"Where will I get the dynamite?"

"I'll get it for you," he said, his voice barely audible. "Wait here."

Jack vanished inside and returned shortly, holding a small bowl of peaches and a knife. He sat beside her. "Found me some beautiful ones down at the market the other day." He picked up a plump peach and carved out a slice. He lifted it to his mouth as a line of juice ran down his hand.

An urge to lick it off rose like a deep hunger in Adah. She looked away, and then his hand was before her, holding out a slice.

"Here," he said softly.

Helplessly Adah opened her mouth and tasted the sweet fruit as he slipped it onto her tongue. She also tasted the slightly salty flavor of his skin. She slowly chewed and then swallowed. It was so sweet, juicy, earthy. "What about the dynamite?"

"You think too much, Adah. I'm going to get it for you. But for now, can you let your burdens go? Let yourself enjoy a moment here and there. Let me worry for you for just a short spell."

Adah allowed herself to be fed, and with each successive bite Jack's hand rested a moment longer, until the peach was nearly gone, and he put his finger on her bottom lip, then gently traced it.

She threw herself into a standing position and took a few steps away then, hands clenching her skirt, but finally ready to face something new—she loved him back. She had to have married the wrong man to know the right one when he came along. Maybe only after unhappiness and loss could a man like Jack Darby make sense. A man through whom she might find hope and redemption. Forgiveness, even.

A new concern had now been added to her life. *Jack.*

One foot before the other. She could do it; she had to walk away. Then she began running, adrenaline surging through her every cell. She was way too scared and shaky to even turn around and wave goodbye. She ran with a kind of madness. A wild dash.

And still it made no difference. She loved him back.

Chapter Twenty-Two

The next day, she went in search of the Branch still. Plunging through the woods and looking for clearings, she focused on land near the creek. It was as hot as blue blazes that day, and the creek was running high from some recent rain. She swatted at gnats that gathered about her head and picked her way among fallen branches, stones, and leaves. The air away from the house tasted of freedom, and Adah drew it deeply into her lungs.

Adah searched quickly, and the still wasn't difficult to find, located on the high side of the creek bed, up away from the water, and partially dug in. There she came upon a cleared spot of packed dirt shaded by a circle of trees and a tarp, under which there was a large barrel made of copper set on planks of wood, the ash remaining from doused fires, some wooden boxes, buckets, pipes, and other equipment she hadn't seen before. She'd never seen a still, but she had no doubt. This was where Jesse and Buck made their moonshine.

Not wanting to linger and hoping her absence hadn't been noticed, she backed away. The still was far enough away to pose little threat to any person, but it was close enough that she ought to be able to run back to the house in only a short time.

She could only imagine the expressions on both Buck's and Jesse's faces when they heard the explosion and knew where it had come from. She smiled despite hearing Jack's words in her head: *You're playing with fire.*

As she traipsed back through the woods, she kept spinning her web. The next step would be to clean up the old house, making it appear as if she were hoping to live there again someday.

Thoughts raced and whirled. She closed her eyes and envisioned Daisy and her leaving, like two threads pulled straight out from a tightly woven trap, finding escape from the matting and floating away free. But she also knew that imagining things did not make them come true. She had to be diligent about secrecy, leaving no trails, and she had to be thorough in her planning. Concentrating so hard during the day left her exhausted and sleeping soundly, as if transported to another place, and although she vaguely remembered having complex, swirling dreams, she awakened with a blank mind.

But as arid days dragged on, something of those harried dreams returned. Adah touched her neck; her pulse was rapid. Could she do this?

On top of all her worries, it was the beginning of the driest season of the year. The grass outside seemed to spark like striking a match and the creaking porch steps sounded like brittle bones breaking. She didn't know when she could count on a hard rain to come, and Jack was planning to buy dynamite in another town, just to be sure that it couldn't be traced back to him or to Adah. But he hadn't had time to make the journey yet. She had to wait.

August arrived so quickly, more wasted days falling away from the calendar. Time was marching on while Adah's plans stagnated. She needed dynamite and wet weather. In the meantime, the life of the farm rolled on. The tobacco plants had to be suckered, and Adah was able to help once again, taking Daisy with her and teaching the girl how to locate and remove secondary stems that had grown from the base or leaves of each tobacco plant. It was one of the most tedious and time-consuming steps in tobacco cultivation, and although Buck had been keeping the colored men on at eighty-five cents a day and pushing them to their limits, Adah made time to be of assistance. As she worked she knew Jesse was always keeping an eye on her, while trying to pretend he wasn't.

Daisy tired of the task after working on just a few plants, and Adah released her to play nearby among the rows. There she ran up and down, waving her arms as if she wished she could fly. Daisy had been having nightmares, suddenly waking with a scream so pitiful and weak that only Adah heard it. It often took a half hour of consolation and gentle touching to calm her enough to send the ghosts of her dreams away and get her back to sleep.

Often Adah stayed awake, finally giving in to sleep again as the stars came out, distant mad explosions showering her into slumber. She imagined Daisy as a beautiful little bird rising out of the ashes of her wounded past, soaring far and away, away from this farm, away from this family, away from this life. It wasn't too late; Adah knew it.

The night before, Adah had gazed down on Daisy and stroked her hair. A sleeping child struck her as the most innocent of beings, a willow in the wind, at its mercy. Daisy's hair was even softer than her skin. Her eyes fluttered under her lids, and Adah could feel life thrumming inside that small body. Was this what people saw when they talked of the miracle of life?

She had no time to ponder such things; she had to focus all her energy on succeeding. She had to set a fire to start slowly in a woodpile down at the still. She hoped to be able to get back to the house and in her bedroom before the fire reached the dynamite and the blast sounded. Jack's idea about lighting one side of a woodpile and leaving the dynamite on the other side still seemed the best option.

But what if the fire didn't catch and reach the dynamite? What if she had to go back and restart it again and again? Every time she left the house posed a risk of exposure, and each time she approached the still, she could be walking up at the same moment the explosion occurred, just as Jack feared. She could be hurt or killed, certainly found out. She remembered being watched when she went out to the barn the night Daisy slept there. She had to hope that the fire would catch on her first try and the explosion would happen at just the right time. And she had to wait for a really rainy day and then wait again for it to stop, leaving the woods damp.

Now, in the fields, she closed her eyes and tried to play out the hoped-for scene in her mind. Buck and Jesse would jump out of bed when they heard the explosion. Of course the dogs would be barking wildly, and then the men would think immediately of the still. They would panic, thinking that others would have heard the explosion and be on their way to investigate or help. They would rush to the still to hide the evidence of their moonshining, probably tossing things into the creek. They would be far away and so caught up in getting rid of the debris that they wouldn't notice Daisy and Adah leaving the house and heading for the road. But would they ask Adah to help them? What would Mabel do?

And then there was the matter of escaping. She would have to wait for the perfect day, then go and ask Jack to meet Daisy and her down the road a ways at a guessed-upon time, then pick them up and take them to the docks. So Jack's face would be the last one she saw before disappearing. This she had to accept, mournful as it was. Yet desire for him ran through her veins during the day and kept her awake at night.

And what if a fire started anyway and got out of control? Her mind conjured up ghastly images. It bothered Adah not a bit to think of all the buildings burning to the ground, not even the house, but she didn't relish injury to any person or creature, including the Branches and the farm animals. And what if the fire spread to other farms?

Adah pushed her hair off her forehead and concentrated as she worked. Even the air felt different—the featherlike wind had a charged feel, a combustible quality to it. Now that she knew Betsy had been trying to get Daisy away from the Branches, Adah was even more determined to make that happen. In addition to saving Daisy, she would also be fulfilling the wishes of Daisy's dead mother. It gave her renewed determination. Betsy had died a violent death because she had wanted to leave with Daisy. She had failed. Now Adah would succeed for her.

As her mind swirled with the details of her escape, she also came up with a plan to make the Branches think that leaving was the last thing on her mind. They needed to believe that her fervent goal was to get Lester's farm back and stay nearby. It worked to her advantage for them to believe she was taking extra interest in tobacco cultivation, and so she asked questions, even those she already knew the answers to. She pretended to be teaching herself about successful farming, as if she hoped to be running a farm on her own at some time in the future.

One night over supper, while everyone ate in silence after a very hot day out in the fields for all of them except Mabel, Adah asked out of the blue, "When will Lester's estate go to probate?"

They all startled at her sudden question, but Adah looked at Mabel first because her face was the one that usually revealed the most.

The woman paled and stopped eating for a moment, her eyes on Adah like a cornered animal peering at a predator about to pounce. Then just as quickly she darted her eyes toward her husband.

Buck wiped fried chicken grease from his mouth with the back of his hand, even though there was a napkin in his lap. He gave Mabel an almost indecipherable nod as if to say *Remain calm.* Then he set a hatred-filled stare on Adah. "We ain't heard nothing about no probate. Not even sure what you're talking about."

Liars. Esther Heiser had told Adah they were awaiting the probate date. "Probate," Adah said and touched both corners of her mouth with her napkin, then lifted her chin. "I've been told it's what happens when someone dies without a will. We have to go to something called probate court, before a judge or someone like that. I've been told it will spell out how much of the farm is mine."

Buck took a bite of chicken and then dropped the drumstick on his plate. "Like I said, we ain't heard nothing about no probate."

"Who you been talking to?" Jesse chimed in.

Buck shot him a look that said *Keep your mouth shut.*

Instead of answering Jesse, Adah just shrugged and tried to act the part she'd cast for herself. She couldn't arouse suspicion; she couldn't let anything show. Everything depended on that. Poker face. They had to believe she wasn't thinking about leaving.

She said, "I guess I'll have to find out myself." Funny how at one point in time she had truly wanted to see a lawyer and hadn't wanted the Branches to know about it. Now it suited her purposes to have them think she *would* see an attorney, even though she had no intention to do so. "Guess I'll have to go see a lawyer about it."

Silence reigned again for a moment, and the tension in the air was like a noxious fume. "You do that," Buck eventually said while shooting a satisfied smile at Jesse.

His expression stilled Adah and dried her mouth. What was the smug smile about? Did they already have an attorney lined up to fight her? Did they have what they thought was a foolproof plan?

She forced herself to breathe in deeply. It no longer mattered. It mattered only that the Branches believed she intended to stay here and fight them, when in truth she was going to escape and do nothing of the sort.

When she saw Jack next, she told him she'd found the still. He just stood there quietly, a look of resignation washing over his face. Then he walked inside and came back holding a gun. It was so small it looked like a child's plaything.

"What have you done?" she asked, searching his face. "I thought you were going to get me a stick of dynamite."

"I will, but first things first." He met her gaze, and she found something of a plea inside it. But he matter-of-factly said, "I told you I was going to get you a gun." Without waiting for her protests, he said, "This is a Colt 1903 .32 caliber—an older model of what's still being made today. It's perfect for carrying in your pocket or a purse." He held it out to her. "It's not loaded. We're going to get to all of that later, but for now, just get used to the feel of it."

She rolled her eyes. "I see you've made a decision for me. And I don't like it."

Jack was acting as if he had something important to do and there was no chance anyone would stop him. "Take it. How could it hurt to have it just in case? Think of it this way: it might save not only your life but Daisy's, too."

Conceding his point, Adah studied the pistol. It was only about seven inches long, not even one inch wide, and about four inches tall. "It looks light."

"It'll be heavier with the magazine in."

Her gaze shot up. "What's a magazine?"

"It holds the bullets." He paused. "I know you have no experience with guns."

She heaved in a hot breath. Every day the surreal quality of her current life was starting to feel more and more normal. "No experience whatsoever. I never thought . . ."

Jack, looking determined, continued: "The advantage to this gun is its size and ability to be concealed. But it's a classic, too, used by the police and even the army. It's a simple gun, easy to fire."

Adah made a closer inspection and then took it from him in one hand. It fit.

He added, "You might find it interesting that Bonnie Parker used one of these to break Clyde Barrow out of jail, and John Dillinger had one on him when he was shot by FBI agents."

She let out a tight sigh. "Yes, those are people I aspire to emulate."

He gave a low chuckle. "Just thought I'd try to make you smile."

She shrugged. "Smiling is rather out of my realm right now. Sorry."

His face fell. "Alrighty, then."

Inside the barn and out of sight, he showed her how to handle the gun, load the magazine that held eight rounds into the butt, retract and release the serrated slide, and apply and release all three safeties. He gave her all sorts of safety instructions. Then they went into the woods, where she could practice shooting at a tree.

Jack showed her how to hold the gun with both hands and how to aim, coming up behind her and resting his right arm on hers, and then his hand on her hand, checking her hold on the gun. "Then you squeeze," he said. But her fingers suddenly lacked strength as she focused on Jack's darker, tanned arm alongside her paler, creamier one. His hand fit over hers like a clamshell protecting the life it held inside.

She looked over her shoulder at him. "What about the shots? People will hear."

Jack's breath was warm on her neck. "They'll think someone is out hunting or practice shooting. I doubt anything will come of it, and you have to practice. Try to hit it about five feet up from the ground."

She took her first shot. She didn't hit the center of the tree trunk, but she did hit it. And she took a few more shots until she had satisfied Jack.

He said, "I knew you had it in you."

Adah had to suppress a smile. "I'm not sure how to take that."

"Let's just say you did well."

Shrugging off an awful feeling, she said flatly, "Maybe I'm a natural."

He told her to trigger the safeties; then he gave her a full magazine to load, and she slipped the gun into her apron pocket.

Her apron felt heavier, but not remarkably so.

By that time the forest seemed to be closing in and the air was steamy. Perspiration gathered on Adah's upper lip. They slowly worked their way out of the woods and walked back to the house, where Adah waited while he went indoors to retrieve a basket of dirty laundry.

She stood on the grass in front, and he came down the porch steps as if he was weary, as if something was weighing heavily on him. As she was preparing to leave, he said in a low-pitched, worried voice, "Where will you go?"

Adah was already backing away. The last thing she had wanted was to hurt this man. There was a silent, gentle wind that day, no sounds except for the occasional cry of a hawk overhead and the whizzing of insects in the air around her. She could hear her feet crunching on the dry ground, and it might as well have been the sound of her bones breaking. She barely eased out, "I don't know."

He looked slapped. "Or you don't want me to know."

Adah gazed down at her feet and then up to the sky, searching for someone, something. If only the ghost of Betsy Branch would appear and help her or bless her.

"It's better if you don't." Her eyes back on Jack, she said, "If by chance the Branches decide to report what I do to the police, they'll question everyone I talked to. You're a customer of mine. They'll try to find out if you know anything."

He looked pained. "And you think I'd talk?"

"No."

His gaze leveled on hers. "So you don't want me to know where you're heading. You want to make sure I can't find you." In his eyes, a plea, even as he spoke of her leaving. Did he think the strength of his love could hold her here? If only it could!

She bit her lip. "I need to try to make sure *no* one can find me."

She watched him swallow hard. "Even me," he said.

Her chest began to ache. She had to make sure Jack didn't offer to run off with her and give up this land he'd saved for and loved so much. He'd found a real home here, and with her, he'd have to live with shallow roots, holding on to a terrible secret, always looking over his shoulder. She was choosing that life, but it wouldn't be right for him. "I'm so sorry, Jack. I didn't mean for anything to happen between us. What can I do? How can I make it better?"

His face was molded with agony, his eyes shimmering in the sunlight, and he spoke like a defeated man, a broken man. "There's no help for this."

And then he simply kept his eyes on hers. She saw pure adoration in them. And she hated to admit it, even to herself, but his face had become the first thing to swim into her consciousness when she awoke in the morning. It had also become the last thing that followed her in dreams as she fell asleep at night.

He said again, "There's no help for this. I'm sick with longing . . ."

With the prismed light and soft hum of nature around them, it was as if they were submerged and alone, in a world all their own.

But then there was Daisy.

Chapter Twenty-Three

Adah, emboldened by her successful trip to town to see Kate Johnson, took the next step in enacting her plan for diversion. She caught a ride into the city, and then another to Les's and her old house on the river. Even though she had been gone from the house longer than usual when she'd visited Kate, no one had mentioned it to her. And today, if the Branches did find out she'd come to the old farmhouse, it would work to her benefit.

The farmer who picked Adah up dropped her off at the entrance to the property. After thanking him, she walked toward the house, which was partly obscured by tall weeds growing along the dirt drive. It would be the first time Adah had to face alone the place where she had killed a walking, breathing man, one she had once loved. A sense of self-preservation slowed her steps. The only time she'd been here before had been in the company of Jesse and Buck, and she had been on a mission to find Lester's money. She simply hadn't been able to let down her guard. But this time she would have no such distractions.

What would it feel like to walk across the same ground where she had dragged Lester's lifeless body to the river? Would she be forced to relive what she'd done? She'd heard that time healed all wounds, but as each day passed, she found that the shame over Lester never left her completely. Other wounds could be treated and healed, but guilt never goes.

A bright-red cardinal flew across her path, and the sweet smell of rolled hay tickled her nose. In a roadside tree, she spotted a bird's nest up high. *All good signs,* she said to herself and pushed on.

At her side, she carried a pail full of cleaning supplies. She planned to remove as many of the ruined furnishings as she could and then start washing down walls and floors. As she drew closer and the house came into view, however, she paused. A pickup truck was parked in front of the house, but it wasn't Lester's old one. Lester's was nowhere to be seen, and a man was walking through the front door.

Adah didn't recognize him.

Continuing forward, she tried to imagine who would have any business here and what their business could be. The house looked the same; a grimy watermark still ringed the structure up high near the roof, and below that was dirt left behind from the sludge after the flood. When she reached the house, she climbed the steps to the open front door, and the same moldy smell wafted out from it.

"Hello," she called out.

The man she'd seen go into the house came to the door and stepped out on the porch while saying hello back at her. He appeared to be in his late twenties, redheaded with a ginger beard, rail thin, and he wore a long-sleeved shirt, work pants, and boots—the garb of a farmer. He also had the quiet, sober demeanor of most farmers she'd known. His hands were lean, with ragged but clean nails. He probably worked the soil but made sure to wash his hands at the end of each day.

When he gazed at Adah, his gray eyes held curiosity but not one ounce of anything negative. "Can I help you?" he asked.

Not sensing anything amiss but overcome with curiosity, she said to him, "I was about to ask you the same thing. May I help *you*?"

He looked confused. Now a woman holding an infant came to the door and gazed out at Adah with a question on her face.

The man extended his hand. "I'm Adam Connor, and this here's"—he gestured toward the voluptuous flaxen-haired woman—"my wife, Cora."

Adah shook his hand. "I'm Adah Branch. This is my farm."

Adam Connor's eyes flew open wide. "*Your* farm?"

His surprised look landed on Adah with a certain harshness, setting off all sorts of warnings in her head, but she remained calm. "Yes, my husband and I lived here before the flood. He drowned . . ."

Adam Connor blinked and said, "Oh . . . now I know who you are. So sorry for your tragedy, ma'am."

"Thank you." Obviously these were nice people, and Adah didn't want to be rude, but her mind was muddled with questions.

"How are you getting along?" he asked.

"I'm fine," Adah answered, but she had no urge to turn this into a social call. This chance meeting started to feel unsettling. Heat crept into her cheeks. She set down the pail on the porch planks and raked the hair out of her face with her fingers. "I'm sorry to have to ask, but I didn't think anyone would be around. Why are you here?"

Again, Adam Connor looked surprised. "The place is for sale. Well, not officially yet, but word has gotten around. Me and my wife and baby been looking for the right place for some time now. We been out here before, and we was taking another look now. We sure are interested, even if it might flood from time to time. More than interested, if truth be told. But we still want to bargain a bit with old Buck. We can afford this one, but not many others. Most of the farms in our price range been underwater before, but—"

Adah's face had knotted, and her breath halted. "For sale? It can't be for sale. I own at least part of it, and I haven't agreed to sell it."

Adam Connor shifted his weight and stole a nervous glance at his wife. Then he looked back at Adah, and his voice lowered. "There must be a misunderstanding. Buck Branch done told us—"

"Buck Branch doesn't own this farm. He's my father-in-law."

"Well, he told us *he* owns the place and he's going to be selling it soon."

Adah's forehead puckered. "But that's not the case. The farm was my husband's, and I lived here for three years with him and his daughter. This was our home."

Again, Adam Connor seemed uncomfortable but steady on his feet, meeting her gaze with a firm one of his own. "I'm sorry for all this confusion, ma'am, but I asked Buck Branch why he was the one doing the selling. I done known this place was your husband's." He glanced away and shook his head, then almost chuckled. "Ole Buck told me it was none of my business why he was doing the selling. Mumbled something about how he'd made things right. Then he showed me the deed. It looked new, and it sure as shootin' said Buck Branch owns this place."

Adah reached a hand toward the porch railing to steady herself. Could this be true? Had Buck managed to get someone in the courts to let him have the farm? Had he bribed someone? There was no telling what the truth was, and it didn't matter. Either way, obviously Buck had figured out a way to get the entire farm away from her.

"Ma'am, do you need to sit down?" Adam Connor asked, his eyes swimming with concern.

His wife handed the baby to her husband, came toward Adah, and placed a hand on her shoulder. Her hands were ruddy, square, and solid, but gentle. "Bless your heart . . . ," she said.

Adah succumbed to the woman's comforting touch; all the while her mind was a jumble of new knowledge and disbelief. "What you said about Buck . . ." Adah looked to Adam again. "Are you sure he told you he owned the farm?"

"Yes, ma'am, I'm sure. I'd heard the sad story of your husband's death, and he told me he's not quite ready to sell yet but was thinking he'd give it up soon. He invited us to come out here and take a look anytime." He gestured toward the front door. "We're ready to buy, but we're waiting, like he asked. In the meantime, we been thinking about clearing things out a bit. Last time we talked to Buck, he told us he'd get rid of that ruint truck sitting here, and sure enough it's gone."

Tight worry all over her face, Cora Connor finally removed her hand from Adah's shoulder and looked deeper into Adah's eyes. She asked quite gently, "I take it you didn't know the farm is in Buck Branch's name."

Adah's brows drew together.

"Well, if that don't smart . . . ," Adam said through a beleaguered sigh.

Adah's knees buckled as if she'd been struck.

"Come now. Sit down," urged Cora and tried to steer Adah to sit on the porch steps.

But Adah couldn't move. This was the last thing she'd been expecting. She'd expected to do some cleaning today and tell the Branches about it later that night, further cementing in their minds that she wasn't interested in leaving these parts.

Instead she'd come at just the right time to run into these people and learn something very valuable. "I'll be alright," she said automatically.

"You don't look so good. You look like you just seen a ghost," said Cora.

A ghost? Yes, of course, a ghost: the ghost of her husband sliding around the corners of this house and the edges of this land, angry and swift. Here he had lived, worked, killed, and died. His presence still hovered and flew wildly about, and now he must have been laughing, Adah thought. That old sinister laugh of his echoed in her head. Adah clenched her fists. What terrible pain!

"I'll be alright," Adah said again and managed to pull in a ragged breath.

Adam and Cora exchanged a knowing glance. When Cora turned her gaze back on Adah, she said, "You poor thing. I'm sure sorry about your husband, too. Worst flood any of us has ever seen. This sure ain't been a good year for lots of folks . . ."

Not a good year, indeed. Her head ignited with a hot white heat, and the sunlight took on a fantastical quality. It was a long moment before she could gather this new information together. She shook her head; she probably looked like a madwoman. In the next half second, she became queasy, as if she might faint.

Adam said, "I can see you're taking this hard. I'm sorry we had to be the ones that brung you such bad news."

The sun hung blindingly in the sky. Adah's best memories of the farm came from her first summer there, when she had stayed out as the night came on, and it was so quiet she could hear the cows tear grass from the ground and then chew it. The air had smelled of greenery and pond water and earth. For a time, it had been beautiful. Over the years, she'd come to think of it as at least partly hers; it had meant something to her, something solid, despite it all.

"Are you absolutely sure?" she asked again.

Adam Connor solemnly nodded. "I know what he told me and what he showed me. Folks in town figured the farm belonged to your husband, and because of his death, it wouldn't be sold for a long time. But Buck sure does hold the deed, and he's almost ready to sell."

She put a hand to her throat. Searching out her voice, she said, "I'm so sorry to have bothered you . . . I just need to catch my breath for a moment, then I'll be on my way. I'm sorry . . ."

"No need to be sorry. And you take all the time you need, ma'am," said Adam.

"It's no bother," said Cora. "Are you going to be okay?"

Adah nodded, laughed ridiculously, and then pressed her temples. The density inside her skull had grown. She let her hands fall; nothing was easing this explosion in her brain. But she managed to gaze around at the land that she now no longer held any claim to. Even though she'd planned to leave the farm behind, this news was a sure sign of Buck's influence in the community.

"I'll be on my way now," she said in little more than a whisper.

"Are you sure you don't need to rest a spell on these here porch steps?" asked Cora.

Adah shook her head again. She took one step back.

Adam Connor, his eyes still murky with surprise and worry, said solemnly, "We don't want no trouble . . ."

"There won't be any trouble. At least not from me."

"Is there anything we can do for you, ma'am?"

Adah glanced heavenward, then looked at the couple again. "There is one thing you can do, come to think of it. Please don't say anything to Buck about my coming here."

"Sure thing." Adam nodded. "We don't aim to get caught up in no family fights."

She said, "There won't be any fight. It's done."

Adam nodded. "I'm sure sorry . . ."

Blinking, Adah said, "I do hope you'll be happy here."

"I have my doubts," said Cora, stepping up to the top of the stairs. "Your husband got swept away here, didn't he?"

Adah nodded.

Cora inclined her head to one side. "I'm thinking this place might be bad luck. But my husband here says it's a bargain we can't afford to pass up." Adah registered the quaver in Cora's voice.

Adah looked at Adam as a warning bloomed to life in her mind. The deaths of two young people had occurred here already, and she worried about more to come. "Your wife is right. You won't find happiness here even if people like me wish it for you. This place *is* bad luck, and you're too nice a people to live here. Please take my word on this. Don't buy it."

Now it was Adam Connor's turn to pale. His eyes never faltered from Adah's as his wife, her arms hanging at her sides, said ever so softly, "Thanks for telling us . . ."

Adah took the remaining steps down onto ground that had turned out to have never been even partly hers. She closed her eyes and stood for a moment, breathing deeply, letting this new realization pump through her, the vessels in her head filling with hot blood and the weight of this. When had Buck gotten the deed changed? How long had he known that ownership of the farm would never be in question? Even though Adah had given up on fighting for it, it had still meant something to her.

So why had they allowed her to stay once the deed had been changed? On any given day, they could have told her to leave. She wasn't blood kin, and she had no home to go back to.

And then there was Esther Heiser. She had confirmed for Adah that the Branches wanted to get her part of the farm for themselves. Did she know they'd managed to get it without Adah's consent? Had she been instructed to hide the truth and make Adah believe she might still get part of it? Had she been a part of the plan, too?

Adah walked off the farm as all of the invisible stars in the sky began falling from the heavens. She had no claim to the property now and probably hadn't for some time. So why had the Branches made her believe otherwise, even referring to it as "your farm" and "your house"? Of course in the beginning, they had wanted her to stay around long enough to perhaps confess and also be nearby, should more evidence about Lester's death surface. They'd always doubted her story about the night of the flood, but there hadn't been much they could do about it in those early weeks. Lester's body hadn't even been found.

Then the body *was* found, which convinced them even more of her guilt. But despite their influence and family history in the area, they hadn't been able to manipulate the police into charging her with a crime. So the Branches had let loose Drucker on her, but what had he really accomplished? Sure, he had scared her, and she'd lost sleep over simply knowing he was out there and making threats. But he'd never taken her in for questioning, and she hadn't heard anything more about the exhumation of Les's body, either. Drucker hadn't really done anything, and it appeared as though she was going to get away with murder.

So, after getting all of the farm and failing to get her charged, why were the Branches still keeping her around? Why?

Now that she'd spent so much more time with them, an obvious answer struck her squarely in the chest. The Branches held lifelong grudges for even the most minor disagreements. And they always got revenge for any perceived wrongs. Convinced as they were that she'd killed their son, they would never want Adah to simply walk away and start a new life. In that case, she would still be alive and free, and Les's death would remained unavenged.

Adah pulled in a deep aching breath. Over the time she'd been with the Branches, they'd learned a great deal more about *her*, too. They'd seen how much she loved Daisy and wanted to protect her. Had they seen that as her weakness and exploited it? Had some of the harshest treatment of Daisy been the slightest bit exaggerated? She filed through all the assorted memories of what seemed like excessive meanness toward Daisy that had gotten worse. They had kept up the pressure on Daisy while at the same time keeping Drucker pushing and prodding Adah.

Why?

Adah clutched her dress. Perhaps so she'd do *exactly* what she was planning to do.

She remembered the day Jesse had trailed her and Daisy to town, and it hit her then that one of the Branches always kept close by whenever she and Daisy were together, especially when they were outside. Why, they'd even given her a chance at making a run for it on the night Mabel had made Daisy sleep in the barn. They could have been tempting her to make a hasty move. Daisy was already out of the house. And Adah *had* gone to her in the middle of the night and *had* thought of snatching Daisy up and making a run for it. And one of the Branches had been watching from the window.

Oh, dear Lord, Adah thought as she stopped walking. The Branches had hatched an elaborate plan. They hadn't succeeded in nailing Les's death on her, but they'd seen an opportunity to catch her committing a different crime and make her pay. They had deliberately made life in their house as miserable as possible for both Daisy and her, knowing that the cruelty would spur Adah into action. They meant to avenge Lester's death, would never let it go, and she had fallen into their trap. They had only to wait it out and bring her to her limits, and then call the police when she tried to escape with Daisy. Or they'd call Drucker. It wasn't far-fetched to imagine that they'd probably made arrangements with some ticket agents who were friends or had been bribed to report it immediately should she and Daisy ever appear at the train or bus station. And they'd had Esther Heiser providing information and assistance to them, whether she knew it or not. Adah had almost confessed her kidnapping idea to Esther. She had revealed too much. And what of Drucker? Had he come up with nothing to help the Branches, thereby making them more determined than ever to exact revenge on their own?

All along she'd been playing into their hands, and she'd been right about one thing. There was too much risk for them in staging another accidental death on their property, just as she'd thought. So they'd come up with another plan. Everything they'd done over the last few months had been staged so that she would eventually kidnap Daisy. And get arrested and convicted for it. That—her life in prison—would amount to some justice in their view.

Adah looked at the teeming fields around her awash in sunlight, the smell of grass and loam in the air, porcelain blue heavens above. A lovely day to bear witness to what she now knew had been waged against her.

A war. One she'd probably never had any chance of winning, and she wasn't winning. Jack had been right. She couldn't fight the Branches. Instead she had been taking steady steps directly into the intricate ambush the Branches had set up. They knew she loved Daisy, that she would do anything for the girl, that she was Adah's Achilles' heel. They knew they could drive her to try kidnapping Daisy and then make sure she was caught.

Only then did she realize she'd left the cleaning pail behind, along with all of her plans and dreams.

Chapter Twenty-Four

As she slowly walked onward, the realization of what she must do sank into her just as rainwater slowly seeped into the earth.

She had to stop. She had to give up.

Her chances of a successful escape had always been as far away as the sea.

They had beaten her; they had won. They would have Daisy, and although the thought of it was so devastating Adah had to gulp hard to recapture her breath and blink away the little white lights swimming before her eyes, it was the truth. The Branches' hatred of Adah and what she had been doing had made it harder on Daisy, the girl's mistreatment carried out to extremes in order to make Adah feel compelled to snatch her away.

The truth didn't change the fact that the Branches were willing to commit acts of cruelty to get their way, even toward their own flesh and blood—an innocent child. But perhaps if Adah gave up, the Branches would stop being so harsh toward Daisy. What kind of people would sacrifice a little girl's happiness in order to get revenge? Adah was still worried they would continue to hurt Daisy. But there was now a glimmer of hope that perhaps, with Adah out of the picture, they would grow to love her and treat her kindly. Or at least humanely.

Adah knew nothing any longer, even who she was. She had traveled from one road to another in only an hour's time. During all the years she had lived on her own, wandering around and setting up camp, then leaving and starting again, she had never felt lost. As long as a road led out of town or a river ran close by, she'd always had an exit. This feeling was entirely new to her. Running up against a wall she couldn't climb or a river she couldn't cross or a place she couldn't escape was unthinkable. Giving up was something she'd never imagined doing, ever. But it was time. She had come to the edge, to the limit of her abilities.

That night, she had to put on the bravest face possible and not look like the cornered and defeated animal she was. If the Branches knew she'd figured out their scheme and she wasn't going to act on *her* plan, they might go ahead and stage another accident and take their chances it would pass muster again. One thing was certain: had she gone through with it, she would have been caught. They had set her up and were onto her. And Adah's imprisonment would only worsen Daisy's chances of a happy life. If Adah stayed around and free, then perhaps she could still exert a positive influence on the girl, even from afar.

She donned a confident mask as she got through the evening, suffering through a near-silent supper, the only conversation centering around the details of Jesse and Esther's wedding, which would be held just after harvest.

Only a few questions remained in Adah's mind: Was Esther in on the plan, or was she an accidental partner who had worked to their advantage? Adah hadn't completely confided her kidnapping plan to Esther. But it had been insinuated. Was that one of Esther's purposes, to get Adah to talk? And had she told the Branches? Had she given them reason to believe their plan was working to perfection?

And yet Esther had also sent Adah to Kate Johnson for letters that Adah was sure the Branches weren't aware of and wouldn't want her to have. Was Esther a participant in the Branch plan who decided to give Adah a bit of what she, too, had wanted, or was she simply another innocent pawn the Branches were playing?

Her second big question: How much did Drucker know? Had his threats been empty all along and his taunting of her meant simply to scare her and spur her into enacting a hasty plan of kidnapping and escape? There had to be a reason he'd never arrested her. Maybe he was supposed to be a key player in catching her had she gone through with her kidnapping plan. How many police and sheriff's officers might have been on the lookout for them had she tried to get away with Daisy?

All along, the odds had been stacked against her; all along, she'd been fighting a losing battle.

That night, she took Daisy to bed with her on the back porch again, and while the little girl slept, Adah stroked her hair and her back and stared into the darkness. She remembered sunny days riding the rails, trees shimmering in the wind, slow-moving waters, and nights made of stars. But tonight everything seemed black.

Ever since the flood, her mind had been functioning in protective mode. Although she had killed, and been trapped at the Branches', there had been a deeper river of thought underneath that told her things would turn out right. She had secretly believed in a simple solution and had envisioned it as a gift coming to her unexpectedly. How else could she have muddled through all the aching loneliness and uncertainty? She had been bested, and by the worst people. What ending to the story could she see now?

She was still lost in a lightless canyon, so deep she could imagine stars falling in as the night lengthened. She was still down there in the dark, and yet a tiny white light appeared.

The next day, she found Jack in the barn grooming the horses he so loved.

He looked freshly bathed and shaved; he wore clean clothes, and his hair was combed and pomaded, as if he had been expecting her. When he glanced up, an immediate smile broadened his face.

But his expression fell as he took a closer look at her. "What has happened?"

"Could we go for a ride?"

He said, "Sure," but first came forward and took her in his arms. "I have the dynamite, in case that's what's worrying you. And it's not traceable to either of us."

Fighting tears, she held him, too, but then gently pushed herself away, for the moment. She was not ready to give it words yet.

And so she and Jack saddled the horses and took the same ride into the woods they had before, on that day that seemed so long ago. Surrounded by dappled sunlight again, they dismounted and stood facing each other, a strange silence there, as if even the insects were stilling their wings and the squirrels were ceasing to breathe.

In that quiet and beautiful place, Adah managed to relay the horrific story of what she had uncovered and come to realize; all the while Jack watched her reveal emotions she'd had to contain until now. Beyond tears, she told him she would be leaving the Branch house as soon as she could.

"Where will you go?" he asked, and she detected only the slightest hint of hope in his eyes.

A quickening throb—a need she'd never known—came from the ground, up through her body, and out of her pores. Once, Adah had protected herself against vulnerability at all costs, but now she was like a newborn entering the world, opening its eyes and breathing for the first time. She faced him squarely. "You once asked me to marry you, Jack," she whispered, breathing shallowly.

She'd been thinking of nothing else. Over the past night, she had been reminded of how small each human life was. How short their frenzied fight to survive. Over in a single blink of time, their existences as insignificant as particles of dust. And how foolish not to take any chance at happiness, to hold on and believe that everything they needed was right here.

A sigh came from the forest. But she didn't turn toward it. Instead she breathed into the aching air. "Is the offer still open?"

He stood in silence, looking stunned, as if realization was dropping into him like a stone falls into a pool of water, rippling the usually quiet surface in ever widening circles. His face went from holding on to a shred of hope to being awash in it. But he didn't rush forward as she had thought he would or hoped he might. In his eyes was love but also doubt. "Of course it's still open. But . . ."

Adah held still.

"You're hurt, you're defeated, and you're giving up. I know I asked you to do that in the past, but I wouldn't want you to be unhappy." He paused, his hands hanging at his sides, his body facing her squarely. "I wouldn't want you to marry me if you'd be unhappy. I'm not sure I'd be happy." A tiny wry smile. "I guess I'm vain enough to want a wife who loves me back, even a little bit. I'll help you get on your feet no matter what, whether you're with me or not. I'll do everything I can to be your silver lining and make our lives good and sweet one way or the other, but I have to know if this is desperation or if it's born from something more than that."

Despite it all, she was still capable of love for a good man. Her notion of love had transformed before her eyes, had come alive by slow degrees, and now rose to the surface of her being.

Adah slowly took a couple steps forward, reached up, and gently placed the first three fingers of her right hand on his lips. "Now that that's decided . . ."

Jack's eyes swam with joy, and he took her fingers into his mouth, then closed his eyes.

The grief and anguish of the past months eased out of her body in his arms. The openness of his desire was something unknown to her—the way he held her head in the palm of his hand, how he whispered into her neck, his breath and lips on her face, the ridiculous joy of it all. Nothing stifled, everything exposed and frank and freely given. Her body and so many sides of her heart had been lost and now found.

And yet she couldn't enter a union without honesty. She pulled back. "There's one thing I haven't told you."

"You don't have to say it."

"Yes, I do."

"You don't."

Later Adah would remember the pulse she saw ticking in Jack's neck, the warmth of his breath, the change in his expression. "I killed him. I killed Lester. It was an accident. He'd hit me and was kicking me and might have kept at it until he'd killed me. I picked up a shovel and hit him in the head, and then he was just . . . gone."

His eyebrows gathered together into one line. "I already figured this out."

"How?" Adah asked, aghast.

"Because you were just so scared—you've been so terrified from the very beginning. I knew there had to be something behind all that."

"And you don't care what I did?"

There wasn't a touch of dishonesty in his eyes. And the look on his face was so sweet, spelling out clearly his devotion, admiration, everything good and real. "Yes, I care. I care what he did to you and what he did to his first wife. You acted in self-defense. The way I see it, Lester Branch got his just due."

"You don't know what it feels like to have killed."

"No, I don't. But I recognize regret and shame when I see it. I see that it killed a part of you, too, a part I'll bring back to life, I promise you."

"I'll never forget what I did."

"You will. I'll spend the rest of my life making sure you do."

"You'll be marrying a murderer."

"I'll be marrying the woman I've waited for my entire life."

He touched her arm, and his callused hand moved smoothly down to her hand, which he cradled and brought to his chest. Nothing else needed to be said with words. They stood like that amidst a bed of clover on a forest floor while the sounds of life around them returned, and creatures darted between the trees.

Jack's face hovered before her—the only one she wanted to study now and forever—and they made plans. Adah asked for three days to gather her thoughts and say goodbye to Daisy; then on the following day they would meet on the courthouse steps at noon to become husband and wife.

The most beautiful sight was the elation that began to spread over Jack's face.

Before she left his farm, she went inside the house to use the bathroom and took note of where soon she would be living. She paused before the open bedroom door. Jack owned a couple's larger bed. Secretly he'd been looking for someone; he'd been waiting for her. The bed was neatly made, the pillows plumped. Already imagining what it would be like to truly touch Jack, to love him unbidden, and let him love her now that she had told him everything. There would be no holding back.

Back outside, as she took steps to leave, he reached for Adah's hand, kissed it, and pressed it against his cheek. "On our wedding night, I'm going to sop you up like a biscuit . . ."

Back on the Branch farm, Adah had to work hard to keep her mask in place, even around Daisy, only letting it fall off at night. She had decided to tell Daisy of her plans on the morning of her leaving—no sense in doing it sooner—and then to assure her that she would always love her, would always be nearby, and would do anything she could to remain as close as possible.

A vibration seemed to be coming out of the ground, but it was coming instead from her body, shaking her to her core. She couldn't imagine what the little girl's reaction would be and hated the thought of her despair, but she told herself she was making the best decision she could. Father Sparrow had once told her that a person gained wisdom when they asked themselves the hard questions in life, and now she stood face-to-face with two she could not answer: Had she done any good in her life? Was she making the right decision?

She planned to tell the Branches nothing. Just walk away, making it easier on Daisy without some big showdown scene. Plus, if they knew she planned on leaving, would they take a final shot at killing her before she left their land?

Adah planned to continue attending the same church, where she could see the girl. If the Branches refused to let Adah and Daisy embrace and talk before or after church services, it would prove a poor reflection on them with townsfolk. And when Daisy went to school, Adah thought that perhaps Esther Heiser might help Adah get work in the school kitchen so she could see Daisy there as well.

Somehow, some way, Adah would remain a part of Daisy's life. She couldn't imagine going forward any other way; she owed it to Daisy and to Betsy Branch. She owed it to herself and to Jack, who wanted her to be happy.

Giving up now was like peeling off her skin. But she had to do it. She had to leave Daisy behind in the Branch house.

Sitting on the back porch, she was determined to remember the sound of Daisy snuffling in her sleep and the sight of her arm around her doll at night. She imagined opening the door on the morning of her leaving and wondering, *Will I ever cross this threshold again? Will I ever spend time with Daisy again?* She wanted to remember every moment she'd spent with Daisy, even the ones that had happened in this place, and yet she knew that after she said goodbye and lived elsewhere, she would slide farther and farther away.

The next evening, Esther came over for supper, and wedding details were ironed out. Adah made a careful observation of Esther, wondering . . . But Esther seemed overjoyed by the prospect of her upcoming wedding, and when she occasionally met Adah's eyes, there was no malice there.

The tiniest of burdens lifted off Adah's shoulders. Esther hadn't wanted to be a stepmother figure, and she had been stern with Daisy, but perhaps in time and without Adah's presence, she would grow to care for the girl. At the very least, Adah was almost convinced that Esther was not a party to the plan for catching Adah. Perhaps Esther could become the silver lining in Daisy's cloud, just as Jack had become the silver lining in Adah's. Given time . . .

After supper, Esther sought out Adah on the back porch as the sun became a blood orange breaking apart along the horizon. For a moment, Adah closed her eyes. She could hear a faraway train clacking on its tracks.

After making sure they were alone, Esther asked, "Did you go see Kate?"

Adah nodded.

"And . . . ?"

Adah was surprised by the question and made a quick decision. There was no reason for Esther to know what the letters revealed. Just because Lester had been violent with his wives, it didn't mean Jesse would be. And there would always be some tiny shreds of doubt about what Esther knew and what she would say to the Branches. "She gave me some letters. There was nothing there. Nothing. But thank you for trying to help."

Esther straightened and harrumphed. "Just as I thought. Nothing but rumors . . ."

Though Adah tried, she could not make herself smile at Esther. Esther was a wise woman, and her position in the community was admirable, but she had lived a cloistered life. As naive as she could sometimes be, Esther deserved her chance at happiness. Adah had tried to warn her about the Branches, and it had done no good.

"Yes," Adah said. "Nothing but rumors. I hope you and Jesse will be happy together." And she truly meant it.

Looking satisfied, Esther continued to peer closer at Adah. "What of you?"

Adah shrugged and said no more. To think that she'd once looked up to Esther, but Esther had in essence sold her soul to wear a wedding band. Would a child of her own bring her happiness?

She gazed out to the sky, now coming alive with stars. Adah had no need to tell Esther anything. Just to be safe.

Only one day remained.

Chapter Twenty-Five

The Branches could not have any idea she was leaving.

Everywhere she went, she felt inquiring eyes following her every move. When she hung laundry on the clothesline, she sensed someone coming up behind her, but when she turned around, no one was there. When she walked the roads delivering laundry, she was certain someone was following her, but when she glanced behind her, all she saw was the dust her feet had churned. In her room at night, she once had the strange sensation that someone was listening with their ear to the door, but when she slid out of bed and silently opened it, the hallway was empty.

She had to wear her mask for only the rest of the day, and then she would rip it off for good the next morning. Such a mix of emotions—she would be marrying Jack tomorrow, and there was the sense that out of the rubble, they would build their own happiness. But she was also leaving Daisy, who deserved everything admirable and decent and worthy, and for whom destiny should have served up those things on a golden platter. Elation and loss coursed through her like leaves of different colors floating in her veins.

When dusk came it startled her with its finality; the last day was gone.

Daisy was crankier than she'd ever been before. It was as if she knew her life was about to change drastically. Adah had a hard time getting her to sleep, but finally the girl succumbed to Adah's comforting touch.

With Daisy sleeping soundly, the night came alive with sounds. Adah could hear the walls settling and insects outside, the howl of a dog far away, the wail of wind that had started to pick up. At the window, she saw that an anvil-shaped thundercloud had blossomed to life in the distance, illuminated by moonlight.

Sleep would be near impossible, and she planned to watch the clock until the relief of morning. It seemed as if time had slowed, and her heart broke with each passing hour. She believed in the power of love. It was the only faith Adah could profess with certainty. However, as each moment drew out, she could feel the girl slipping through her fingers like fine sand sifting to the ground. How long would it be before Adah saw her again?

Her body nearly gave way as she pulled the needlepoint bag out from under the bed and packed it with the things she had been mentally planning to take with her: all the money from Lester's cash box that she'd hidden beneath the mattress, the clothes she'd been given, the gun Jack had given her, and lastly the deck of tarot cards he'd also given her.

Holding the deck in her right hand, she paused and drew a breath. An urge came over her, and she looked down at the cards. Never had she done a reading on herself. Adah passed the deck into her other hand and then back again. Struck with certainty and curiosity, she removed the rubber band that held the cards together and then shuffled once, twice, three times. Then cut twice with her left hand, gathered the cards back together, and turned three cards over, faceup.

She stared with wide-open eyes, then studied the cards again to be certain she was seeing straight.

It was not what she'd expected.

Thunder roared out of the sky and shook the house. Adah looked at Daisy and found her still asleep. Once Daisy fell into slumber, only a bad dream could usually awaken her before morning, and Adah was grateful for that as she heard another huge rumble of thunder, even closer and louder.

She went to the window and pulled the curtain aside. Lightning was brightening the sky in bursts and sprinting across the black expanse, touching the ground like some spidery creature dancing a jig with its white-hot legs. It was beautiful, a display of the power of nature, more dramatic than a fireworks show.

She left the window, lay down next to Daisy, and tried to close her eyes.

There was a moment of pure silence, in which she heard the thumping of her heart.

Then a monumental cracking noise came from outside, as though the sky had broken in two. Adah jumped up, returned to the window, and saw in the distance, perhaps a farm or two over, that a structure was burning. It must have been struck by lightning.

With those cracks of electricity still illuminating the landscape in eerie silver-blue light, she could see the top of that faraway structure releasing a burst of fizzles. And then even farther away, a plume of smoke. This was an electrical storm like no other; it was striking nearby buildings, and it raised all the tiny hairs on Adah's arms.

Then a boom and a crack that actually did move the house, as though it had come from the earth and not the sky. Now the dogs were wildly barking. Several minutes passed with only the sounds of the storm and the dogs before she heard footsteps on the wood-plank flooring in the house, and then Buck's voice. A band of light stretched beneath the door; the hallway fixture had been turned on.

She thought she heard him say, "The barn's hit."

As if by miracle, Daisy was yet still sleeping through it all. Wearing only her nightgown, Adah went to the bedroom door, flung it open, and took a step out. Jesse was already flying down the steps like a man running for his life, and Buck was hitching up his pants.

He took quick note of Adah and commanded, "The barn's afire. Throw something on and come help." Adah nodded and watched Buck lumber down the steps. He darted a panicked glance back at her as he reached the bottom of the stairwell. "What you standing there for? Go on and git yourself decent. We need your help."

Buck disappeared out the front door, and then something new reached in and grabbed hold of Adah's heart with a trembling fist. Instead of following Buck's orders, she ran to the window in the hallway that looked out over the farm's outbuildings and saw what Buck had seen. The roof of the livestock barn was afire. Licks of molten light glowed brighter as the wind blew in bursts to spread the flames.

As the calamitous scene played out before her, a spark went off in her head. It was a distraction, not unlike what Adah had planned for her escape. Here Mother Nature herself had taken matters into her own hands and had chosen the livestock barn instead, causing the diversion she'd desperately sought. Buck and Jesse would be frantic to save the livestock, especially the horses. They also kept hogs and chickens and a couple of goats. Not to mention that the fire could spread to the house or other outbuildings. They would be completely caught up, as would everyone around, including the police.

An act of God's, not hers. Was this the easy solution she'd once envisioned? Was this the gift she'd imagined coming toward her? Did life really answer our prayers, only not in the ways we expected?

Thunder boomed again, and fiery light once more exploded in the sky, this time like a flower with narrow electrical petals. For a moment, everything in the landscape was distorted. Now there were several fires in the distance, and the barn roof was burning right in front of her. Everything amiss, chaos would reign as everyone tried to douse the flames on their stricken and burning structures. All in disarray. Swayed by a wave of vertigo, she reached for the wall to hold herself up.

She had but one moment to decide, one moment to leave, or she would miss her chance—one moment to choose the course of the rest of her life and Daisy's. Did luck really fall on people like her? Of course she knew it could. She'd seen Lady Luck sprinkle her gifts about like little trinkets left on a table. Occasionally one had landed in front of her, having taken the form of Father Sparrow, the Nash brothers, or Jessamine. And Adah realized that if a gift landed in front of you, you had only to pick it up, roll it in your hand, and pocket it. Quick, before someone else stepped up and snatched it away. Why was she hesitating? Only fear and doubt and a man named Jack stood before her and destiny.

But there was never any real doubt about what she would do.

Adrenaline surging through her every cell, Adah ran back into the bedroom and threw a dress over her nightgown, stuffed her feet into shoes, then awakened Daisy, who was resistant and complaining.

"Where are we going, Mama?" the girl asked.

"Shhh," Adah said. "I'll tell you soon." She pulled one of Daisy's dresses on over her pajamas, shoved on her shoes, and lifted the girl onto her hip, gently urging Daisy to lay her head on her shoulder; then she grabbed the bag she had packed and headed for the stairs.

At the bottom of the steps, the front door called to her, and its promise of freedom beyond was something she could taste. Adah hitched up Daisy and headed for it.

"Oh no you don't."

Mabel's voice. It hit Adah flat out.

Her mother-in-law moved in front of the door, blocking Adah's exit. She stood braced in a wide stance, her face suffused with anger. She was shaking her head without speaking, and the room lit up with the power of her rage. "You leave if you want, abandon a ship in trouble. I've expected something like this. But you ain't taking Daisy with you."

Daisy had come fully awake but said nothing as Adah lowered the girl to stand beside her. It was as if even the very young could discern when something life changing was happening, and it held Daisy still and silent. She stood clinging to Adah's left leg as though it were a life raft.

There was only one thing to do. Barely breathing, Adah moved the needlepoint bag in front of her body, reached her right hand inside, and felt for the cold, hard metal. She pulled the pistol from her bag, lifted it in one swift movement, and aimed it at Mabel's eyes. She planted her feet on the floor with steadfast care. Then slipped off the safeties and retracted the slide.

Mabel flinched but made no other move. Adah could read how shock was hitting Mabel, how her cold-chambered heart had been pierced with new fear, how it surrounded her as if in a black vapor.

Adah was afraid her hands would be shaking and weak around the barrel, but they were steady and strong, like the small bones of her body.

"Listen to me, Mabel," she began. "People around here already suspect that perhaps Lester killed Betsy, and that you and Buck, maybe Jesse, too, helped him cover it up by staging an accident on this farm. I'm not sure you were aware of that, and I'm also pretty certain you didn't know that Betsy and her mother were corresponding in secret."

Mabel's face didn't move, but her eyes looked stunned and filled with imaginings. Probably she was remembering the day she was party to concealing a murder.

A chill traveled up Adah's arms all the way to her chest, but she continued playing the cards she had, the same ones she would've left in a letter had she gone through with her original escape plan: "Betsy had revealed that Lester was hitting her and she was planning to leave him. There's proof, in letters, and someone nearby in town has possession of them. If released to the newspaper and the police, they will place serious doubt on your story. Maybe the police will even take a new look at the case. But even if they don't, your reputation as a family will be ruined."

Adah had to stop to breathe as she took note of Mabel's pale, stunned expression, horror in her eyes.

"I'm leaving here now, and if anyone comes after me and Daisy, someone nearby will make all of those letters public. The moonshining could be exposed, too. Your lives will never be the same, and I know how much appearances mean to you."

Mabel lifted her chin. "All I have to do is step outside and shout for Buck. They'll stop you."

"But you won't," Adah said. "I'm holding a gun on you. Don't fool yourself into thinking I won't use it. And even if I don't, I doubt you could get Buck and Jesse's attention in time. I'll be gone as fast as that lightning has been traveling. And if you report me or try to find me, everyone in these parts will know that your son was a wife beater and probably a murderer, too. Is that what you really want?"

Mabel stood paralyzed, as if searching inside all the hidden crevices of her brain for answers, to no avail. Then a more defiant look appeared on her face; she would not give up easily. But Adah had to make her do just that. Time was of the essence.

Huffing now, Mabel said, "How can I just let you go?"

Adah answered, "You just do. Tell everyone the storm and the fire scared us to death, and you let me take Daisy to start a new life. You can tell everyone it was amicable and that we send letters back and forth. You can save your standing in the community, and you don't really want Daisy anyway, now, do you?"

Again, Mabel didn't answer.

"In your heart of hearts, you know Daisy is better off with me. You do love your granddaughter, I know it." Adah gestured with the gun. "Now move aside."

Mabel stood petrified, and Adah feared for one moment that the standoff would last too long. She couldn't really shoot Mabel, but Mabel had to believe Adah's threats—all of them.

After what seemed like interminable seconds, Mabel licked her lips like a madwoman but then moved aside, just as Adah had told her to. Mabel truly cared more about appearances than reality and much more about those things than her granddaughter. She would make sure the men did what she wanted.

"Thank you, Mabel," Adah managed to say. She replaced the safeties, put the gun back into her bag, lifted Daisy, and headed for the door. Flung it open and took one look toward the barn, where in a flash of lightning and the glow from the fire, she could see Buck and Jesse pulling animals out of the barn in a frenzy. They would never notice a fleeting shadow on a night like this one. The darkness between bolts in the sky was as impenetrable as the depths of the river.

Her back turned, she started walking, then moving as fast as she could while carrying Daisy. She half-ran down the front-porch steps, then sprinted across the drive and onto the grass. She left behind the light cast by the house and the burning barn, then headed out and away and onto the road, keeping up the pace while kicking up gravel behind her. The storm snatched away all of their sounds. And then she realized that instead of running away in the midst of a deluge, and despite lightning still spidering across the sky and tiptoeing across the land, not one drop of rain had fallen.

Adah eventually had to stop running and settled into a brisk walk, still breathing raggedly, heavily. For the first hour or so, she worried that the Branches would come after her despite the barn fire and her threats to Mabel. What if Mabel had changed her mind after she let Adah leave?

There was commotion all around. Many people were out on the roads, either driving away from danger or going to help others. A car stopped and Adah saw Florence Wainwright and a young man who must've been her son inside. They told her they hadn't been hit and were driving to check on friends nearby. They had appeared before Adah as if by another gift from God.

Florence made no comment about Adah's and Daisy's attire—pajamas and nightgown hanging out from under their clothes—or the bag Adah carried, and when Adah asked for a ride to the docks, neither Florence nor her son asked one question. As Adah and Daisy hopped into the car and they drove away, Adah couldn't help turning around in the seat to look for Buck's car or the pickup truck, but the road behind them was empty.

It was clear to anyone who saw her what Adah was doing. How fortunate that she and Florence had met at the funeral and had understood each other perfectly.

Then a squad car was coming at them from the opposite direction, lights flashing, sirens howling, and Adah stopped breathing. It was all over now. When the headlights of Florence's car lit the figure inside the oncoming vehicle, it was just a black silhouette, but as the car passed by, Adah recognized Manfred Drucker through the driver's side window. His hands were clenching the steering wheel, his body leaning forward as if he could power the automobile with the strength of his determination.

A huge swell of nausea made her eyes water as she waited for Drucker to turn around. If she'd seen him, he could've seen her. She would be caught and trapped. But Drucker simply kept driving. He was probably headed out to check on his old friend Buck Branch, who was fighting a fire and whose inattention had allowed Adah and Daisy to escape.

The rest of the way, Adah could scarcely believe it. They were going to get away.

Florence spoke only once more, when Adah and Daisy stepped out at the docks, saying simply, "Good luck."

Flooded with elation, Adah searched the dockside. Even if the Branches decided to come after her, they would look at the train station or the bus station in the morning. They'd never know that Jack had given her this escape plan instead. After she had bribed her way on board a loaded barge heading out at dawn, exhilaration poured through her. She had outfoxed them. In the end, aided by a big dose of Lady Luck, she had bested the Branches.

On board and safe, her only regret: *Jack.* The man who had appeared before her, cracked her shields, and stepped inside . . .

Oh God. She did not mean to think of him.

Epilogue

At the train station the next day and on the other side of the river, the man in the ticket booth asked Adah where she and her daughter were heading.

"West," Adah answered. "Any train heading west."

On board a fast train an hour later, Adah held still. She had never been this far west; each new step was into uncharted territory, one step farther from the past. More clapboard houses, more farms—some dirt poor—more small towns, each with its own flavor. One sign read, "Josephine's Chicken, Best in Country." Work lines, food lines, and power lines. Copses of trees. Deserted factories. Dogs, mules, and cats. A man cranking the engine of a very old truck to life. Another man on a bicycle. A church steeple. Stained glass. Then stretches of seemingly empty land.

The clacking rhythm of the train broke thoughts free from her brain, and Adah relived the moment when she'd turned the third tarot card the previous night. The first two cards had not been very revealing, but the third and most important one had been the six of swords, which showed a woman and a young child being rowed across a body of water toward land. The woman's head was covered, implying her sadness, but she was moving away, toward a place of peace and tranquility. The woman was leaving, going somewhere distant and new, into a different life, a child with her.

No doubt remained going forward: once in a blue moon, the cards foretold the future. Once in a blue moon, they held true.

Although she labored to keep her sorrow curled inside, there were too many moments when it pushed itself out beyond the boundaries she'd tried to build. When she looked at Daisy, she could keep it separate, outside. But when she gazed beyond the window and thought of him, it burned to life inside her.

At night a sea of stars swam overhead, and the air was warm enough to lower her window and breathe. They would take new names as mother and daughter and live with their secret. She would find a small safe place and hope for peace of mind. She would do honest work and get Daisy a pet—a cat or dog or bird. Perhaps a rabbit. They would find a cozy home with a garden, where they would grow vegetables and flowers. She would cook again. There would be their lives before and their lives after. They had crossed over and now could be any people they wanted to be. She indulged in her fantasies, convinced she would make them come true but also hoping to bury the flame of regret, the fear of having made the wrong choice.

Adah's torment was a vision of Jack, and her mind replayed the scene over and over—his waiting on the courthouse steps and worrying, fretting, and hesitating, looking at his pocket watch, until it dawned on him that she wasn't coming and she had changed her mind without explanation. Later, of course, he would learn that there had been a fire on the Branch farm and that Adah and Daisy had left town. Then he would figure out she had taken the opportunity to flee, disappearing like fog burns off the river in the morning, leaving him behind. He would figure out she had chosen Daisy over him.

She would stop somewhere along the way and send him a letter, explaining what had happened. Would he understand? Would she ever see him again? Would a path ever reveal itself?

She closed her eyes, opened them again, and raised her window. She could see Jack's face in the reflected light on the glass, as if he were still looking for her even then. But she couldn't think of that; instead she made herself imagine him with his horses, walking in his cornfields, and after a hard day's work, sitting on the porch looking out on the land he so loved.

Jack had once said that forgetting was the only way to get past all the bad things in life, and Adah hoped that he would forget about the short chapter of his life that had featured her. If not, when he looked back on the season of romance, would he feel grateful or regretful? Would he view it as luminous and lovely or colored with confusing shadows and shades? There would be pain in his heart, as there was in hers, and she knew that hurt could cripple and bring one down to a place where *up* seemed impossibly high and out of reach. Would he ever seek love again, or would he keep the possibilities at a distance, beyond the reach of his arms? She had to hope that she and Jack were the kind of people who believed that each and every life, even their own, was worth fighting for and living for through thick and thin. They were survivors.

And yet she was not ready to lose the spell Jack had placed on her or bid farewell for good. She had the feeling that he would walk with her throughout the rest of her days on earth and find a soft place in her memories that she could sink into from time to time.

When morning broke, and with Daisy still soundly asleep with her head in Adah's lap, Adah set her hand on the girl's back, feeling her breathe. She gazed beyond the window, where bright-red and orange slabs of light were beginning to emerge from blue and lavender shadow as the sun wheeled up beyond the horizon. She breathed in and out and watched the day break as she imagined people before her had done for millennia.

Her heart beat at the same slow, steady pulse as the hearts of people before her had, all those other people who had raised children. She could've been here a thousand years earlier, and the feelings would have been the same. Adah lost herself for a moment in the newness of freedom, the joy of it, drawn to the wonder. It was worth everything. Two small shadows would emerge from the dark and into the light of liberty. A new life awaited them. As each new year was added, she imagined one from the past could fade away. She had to believe the past could be buried, especially when the future loomed free.

Would Daisy recover from all she'd seen and experienced? Perhaps enough care and love would accomplish that. Would Jack forgive Adah in his heart? Would he forget his sorrow, given time? Adah hoped to overcome the haunting of Lester's death. Could sorrow and pain some-day lose their power, falling into the fathoms and fathoms of former seasons and distant memories?

She let out a hard-held breath. Had she made the right decision? The last question lingered unanswered for only a moment, until Daisy heaved in a big sleeping breath, and a soft little smile appeared on her lips, as though she was entering the first scene of a bright and sweet dream.

Adah moved her hand to Daisy's head and stroked her hair, then became utterly still.

Her hands were lined and scarred and looked older than her thirty-one years. They had read cards and cooked and scrubbed and carried wood. They had turned the pages of books, touched love, and been betrayed by it. They had touched death, too.

Now they held a human life.

ACKNOWLEDGMENTS

My thanks always to my agent, Lisa Erbach Vance of the Aaron M. Priest Literary Agency; my editor, Jodi Warshaw, at Lake Union Publishing; and editor Amara Holstein for her insightful and helpful input. The entire team at Lake Union continues to help me improve my work, and I will always be grateful.

Thanks to Brent E. Taylor at West Kentucky Community and Technical College for his fine historical review, and John E. L. Robertson, author of *Paducah, Kentucky: A History*, who took the time to speak with me. My gratitude to Nathan Lynn and Susan Baier of the McCracken County Public Library for help with historical details and assistance in finding a reviewer, and George Dearen of Campbellsville, Kentucky, for his firsthand experience with and willingness to share information regarding tobacco farming.

A special thanks to Pat Taylor, author of *Paducah's '37 Flood Rivergees*, who sent me the January 25, 1987, fiftieth anniversary issue of the *Paducah Sun*, containing many first-person accounts of the flood of 1937. And finally, thanks to my family, friends, and fans, especially my dear neighbors and friends in Kentucky. I apologize in advance for creating the Branches—you are nothing like them!

BOOK CLUB QUESTIONS

1. In the opening chapter of *The River Widow*, Adah kills Lester in self-defense, and yet she refers to herself as a murderer throughout the book. Today, would you consider Adah a murderer, and why or why not? Do you feel sympathy for her despite what she has done?

2. In the 1930s, domestic abuse had not yet been named or described. In those days, Lester would have probably been called a *wife beater*. How have views regarding domestic violence changed in the last eighty years? Is Adah justified in feeling that, had she confessed, she would never have received fair treatment by the justice system?

3. After Adah survives the flood, she faces a moral dilemma. Flee or go back for Daisy? At surface value, Adah would probably not have been considered a righteous or ethical person, and yet she makes an unselfish choice that could've resulted in her demise. How does her decision affect the way you feel about her? Do you think you would've made the same choice?

4. In the aftermath of losing Lester, the Branches are highly suspicious of Adah's story and aim their rage at her. As the reader knows, their suspicions are fundamentally correct. They don't know the circumstances,

but Adah did kill their son and brother. What are the beliefs that drive the Branches toward exposing Adah and enacting revenge? While reading, did you ever feel any sympathy for them? If so, why?

5. For some time, no one is willing to help Adah. How do you feel about the attitude of the townspeople, who prefer to look the other way? Do you see them as basically good but too fearful to risk themselves? Or do you see them as basically selfish and hiding behind the social norms of the day? Which attitude do you think is most typical of human behavior?

6. Adah has very different relationships with each of the other characters in the book, among them Daisy, Mabel, Esther, and Jack. How do each of them view Adah and define who she is? How is she changed by each of these relationships?

7. The events depicted in *The River Widow* are triggered by the Ohio River flood of 1937. Had you heard anything about the flood before reading this book? Considering recent natural disasters, have you ever thought that humanity could be seen as constantly in battle with nature? If so, why?

8. What do you think of Jack? Why is he drawn to Adah? Why is she drawn to him? Had they met under different circumstances, would the same pull have existed? If Adah had not asked for Jack's help, would the love between them have developed anyway?

9. How would you describe Adah's relationship with Esther? Antagonistic? Trusting? Suspicious? How do you feel about Esther's determination to get married, have her own child, and turn a blind eye to the Branches' sordid history and reputations? Would you have been able to make such a choice?

10. Discuss the theme of secrets in *The River Widow*. Many of the characters are hiding something. In what ways does this drive each character? Is Adah's secret portrayed differently from the secrets of others, such as the Branches or Esther?

11. In the end, Adah has to make another life-altering choice between marriage and safety with Jack or escape with Daisy. Clearly she loves them both. How does maternal love motivate Adah? How does romantic love motivate her? Do you like her more or less because of the choice she makes?

12. Would Jack and Adah have been happy had she stayed and married him, or would Adah have been haunted every day knowing that the Branches had custody and were possibly still harming Daisy? How would the relationship with Jack have evolved, and would it have endured the test of time?

13. The ending of *The River Widow* may be described as bittersweet, in that Adah loses Jack but saves Daisy. How do you feel about such endings? Do you find them satisfying? If you were the author, how would you have written the ending?

14. The author leaves a small sense of hope that Adah and Jack could be reunited someday. Would you want Jack to give up his farm and join Adah in a life of hiding? How do you imagine the future for Adah, Daisy, and Jack?

ABOUT THE AUTHOR

Photo © 2015 Whitney Raines Photography

Ann Howard Creel was born in Austin, Texas, and worked as a registered nurse before becoming a full-time writer. She is the author of seven books for children and young adults as well as five adult novels, including *The Uncertain Season*, *The Whiskey Sea*, and *While You Were Mine*. Her children's books have won several awards, and her novel *The Magic of Ordinary Days* was made into a Hallmark Hall of Fame movie for CBS. Creel currently lives and writes in Paris, Kentucky, where she is renovating an older house. Follow her at www.annhowardcreel.com.